Mike McPheter

CARTELS AND COMBINATIONS

MIKE MCPHETERS

CARTELS AND COMBINATIONS

BONNEVILLE BOOKS
SPRINGVILLE, UTAH

ISBN 13: 978-1-59955-487-7

Published by Bonneville Books, an imprint of Cedar Fort, Inc., 2373 W. 700 S., Springville, UT 84663
Distributed by Cedar Fort, Inc., www.cedarfort.com

LIBRARY OF CONGRESS CATALOGING-IN-PUBLICATION DATA

McPheters, Mike, 1943-
  Cartels and combinations / Mike McPheters.
     p. cm.
  Summary: A young Mormon woman is abducted by members of a drug cartel, who
hold her as ransom for the return of the sons of the cartel's leader.
  ISBN 978-1-59955-487-7
  1. Drug traffic--California--San Diego--Fiction. 2.
Narco-terrorism--California--San Diego--Fiction. 3. Mormon
youth--California--San Diego--Fiction. 4. Kidnapping--California--San
Diego--Fiction. I. Title.
  PS3613.C58745C37 2010
  813'.6--dc22
                                        2010034925

Cover design by Danie Romrell
Cover design © 2010 by Lyle Mortimer
Edited and typeset by Megan E. Welton

Printed in the United States of America

10 9 8 7 6 5 4 3 2 1

Printed on acid-free paper

Subsequent to my retirement from the Federal Bureau of Investigation on November 7, 1998, my children presented me with a framed Certificate of Appreciation that read, "We honor you this day for teaching us children the true meaning of Fidelity, Bravery, and Integrity." Few things in my life have meant more to me. It is to them—Marni, Shad, Tylee, Shayna, and Justin—that I dedicate this book.

Also by Mike McPheters:

AGENT BISHOP: TRUE STORIES FROM AN FBI AGENT MOONLIGHTING AS A MORMON BISHOP

CONTENTS

CONTENTS

ACKNOWLEDGMENTS

SWITCHING FROM WRITING non-fiction to fiction can be a monumental undertaking. My personal editors, Darcy Creviston and my daughter, Marni Wilks, along with the editors assigned from Cedar Fort, Inc., have helped me tremendously in making this leap. In addition, Marni, Leah Bowman, and my dear wife, Judy, have read as I have written and provided useful and encouraging commentary. I extend my love and appreciation to all these wonderful guiding influences.

In addition, I owe a debt of gratitude to Lee Nelson, whose writing I treasure, and David Ridges, whose doctrinal commentaries buoy me up spiritually, and to my friends from various branches of law enforcement who have expressed for the readers their commentary on the back cover: Leon Fish, Jim Tilley, and Ted Livingston.

FOREWORD

IT WAS ROSA, my friend from Mexico, who strengthened my commitment to write about the Mexican drug cartels, the porous nature of our borders with Mexico, and the imminent threat these problems pose to our country.

Rosa's father worked at a gas station in a small Mexican town. He was finishing up work one day when a carload of drug traffickers came in and insisted he sell them gas. He told them the station was closed, that he was not the owner, and that he didn't have the authority to reactivate the pumps. They shot him in the head and drove away laughing. Rosa's brother suffered a similar fate.

Rosa explained that her family, like thousands of other Mexican citizens, had migrated to the United States to escape the increasingly violent threat of drug cartels.

The devastating results of these wars being waged by drug cartels are no longer limited to Mexico. According to recent reports, nearly 25,000 people have been killed in drug-related violence in Mexico since President Felipe Calderón declared war on the drug traffickers in 2007. That is almost five times the number of US fatalities in the Iraq War. Although President Calderón has deployed 45,000 troops and 5,000 federal police to fight the cartel threat, and most of these murders were perpetrated south of the border, an increasing number of murders are taking place in the United States. Cartel-linked crime is spreading north, while American money for drug sales and guns purchased in the United States flows south.

On June 16, 2010, I read an article entitled, "Uptick in Violence Forces Closing of Parkland along Mexican Border to Americans." Sheriff Paul Babeu of Pinal County, Arizona, told Fox News that officers were forced to close an eighty-mile stretch of Arizona north of the Mexican border—including part of the Buenos Aires National Wildlife Refuge—to Americans, due to an increase in recent months of violence against law enforcement officers and US citizens, drug smuggling, human trafficking, and other illegal activity.

"It's literally out of control!" Babeu stated. Babeu and Senator John McCain demanded support troops from the federal government to secure the borders, but adequate help hasn't been forthcoming. In fact, as of June 2010, President Obama had suspended construction of the border fence. Signs have been posted warning Americans not to cross into the closed-off territory south of Interstate 8. Babeu said he was in desperate need of more resources to help counter the violence from Mexico. "We need action. It's shameful that we, as the most powerful nation on earth, . . . can't even secure our own borders and protect our families."

It seems to me that, in essence, we are being forced to turn back 3,500 acres of American soil to Mexico's drug cartels.

As a retired FBI agent and as an American, I don't like it!

The cartels, which now do $40 billion a year in the drug trade with the United States, employ American street gangs, such as Barrio Azteca, MS-13, and the Mexican Mafia to do their bidding as collectors, enforcers, and distributors. The gangsters even entice naïve American teenagers who, when offered a taste of "real money," tape bundles of marijuana and cocaine to their bodies underneath their clothing and try to walk them across the border. While there are undoubtedly those who make it across, fifteen-year-old kids who wear baggy sweatshirts in sweltering hot weather look far too suspicious not to be apprehended. Not only do these youths lose out on what they think is a quick profit, but they also rack up a criminal record.

On April 20, 2009, Senator Joseph Lieberman, Chairman of the Homeland Security and Governmental Affairs Committee, and Senator John McCain jointly proclaimed that Mexican drug cartels have displaced the Mafia as the number one organized crime problem in our country. Senator Lieberman stated, referring to the cartels, "This is literally a war: they're fighting for the turf!" He indicated that the cartels are operating in two hundred thirty United States metropolitan areas.

Recently, Arizona has enacted legislation to address the cartel threat by strictly enforcing existing federal immigration laws as a last-ditch effort to protect their state against the onslaught of violence and property damage from Mexico. Arizona's efforts have met with resistance both from the federal government, whose laws they are trying to enforce, and from other liberal elements.

Once they are in the United States, many of America's twelve million illegal immigrants do the bidding of drug cartels by aiding in the transportation and distribution of illegal narcotics while soaking up millions of dollars in taxpayer-provided social services. Unfortunately, there is no sure remedy in sight, considering the average per capita income in the United States is $30,000 annually and in Mexico only $4,000.

Although current law prohibits the disbursement of Social Security benefits to illegal immigrants, many still receive these benefits due to bureaucratic error or deliberate fraud, the full extent of which is unknown. Undocumented workers receive emergency medical care for labor and delivery, short-term emergency disaster relief, immunizations, and the testing and treatment of communicable diseases. They also benefit from community programs such as soup kitchens, crisis counseling, and housing assistance. The cost of these services has brought California and other states to the brink of bankruptcy.

The willingness of the government to cater to illegal immigrants has its basis in vote-gathering. Since the Hispanic vote trends Democrat, courting the vote of the demographic with the highest birth rate is an overt attempt of a liberal administration to perpetuate a one-party system in this country *ad infinitum*.

This book raises no argument with those immigrants who have jumped through all the hoops to enter the United States legally. It is to them that the beloved lady we call the Statue of

Liberty extends the torch of freedom, saying, *"Give me your tired, your poor, your huddled masses yearning to breathe free, the wretched refuse of your teeming shore. Send these, the homeless, tempest-tossed to me, I lift my lamp beside the golden door!"*

American employers, addicted to cheap labor, have brought much of the current immigration crisis upon us by knowingly hiring illegal immigrants, just as millions of drug-addicted American citizens have created the market for marijuana, methamphetamine, opium, and cocaine, thereby providing drug cartels their existence. Mexican drug traffickers entering our country with their illegal products, supported by a ready-made structure of illegal immigrants to distribute them, are only catering to our growing appetite.

Programs have been established in the past—especially during wartime, when there were worker shortages in the United States—to bring in Mexican workers on a temporary basis and then have them return to Mexico when sufficient manpower was reinstated. These programs failed. For undocumented Mexican workers, it has always been worth the risk to stay in America illegally and take whatever wage is offered.

How have the drug cartels gained such power among the people? Elder M. Russell Ballard, a member of the Quorum of the Twelve Apostles of The Church of Jesus Christ of Latter-day Saints, made the following statement:

> The Book of Mormon teaches that secret combinations engaged in crime present a serious challenge, not just to individuals and families, but to entire civilizations. Among today's secret combinations are gangs, drug cartels, and organized crime families. The secret combinations of our day function much like the Gadianton robbers of the Book of Mormon times. They have secret signs and code words. They participate in secret rites and initiation ceremonies. Among their purposes are to "murder, and plunder, and steal, and commit whoredoms and all manner of wickedness, contrary to the laws of their country and also the laws of their God" [Helaman 6:23]. (In Conference Report, Oct. 1997, 51; or *Ensign*, Nov. 1997, 38).

It is true that cartels, with these secret combinations at their foundation, can challenge and supplant governments.

An interesting approach, touching on how those secret combinations could have been passed on to and implemented by the major drug cartels of Mexico, is discovered in the account of the Maya and the Red Maya. This fictional account in no way implies accepted doctrine of any church.

Ruben and Tito Guzman will introduce the reader to the history and modernization of drug trafficking. Gangster organizations in Mexico currently compare in structure to multi-national corporations in the United States. Their operatives no longer appear only as common gangsters with gold teeth, brightly-colored shirts, and .45 caliber pistols hanging in shoulder holsters. Instead, they utilize high-powered computer technology, some of the best chemists in the country for their methamphetamine operations and other state-of-the-art technology, with brilliant attorneys overlooking their operations.

In spite of all the allegations of impropriety and bribery attributed to the Mexican authorities, the Mexican government deserves credit for its effort in facing monumental challenges with the cartels. With a population of over 100 million people, Mexico has the fourteenth largest economy in the world. Its army is still a patriotic and powerful force, even as the cartels bombard its constituents with bribes and hire away their personnel with higher wages. Mexico City is a strong, stable metropolis with modern innovation and increasing hope for the future. The twenty million people who reside there resent being intimidated by drug runners.

I reiterate that the thousands of murders committed by drug cartels each year have nothing to do with the many legal immigrants in this country who are, by and large, peaceful, law-abiding citizens. Instead, this violence is the diabolic work of profit-crazed drug dealers bent on having their way with victims on both sides of the border.

Characters in this book such as prosecutor Enrique Guzman, FBI chief "Big Bob" Brady," and Homeland Security coordinator Mark Madden underscore the trend of a younger generation to rely increasingly on the "gray panthers" of the baby boomer generation to unleash their reservoir of experience in confronting the drug menace. These men and women are summoned out of comfortable retirements to lend their strength to resisting the threat at the border. Those of us in our fifties, sixties, and seventies take pride in the commitment of these people and others like them in law enforcement who are ofttimes regarded as "over the hill" who come through when the chips are down.

The last question and probably the most important to be posed in this book is this: What causes people to go from good to proudly indifferent to bad to hopelessly evil to the point of gladly following secret combinations found at the foundation of the drug cartels if granted access? The answer may lie in the shadow of ancient scripture, which I will help you discover.

I will take you back and forth through the course of recent American and Mexican history through Enrique Guzman's discovery of a leather-bound journal, stained with the blood of his father—a journal that also contains the account of unlikely heroes committed to saving the life of a young woman who has fallen into the grasp of bloodthirsty drug traffickers.

The dialogue you will discover in Miguel Guzman's journal is no more than a mechanism to convey understanding.

CHAPTER ONE
THE KARATE MATCH

SAN DIEGO, CALIFORNIA
10:15 SATURDAY MORNING, SEPTEMBER 25, 2010

SWEAT CASCADED DOWN seventeen-year-old Elena Guzman's olive face as she circled her taller opponent with light Caucasian features and blonde hair—the same girl who delighted in ribbing Elena about her Hispanic ethnicity.

"Come on, Taco Time! Let's see whatcha got!" the tall girl snarled as she waved her fists at Elena mockingly, trying to get her to come closer. "You and your Mexican buddies have been talkin' a lot of smack lately about how you could beat me. Well, let's see it!"

Ann Langley was the local girls' karate champ and figured she had reason to brag. No one had ever put her down. Few would even try. However, in club competition, Elena had come the closest.

I've about had it with her! Elena thought as she kept circling, looking for an opening to deliver a swift punch while at the same time trying to stay out of Langley's range.

The local *dojo* was teeming with spectators. People from the surrounding Hispanic community in the Clairemont Mesa area of San Diego had heard about Ann Langley's disparaging attitude, not only toward Elena, but toward others in the Mexican community.

Langley's seventeen-year-old twin brother, Irv, had been

1

arrested with two other American teenagers. They were trying to make some fast money by taping bundles of marijuana to their midsections and walking them across the border from Tijuana into the United States. This was a new attempt by the Vultures drug cartel from Culiacán, Mexico, to find successful ways to get their drugs into the country.

Irv and his naïve friends were easily intercepted by border authorities, who smirked at the youths' tentative attempts not to draw attention to themselves as they crossed, wearing bulky sweaters to cover their "cargo" in the heat of the summer, their faces plastered with sheepish grins. The arrests and drug recovery were slam dunks.

It was Elena's father, Enrique Guzman, the federal strike force prosecutor who supervised drug cartel prosecutions, who had the last word on Irv Langley's prosecution. Ann Langley was incensed at the thought that Elena's father was prosecuting her brother. Nothing could have exacerbated the ill will between the two girls more. Ann also resented the fact that Elena was the one girl in the *dojo* that could keep up with her progress toward the black belt. She hated the fact that Elena could actually compete with her, even though she wasn't nearly as big or strong.

Theirs was a grudge match in the truest sense of the word.

The *senseis,* or master instructors, had allowed the match, mistakenly thinking it might lead to the girls' reconciliation. The match was to be well supervised so as to prevent serious injury to either girl. They reasoned that since the girls hated each other so passionately, this would be a way to work out the poison. Then perhaps their girls' karate team could achieve some much-needed team unity.

All the indications were that Ann Langley would be the clear winner. Elena was getting hammered. Her petite build, long dark hair, and fine features portrayed femininity, not the toughness requisite for exacting punishment in a *dojo*. Nevertheless, she was fast—very fast—and had been striking well with her feet in sweeping, circular arcs. Even though her span was limited for delivering kicks and punches, she was intermittently making good, solid connections.

Suddenly, however, Elena took another huge hit off the Langley girl's left foot as the taunting continued. "Whatsa matter, Mormon Mex? Isn't Papa Prosecutor around to hold his little girl's hand today? Oh, but he's too busy chasing down teenagers, right?"

There it was again. The "Down on Mexicans" trash talk. Ann was really kindling that fire now. Waves of anger raged within Elena.

Langley wouldn't shut up. "Come on, fruit picker! Let's see some real action. Your mama could do better!"

Elena's thoughts drifted to other instances of racial harassment directed at her family over time, specifically at her Uncle Hector. She envisioned him again, sinking slowly into the water. At first his entire hand was above the surface, then only his knuckles and forefinger, and then nothing! He was gone.

That was all it took.

The head *sensei* had been ready to call the match after Ann Langley delivered yet another telling blow to Elena's upper torso when it happened.

Elena was supercharged by the anger within her, emanating from the vision of Uncle Hector. It was the same hatred over race that Ann Langley was choking her with. It was the verbal abuse about her father. It was the jab at her church.

"Here's a little something from the fruit picker, Langley!" Elena shouted as she spun and came from the side and behind with a perfectly executed roundhouse kick that swept the Langley girl's feet out from underneath her, sending her sprawling.

The audience was silent . . . dazed. Elena had demonstrated a deftness and raw energy that no one would ever have expected from the smaller Hispanic girl. Everyone just stared at Ann, lying on her back, looking up with a puzzled expression, and wincing from her impact with the mat.

The match was over.

Suddenly, the Hispanic crowd went crazy. The other spectators immediately joined them, and soon, all were wildly celebrating Elena's victory. Elena walked into the dressing room, changed clothes, and left without comment.

Elena was not one to hang around the *dojo* for handshakes and kudos. She'd asserted herself by beating Ann Langley only because she had no other recourse to escape the harassment. She was sore, tired, and just wanted to be alone. It had been a long morning. She drove away in her old, pale blue Camaro, the tournament trophy that everyone thought Ann Langley would win on the front passenger seat.

As she drove, Elena grudgingly recalled the deal she had made with her parents.

I can't believe I'm almost eighteen years old and still have to negotiate with my parents for a little tattoo of all things!

The deal had been cut based upon another of Elena's questionable requests. This time she wanted a second tattoo, a budding red rose, five inches long, to be placed below her right shoulder blade. Two years before, at age sixteen, she had bargained with her parents Enrique and Belinda for an even smaller tattoo of a sunflower on her left ankle.

To obtain the second tattoo, Elena had promised to attend a youth conference at the nearby church in the Clairemont Mesa area of San Diego. The activity the night before hadn't been anything exceptional. The music was mellow, not the hard rock that she preferred. However, some of the Mormon boys were good dancers, fun to be around, and not bad looking. The boys were attracted to Elena's long dark hair, olive complexion, outgoing personality, and slim but shapely figure. Elena had pressed her parents to allow her to begin dating when she was fifteen. When they refused, civil war broke out, but she lost.

Attending church was "hit and miss" for Elena. Her parents faced an uphill battle each Sunday, trying to cajole her into going. Whether she attended usually depended upon who became most fatigued first: them from prodding her or her from resisting. Church was only a sideline to Elena and usually buried among many other interests. Living on the edge and discovering for herself what life was about from many different angles was more to her liking.

Why was she angry so often? The anger always came back to roost. Much of it had to do with her parents, Enrique and Belinda

Guzman, and the restrictions they placed on her. The fact that they insisted she go to church played a part in the resentment. But she was especially angry for having to take heat for what her dad did for a living: putting people away on drug charges.

Elena liked the Hispanic crowd every bit as much as the Anglo kids she hung out with, most of whom were not of her faith. Her Mexican friends had relatives who were *narcotraficantes*—drug traffickers—who her father had put in prison. The fact that her father was a prosecutor didn't help her image with her Hispanic peer group. She had, in fact, received numerous threatening calls and intimidating written notes, just as her parents had. She sensed that things were heating up more in recent weeks. She couldn't quite understand why, but felt something was about to happen.

Elena's thoughts turned to her older brother, Miguel, who had now been dead two years. As an act of vengeance against their father, Miguel and his wife were killed by drug traffickers from the Vulture cartel shortly after they were married. She had almost come to grips with Miguel's death. Almost.

Her brother's death was the other "demon" that plagued Elena, and the horrific event from two years ago played out once again in her memory.

＊＊＊＊

Friday was Miguel and Mary's date night. The couple was en route to a nice restaurant in Coronado when a black sedan with four Hispanic men pulled up beside their car. The leader, a fat man known as "El Gordo" rolled down the passenger side window, leveled a fully automatic M-16 rifle at them, hollered the words, "*Un don para el fiscall*"—a gift for the prosecutor—and sprayed their windshield with .223 caliber rounds before speeding off. Miguel's car sideswiped a concrete barrier on the side of the highway, rolled over, and burst into flames.

Elena's mother, Belinda, was so grief-stricken she was unable to communicate with anyone, including Elena's father, for the next three weeks. Finally, in a subdued voice, she muttered to her husband, "We've lost him, Enrique! We've lost our only son! And our daughter-in-law. We've lost them both!"

Enrique's heart was drained of emotion. *I have to quit this job!* Enrique thought through unfathomable grief. *They'll come again. They'll come for Belinda, for Elena, and for me. I have to quit!*

The authorities successfully identified the three men who killed Miguel and his wife as being employed by the Vultures out of Sinaloa, Mexico. According to police reports, they had been in the Tijuana area to oversee cocaine shipments into the United States.

Due to their air flights and shiploads being more frequently interdicted, Colombian *narcotraficantes* were finding it increasingly more difficult to bring their drugs through South Florida. They began looking for alternate routes, and the ones that made the most sense were through Mexico, where they found willing partners in the Vultures, who took on the shipments for a fee.

The Vultures had become aware that a federal prosecutor named Enrique Guzman was about to file charges against several of their members. If that happened, their members would all be going to prison, which would be extremely bad for business. Enrique Guzman had to be stopped, and the killing of his son and daughter-in-law was only the beginning. However, lengthy sentences were eventually dealt out to the perpetrators. Only one got away: the fat one they called El Gordo Diaz.

Elena remembered how as the months went on, her father's grief over the death of his son had escalated into raw anger, anger that Elena caught hold of also. Her father sought vengeance and was even more committed to going after the drug lords.

The harder Elena's father pressed the *narcotraficantes,* the greater was the volume of threats against her family and the more negative were the social implications for Elena from her peers in the Mexican community.

****

As Elena pulled into a gas station for fuel, a friend from the *dojo,* Manolo Barto, pulled in next to her, exited his car, and walked up to her with his usual swagger.

"Hey, *hermosa,* you sure put away that Langley chick!"

Elena rolled her eyes at being called "beautiful" by nineteen-year-old Manolo, a skinny kid with shoulder-length hair. Manolo was born an "anchor baby" in San Diego to illegal immigrant parents. His birth gave them access to social services and many privileges of American citizens, since they now had a child born on American soil. Elena enjoyed her Hispanic traditions and culture but was angered by the illegals who refused to jump through all the hoops for their citizenship, as Elena's family had. She knew people like Manolo took unabashed advantage of American services while still corroborating with Mexico's drug cartels. They were the ones who earned Hispanics a bad reputation. Manolo was brazen in bragging about how his family could "juice" the stupid *gringo*s. Even though she liked Manolo and hung out with him occasionally, she had become increasingly repulsed by him.

Elena was quite sure Manolo was one of the American youth recently recruited by the cartels to walk drugs across the border. In fact, another friend had told her Manolo was involved with Irv Langley the day he was arrested. Apparently, Manolo had barely avoided apprehension. She knew Manolo's desire was to suit up with some drug trafficking organization that would keep him in "fast money."

The day before, Manolo had been spouting off again about how his family had "outfoxed" the *gringo* system by obtaining medical assistance and food. His new claim to fame was that he was going to be trained by the *Pelones,* a militant group comprised of former military operatives who had gone to work for the drug cartels.

"So, my sweet Elena, I hear you're going to college this fall . . . some Mormon college in Idaho, BYU-Ida-Ho-Ho-Ho, or something like that?" Manolo awaited a response with a condescending smile.

"Back off, smart mouth! College is one place you'll never end up, loser! And besides, I don't even know if I'll get in . . . probably because I hang around too much with deadbeats like you."

Elena did little to hide her hostility. For her, BYU-Idaho was only a place her parents wanted her to go and was not even her number one choice. She was actually more interested in attending some local junior colleges with fewer restrictions but had reluctantly undergone an interview with her bishop and sent in an application—just to keep Mom and Dad happy. After all, they would be bankrolling her education.

"Easy, wild woman, easy! You know me. I just like to play around with your heart, magnificent man that I am." Manolo couldn't hold back a grin.

"I only hang out with you because no one else will. You totally know that, right?" Elena had struck a chord with Manolo.

"Come on, Elena. You know you hang with me because you're in love with me. Tell the truth!" Manolo reared backwards, chuckling, as Elena slugged him in the shoulder. His skinny, 160-pound frame buckled considerably under Elena's playful punch.

Elena wasn't about to hold back. "Yeah, sure. Whatever! So I hear you're still using. Is that true? Still doing the drug freak stuff? The truth now, Magnificent Man."

"Now, now, sweet lady, let's not get into my personal life. You know I can do no wrong." Manolo wouldn't look at Elena straight on.

"You were there, weren't you? You were there with Langley's brother, hauling weed over the line, weren't you? Come on . . . the truth!"

"Hey, *hermosa*, let's talk about something else, like eloping or stowing away on a cruise ship to the Virgin Islands. Whaddaya say?" It was obvious Manolo's tongue was not to be loosened.

Elena decided it was time to pick her bone. "You know the difference between you and me, Manolo?" Elena asked.

"Absolutely! That's why I love you so much, Lady." Manolo tossed his head arrogantly.

"That's not exactly what I'm getting at, bonehead, and you know it. My family came to this country to work and make something of ourselves, not to smuggle drugs over the border for the *narcotraficantes*."

Manolo jammed his hands into the pockets of his low-slung jeans. "Hey, you misjudge me," he said, but Elena knew she'd hit a hot button. The dart had finally pierced Manolo's skin.

"All right, Little Miss Righteous, since we're getting it all out here, I'll impart a few truths to you. When I haul stuff across the line, I'm just giving the *gringo*s what they want . . . what they crave. They want all we can give them. It's their choice!" Manolo's voice grew high pitched to the point of shrill.

Elena responded, "Oh, so that justifies it! Sure. I suppose you're going to tell me all about the stupidity of the *gringo*s. By the way, you're one of them, anchor baby. Once your folks swam the river and had you over here, you started getting all the freebies, right? Hot lunches. Hot breakfasts. Free medical attention. Free social services. Free this. Free that. Then you turn around and traffic drugs over here to show your appreciation, right?"

Manolo's arrogant smile disappeared. He knew how angry Elena could get; he had seen it many times before. Her anger mystified him. He saw nothing wrong with taking advantage of the system, and he didn't think Elena really cared that much about what she was saying. *She just likes being angry,* he thought.

He lowered his voice and his face grew serious. "Listen, you need to simmer down about the arrest of the Langley kid and the others. The cops went up the line once the Langley kid started singing and traced the action to the Vultures, who were overseeing the 'walkovers' in San Diego. Six of them were arrested and are in the San Diego County Jail. And two of them are the sons of El Gordo." Manolo was finally wearing a serious face.

"So, what do I care?" Elena asked.

"Word on the street is that heads will roll until El Gordo gets his sons out of jail, and he's really mad at your dad for holding them on such a high bail—one hundred and fifty thousand dollars each. In fact, the buzz is that your dad is on El Gordo's radar. Take it for what it's worth, that's all."

Elena flinched. Manolo had talked a lot of smack before, which she normally disregarded, but his words caused a knot to form in her stomach. She knew all about how the cartels killed people, decapitating them and leaving the heads on the lawns of their relatives or leaving their headless bodies hanging off an interstate overpass. She knew what El Gordo had done to her family. Manolo had definitely gotten her attention.

"Just where did you hear all this?" Elena demanded.

"It's just out there, *hermosa*. That's all I have to say. So there you have it. You jab me about getting 'freebies' and all, and I help out your old man." The smile reappeared. "I told you I was a beautiful man." Manolo got back into his car and quickly accelerated, peeling off rubber. That was his trademark.

He liked to play the big man, she knew that, but what he said had gotten to her.

As she walked away, her stomach reeled. El Gordo Diaz had brutally killed her brother and his wife. What would prevent him from going after her dad, her mom, or maybe even her?

Elena knew she couldn't really trust Manolo. There were rumors circulating that he was trying to get his hands on some easy money by being recruited into one of the drug cartels. She believed Manolo could be bought and that there was little he wouldn't do for money.

She was right.

★★★★

The night before, Manolo had received a phone call. "Hello, who is this?" he asked.

"It's Aurelio . . . Aurelio Flores. Two of our men vouched for you, so you're in for the training for one of our new job openings. If you're still interested, report to the training compound out of Culiacán tomorrow. If you make it through the training the *Pelones* put you through for those two weeks, you'll join up with us. As you know, El Gordo sees to it that the Vultures are paid very well."

Manolo responded enthusiastically, "You got the right man!"

Flores snorted, "We'll see! Now, are you sure you've given us all the information on Elena Guzman? Correct address? Relatives' addresses? The description of her is solid? Do we have it all?"

"I've told you everything I know. I have decided, however, that I think the information is worth a little more than—"

"You got a thousand in cash!" Manolo was silenced by the icy voice on the other end. "No questions asked. That's a lot of money just for some addresses and a car and house description. That's a *thousand* dollars, Manolo! As in one-zero-zero-zero. If you get too greedy, you can forget training with the *Pelones* and any future with us. The Vultures believe that a man is better off not to press his luck."

Manolo realized his bluff had been called. "Okay. Okay. I'm good with the thousand. You're just going to hold her. You're not going to hurt her, right?"

The phone line went dead.

* * * *

As Elena drove toward the church, two dark sedans followed her—one several car lengths behind her and another paralleling her on the next street over.

CHAPTER TWO
UNCLE HECTOR

AS ELENA CONTINUED toward the chapel for the youth conference, she noticed a flurry of splashing in Lake Lucent caused by the cavorting of a drake and hen mallard.

Not seeing the ducks as they made their quick exit into the bushes when her Camaro passed them, she caught only a glimpse of the water being disturbed by something.

Then, in her mind, she saw it again! The frantic hand descending below the surface of the water. Then the knuckles and tip of the forefinger. Then nothing. Just the ripples, going out in every direction. He was gone. In her mind's eye, she saw him spiraling down into the dark water, bubbles emanating from his mouth rising as he sank lifeless and still into the depths of the lake.

Her grandpa, Julio, who she called Abuelito, had told her all about what had happened. It was an image that would never leave her, much as the vision of her brother's car, bursting into flames.

She remembered the story . . .

****

In 1970, Julio and Maria Guzman, with their sons Enrique, Ruben, and Hector, entered the United States from Mexico legally, hoping to become US citizens. They drove across the border in an old, rusted pickup truck and the shirts on their backs to find work in the fruit orchards in the farm camps near Payette, Idaho, an area commonly referred to as "Treasure Valley."

Eighteen-year-old Enrique and seventeen-year-old Ruben fared better than their younger brother, Hector, who was then only fifteen years old. Enrique was smart and learned English easily by listening to radio broadcasts. Ruben was athletic with wide shoulders and an unyielding personality. His trademark was industry and could easily outwork his older brother and father. He lived on the edge and had a tendency to get into trouble. But Hector was scrawny, introverted, and totally traumatized by his new environment.

The family harvested the fruit orchards for local farmers in the summers. Although they earned only a pittance for their work, it was many times more than what they could earn in Mexico even in the best of times. During the off-season and winters, they took whatever work they could find—pruning trees or working in hotels or other odd jobs—just to get by. Then, at the first hint of spring, they would look for tree spraying work back in the orchards.

Though they struggled financially in America, the Guzmans had no desire to return to Mexico and the extreme poverty they had left behind.

To become more Americanized, avoid discrimination, and better themselves, the Guzmans studied English whenever there was an opportunity to do so in free community programs but assimilated it mainly through mimicking words and expressions they heard around them. They believed that deserving American citizenship meant working hard at learning the language of Americans. Each time they paired up to work with Americans in the fields or in the fruit orchards, they would try to learn new words or expressions from them.

As it was with most of the immigrant families, acceptance came slowly for the Guzmans. Hector especially had a hard time adapting to life in the United States. Because he found great difficulty learning even the basic fundamentals of English, he became the butt of a lot of teasing by American teenagers. He was constantly goaded by his peers, who considered him easy prey since he would retreat rather than stick up for himself. He was continuously referred to as "dirty spic" or other degrading names. Because he was quiet and afraid to defend himself, he was routinely targeted for harassment at school, and life was miserable for him. His parents grieved for him but didn't know how to alleviate his suffering. They feared that reprisals from the parents of the tormentors would just make Hector's road stonier.

One day, his older brother Ruben, was driving a tractor with a trailer attached, hauling in fruit. His job was to stop at the end of each row of trees, load the stacked bushels of Red Delicious apples, and proceed on to the next row.

He worked through the morning until just before noon and managed to heft another dozen bushels of fruit onto the trailer when Hector stumbled out of the trees and onto the service road. Ruben was stunned when he saw his brother appear, holding his hand over his left ear.

"What happened to you, little brother?" Ruben asked, pulling his hand away from the ear to see dark blood oozing from it.

Hector was crying as he blurted out, "It was the Allen boys again! They won't quit. Every day they're after me for something . . . being a 'spic' or a 'dirty Mexican,' or a 'loser.' Or just for being 'chicken,' which I know I am." Hector sobbed uncontrollably.

Ruben knew how Hector struggled and wished he could help him. As his younger brother became more and more emotional, Ruben looked around the orchard, his angry eyes searching for the Allen brothers. He had caught Jimmy and Ronnie Allen before, with three other teenage boys, in a remote part of the orchard, ripping off Hector's trousers and briefs, forcing him to run through the orchards naked, exposing himself in full view of the other workers. This was after they had whipped his bare buttocks with tree branches. Ruben taught the Allens a lesson he thought they would never forget, leaving them both with blackened eyes, bloodied lips, and swollen jaws. Apparently his actions only increased their bitterness toward Hector, who they could corner at will in some remote part of the orchard.

Ruben shook his head as he stared at the blood oozing from

Hector's ear and running down his T-shirt. *They'll pay!* Ruben thought.

This attack was just the latest instance where Hector couldn't or wouldn't defend himself, much to Ruben's chagrin. Hector was drowning more, day by day, in a sea of abuse. His self-esteem was mostly diminished. He was a boy trying to become part of an ugly, deprecating environment that surrounded him. He was a boy without skills, without self-confidence, and with no place to go. Sometimes the police would investigate the attacks on Hector; sometimes they wouldn't. If the complaint was called in and the perpetrators weren't taken into custody, life became much worse for Hector.

"Hey, brother, that ear looks bad," Ruben said, tilting Hector's head and taking a closer look at the bloody wound. "We've got to get you to a doctor . . . right now!" As he wrapped his fingers around the handle of a switchblade knife he carried tucked in the front of his pants, he swore to himself, *I'll take care of the Allen boys later!*

"Come on, Hector!" Ruben was adamant. "*Vamos!*"

"No, Ruben," Hector answered. "I'll just clean up. I still need to pick the other two rows. I'm okay. I just can't hear very well." He tenderly touched his left ear, wincing with pain. "Let's just go eat. We'll come back after lunch, I'll just work my rows and stay away from the Allens. If they come after me, I'll run. Let's go, brother!"

Although Ruben and Hector were four years apart in age, they had always been close and had stood up together against a wall of racial harassment more than once since they had come from Mexico. Ruben loved his younger brother and was always there for him, fighting his battles and getting him out of peer predicaments that he, Hector, hadn't created but always seemed to befall him, just like other Mexican kids who preferred not having to fight to be accepted.

As the two drove off in the dilapidated old truck the orchard owners supplied for running errands, they talked about their older brother, who was studying at the University of Idaho. The boys took great pride in Enrique's accomplishments and hoped that if Enrique could be successful, maybe there was a slim possibility for them too. They discussed their parents, who both worked with them in the orchards, and their mother's cancer, which went untreated for lack of money.

The brothers arrived at Joe's Burgers and Fries in downtown Payette. Ruben ordered their lunch while Hector went into the restroom and washed the blood out of his ear. While they were eating, Ruben asked Hector what had happened.

"What did they do to you, *Hermanito*?" Ruben demanded.

"Ronnie, the fat one, he held me down. He weighs about two hundred and fifty pounds. Then Jimmy, the smaller one, stuck a metal pipe in my ear and kept yelling into it, 'Spic boy, can you hear this?' Then he kept blowing this whistle he had carved into the pipe. It felt like someone was sticking a hot needle into my ear! Then I felt something rip open deep inside my ear, and now I can't hear out of it. I'll see a doctor, if Papa says we can afford it."

"You'll see a doctor anyway. I'll find a way to get the money. You hear me, Hector?" Ruben left no room for argument.

Hector felt obligated to say, "Yes," but knew how Ruben would get the money. He had already been arrested twice for theft. Once in Payette, Idaho, and once in Vale, Oregon, not far away. He was lucky not to have gone to prison, although he had had to serve a week in jail in Vale.

After the young men had downed their burgers, fries, and sodas, they headed back to their work areas.

"Listen, little brother, if those Allen boys come near you this afternoon, you run toward the tractor that I'm on. You come *rapido*, okay?"

"Okay," Hector promised. "The bleeding has stopped. It just hurts really bad." There were several moments of silence that passed between them. Hector's eyes reddened with tears of humiliation. "You know, brother, I'm so ashamed. I just don't have the stomach to fight back. I never have! What's wrong with me?"

Ruben glanced over at his younger brother. Hector's eyes reflected a profound kind of discouragement and hopelessness that Ruben had never before observed in his little brother. It troubled him deeply. The sadness in Hector's countenance haunted Ruben after he dropped him off at the orchard. He vowed silently to not go far from Hector's rows.

****

As Elena considered the Allen brothers, she thought of Ann Langley. *Ann would have made those losers a great sister!* Elena smiled inwardly. She continued to recall the story, as told by her grandfather.

****

Roughing up the cowardly little Mexican gave the Allen boys a sense of power that they didn't enjoy in any other part of their lives. While stuffing their faces with cheese sandwiches, candy bars, and doughnuts, they had come up with yet another "treat" for Hector.

Ronnie, the fat fifteen-year-old, was always enthralled with his older brother's assaults on Hector Guzman. Eighteen-year-old Jimmy Allen dropped out of high school long before he was old enough to do that without parental consent. He could neither read nor write, and his parents had never tried to make him go back. Ronnie was content to follow his lazy, older brother's example. Their parents were both alcoholics who never owned a home or held down a steady job but somehow felt superior to what they called the "Mexican trash" who came into town to steal their jobs in the orchards and fields.

The Allen boys' parents took work in the orchards when there was some available and if they were sober. They encouraged their boys to follow the same lifestyle.

Just like their parents, Ronnie and Jimmy resented people who tried to better themselves: people like the Guzmans. When Ruben wasn't around, they always sought ways to tear Hector down physically, verbally, and mentally. He was treated the same way by the kids at school when he first tried to attend. It was easy for Hector to give up on an education because life at school soon became impossible.

Jimmy Allen smiled crookedly as he related yet another scheme to make life unbearable for Hector. "Okay, this is what we'll do when ol' spic boy gets back from lunch," he told Ronnie. Jimmy stood only five feet six inches but was barrel-chested and quick. He continued, totally enthralled with what he believed was his wit and ingenuity.

"Right at the afternoon break, after everyone goes back to work, when the Mex wimp is still at the top of his ladder, picking, you drag over that hose." Jimmy signaled toward the high-pressure hose coiled near the water pump. "You turn the hose on full blast when I give you the thumbs up and we'll see how well Hectorino can do the Fandango twelve feet up in the air, while I'm supplying him with a little liquid."

Guffaws were filling the air as fat Ronnie held his stomach while spitting out the last part of an unfinished doughnut. Once he regained his composure, he asked, "Jimmy, how do we keep him up there on the ladder when the break bell sounds?"

"No problem," responded Jimmy. "I won't let him get down. Every time he tries, I'll kick the ladder. Nobody'll see that, and he'll get the point." Jimmy was grinning at how clever he was.

Right at 2:30 P.M., the break bell rang. Scores of orchard laborers headed for the water hoses and fruit baskets set up on the ends of their rows.

Hector, who was amazed that the Allens hadn't approached him once since the break, took one step down from his twelve-foot ladder before he suddenly realized he was fighting to keep his balance, as Jimmy began kicking the metal rungs at the ladder's base. From the corner of his eye, he noticed Ronnie running toward the water pump. As the ladder continued to wobble back and forth, he began pleading with Jimmy Allen, but to no avail.

"Come on, Jimmy! Stop! Please! No more!" Hector yelled in Spanish, knowing he wouldn't be understood and realizing his balance had already been compromised due to his eardrum being shattered just a few hours before.

Jimmy kept shaking the ladder, laughing and kicking it harder, as he observed Ronnie pulling the water hose over to him and gleefully taking note of the fact the other workers had completely disappeared.

"Jimmy, I'm going to fall! Please, don't . . . " Hector shouted, as he dropped his bushel of fruit and held on to the top rungs of the ladder to avoid a sure calamity. Suddenly, he felt the overwhelming pressure of a piercing stream of water pummeling first into his chest and then into his face as Jimmy held the nozzle at an angle that would maximize the force of the liquid tearing into Hector's mouth and eyes. Not only could he not hear but now he was also blinded. He lifted one arm in an attempt to block the powerful blasts of water pushing his head back, then raised his other arm to reposition his hold on the top rung of the ladder. When he did that, his fingers slipped off the wet surface of the top rung, and he felt himself plummeting downward, almost as if it were in slow motion, careening over into a somersault, ten feet down onto the ground.

He landed heavily on his stomach, his fall only somewhat cushioned by the apples that had spilled out of his picking bucket. Even then, his forehead struck a sharp rock, opening up an ugly gash.

With the wind knocked out of him, he lay for a few moments gasping for breath and groaning. When he finally tried to get to his feet, he found himself looking up at the grinning faces of Jimmy and Ronnie Allen. He could see, but he couldn't hear anything . . . not their taunting laughter nor their racial slurs.

Then he passed out.

As the Allen boys continued their enjoyment, standing over Hector, Ruben rounded the corner of their row on the tractor in a fury, with an eight-inch switch blade open and extended out in his right hand.

When Hector finally regained his senses a few minutes later, his body was racked with pain that he had never felt before, from head to toe, but the thing that bothered him the most was that he still couldn't hear . . . from either ear. A dozen orchard workers were standing over him, looking down, and asking what had happened. He thought the lips of one older woman were forming the word *Pobrecito*, but he couldn't be sure. That same elderly woman gently wrapped his head with a torn white T-shirt and rinsed his face with water from a canteen, cradling his head in her arms. She held the wrapping tightly to maintain pressure on his wound and stem the bleeding.

Finally, when it became apparent the bleeding had stopped and Hector could get back onto his feet, the laborers trickled back to their work, having witnessed just another act of hate and prejudice—the kind of act that had become part of their steady diet in their quest to infiltrate a new and hostile environment. With sincere empathy, they uttered the words, *Ay, Pobrecito!*

Hector took the wrapping from the woman, slowly got up onto his feet, thanked his benefactor, and told her that his brother would take him to the hospital. Then, she too walked away to notify Hector's parents, who were working the far end of the orchard.

Hector realized his hearing was gone, probably for good. As he passed by a mirror tacked onto a fruit tree near a wash basin, he looked at the ugly gash down the side of his head and face. He had never considered himself handsome or attractive to any young lady he had met. It was extremely painful to realize that now he never would be. He also knew that deep down he didn't have the strength or the commitment to fight back, not just against the Allens, but against others like them at the schools that he would like to attend some day. He was through trying.

Hector left the orchard before Ruben ever got back. For the first time in his life, he was determined and fully committed, as he headed toward the steep banks of the Snake River.

His body was found two days later, tangled up in some bushes, five miles downstream.

★ ★ ★ ★

The bodies of Jimmy and Ronnie Allen were discovered the day after Hector was found, approximately one hundred yards beyond the west end of the orchard. Ronnie was still attached to a chain behind the tractor. Jimmy's body had multiple stab wounds. Ruben had disappeared.

Hector's parents were devastated with the loss of one son and the disappearance of another. They continued to work, saving all they could while living in the labor camps to help finance their oldest son Enrique's education. When the day came that they were finally able to purchase a run-down, three-room home in Payette, they concentrated all their energy on supporting their oldest son's desire to attend a university and trying desperately to forget.

****

Resentment clouded Elena's countenance. *How could all of this have happened to my family?* she thought. The more she thought about it, the angrier she became. And what of Ruben? What had happened to him? Later that night, after youth conference, she would do some cooking and cleaning for her Grandfather Julio and find out more about what became of her Uncle Ruben. Then her thoughts went again to the haunting image of Uncle Hector's open hand, sinking into the dark current of the Snake River.

The specter of her Uncle Hector's death faded as Elena pulled into the meetinghouse parking lot, exited her car, and walked without enthusiasm toward the back of the building, where chairs had been set up on the lawn for Saturday's final session. Elena was late, as usual, and Erwin Granger, the elderly stake patriarch, had already started speaking. Elena figured even her tardy attendance would count as a "token appearance," and her parents would never know she'd been taking on Ann Langley at the *dojo* instead of attending the morning sessions.

As Elena listened that afternoon, one thing the old patriarch said stuck with her: "It doesn't matter what happens to us in this life. All that matters is how we respond to what happens."

Following Brother Granger's address, time had been set aside for the youth to bear their testimonies. Elena had no intention of saying anything and planned on just waiting it out until she could reasonably leave. But as she sat there, listening to the other youth talk about their faith in the Savior and the love they had for the Church, she actually felt an unusual stirring—something she could not remember feeling before—that somehow warmed her and made her emotional. Brother Granger's remarks seemed to have set the stage for an outpouring of something unexpected and powerful.

Although she had attended church sporadically, Elena had

never experienced anything quite like this. Suddenly, she was actually standing and expressing her feelings, stumbling clumsily from phrase to phrase.

The words came out slowly and with trepidation. "My name's Elena Guzman. I've never done this before. I don't really know what I believe. I only know I feel something really good today—something I've never felt before. That's about it. Thanks." As she sat down, Elena was amazed that she had done it! She felt embarrassed and proud of herself at the same time.

But the thing she had experienced—the curious feeling that made her feel like crying and compelled her to say something—had awakened a strange, new sentiment within her.

CHAPTER THREE
GENESIS OF A DRUG LORD

SAN DIEGO
4:30 SATURDAY AFTERNOON

ELENA DROVE UP Abuelito's driveway with a smirk on her face. Her parents had fallen for it again. They always did. The new tattoo was a sure thing.

Elena was her old self again. *That wasn't really me,* she thought as she reflected back on the youth conference. *I wouldn't have even been there if it hadn't been for the tattoo deal. No way I would have gone otherwise!* After all, the loss of her brother, Miguel, had haunted Elena for the last two years. She had come to doubt God because of that loss.

Still, the memory of that warm feeling as she gathered with the youth and listened to Brother Granger lingered with Elena. Listening to other youth stand and talk about their appreciation for the Lord and for their families caused Elena to consider for the first time the love and devotion her parents had shown her.

As Elena knocked on her grandfather's door, eighty-eight-year-old Julio Guzman used his cane as he moved to the front door. He opened it and grinned happily when he saw who it was.

Once a month, Elena came to Abuelito's house. She cooked his favorite dish, cleaned his house, stayed overnight for a long visit, and then did his laundry the next morning and took him to church if he asked her to. Her grandfather, an old widower in poor health, was a retired immigration attorney who lived five miles away from the meetinghouse and had given up driving several years before.

"Hi, Abuelito!" Elena greeted him warmly and came inside, toting a box of cleaning supplies and laundry detergent. The old man had aged well and still maintained a winning smile and vivid dark brown eyes—eyes that always seemed to twinkle for his granddaughter. As he greeted Elena with a kiss to the forehead, she realized how special he had been to her.

After setting her supplies on the kitchen table, Elena hugged Julio. "How about I make you some of your favorite tacos, and we'll visit, okay?"

Abuelito had always accepted her for what she was: no more, no less. Although he was aware that his granddaughter was prone to live on the edge a little, he loved her just as she was and often expressed that to her.

As Elena prepared the tacos, she reflected again on what Brother Granger said about responding to challenges, about how a person's response to her challenges was more important than the actual challenge. *Whoa!* She thought. *I'm not sure if I buy that.* Her thoughts turned again to her brother and uncle.

Abuelito picked up a worn, leather-bound journal, plopped down on a sofa, and began reading as Elena started cooking.

Elena removed some tortillas from a clay pot she had warmed them in. Next, she began to prepare *tostadas de ceviche,* Abuelito's favorite dish. She tossed in shrimp, crab, tomatoes, onions, and cilantro.

Once the food was ready, Abuelito removed a Bible and a Book of Mormon from the table, along with a leather-bound volume with the words *Historia de la Familia Guzman* engraved upon it. Elena couldn't remember ever eating a meal with Grandfather Julio where he hadn't read from his precious volumes of scripture and family history. He had used this ritual to drive away his loneliness and to fortify his spirit over the years since her grandmother passed away.

As was customary, once they were both seated, Abuelito bowed his head and pronounced a blessing. Then the eating began in earnest. Abuelito craved his granddaughter's tacos and was overjoyed that she'd made so many. After finishing their dessert, Elena asked what she had been anxious to know.

"Abuelito, what happened to Uncle Ruben?"

"Your father never spoke of him?" Abuelito asked.

"Very little," responded Elena. "He always says Ruben's ways are not our ways and sort of leaves it at that. I've got tired of pressing him about it and always getting the same answer. He just doesn't want to talk about it."

Abuelito knew the flames of Elena's curiosity had been fanned. He slowly turned the pages of his leather-bound journal, looked seriously at Elena, closed the journal, and said, "Elena, things weren't right with Ruben. Are you sure you want to hear this?"

"Well, if I don't hear it from you, I never will. Papa just won't talk to me about it . . . or to anyone else, as far as I know."

"He's a prosecuting attorney, Elena. Your Uncle Ruben was a drug lord. What would his life be like if he advertised that he was in contact with a drug lord? He couldn't have a lot to do with Ruben, but you know what? He did stay in touch with him . . . right up until Ruben died." Abuelito's eyes were fixed on his granddaughter's face.

Elena gasped. "He died? When . . . how did that happen? I never heard anything about it."

"Ruben's heart problems started two years ago. He died last year. Your father and I have had contact with Ruben off and on for many years, but we weren't notified of his death until his son, Tito, who now runs his business, called a year ago, to let us know Ruben had been cremated. Your brother, Miguel, met Ruben on his mission in Mexico and also had contact with him and Tito until he was killed.

"It was better that way, with his work, you know, that your father didn't have a lot of contact with Ruben."

There it is again, Elena thought. *Everything centers around Papa's work. It's the prosecutor this and the prosecutor that.* Elena sometimes wished that her father could be a mechanic or a baker.

Abuelito continued. "Your father and Ruben called each other a couple times a year. Your father kept trying to talk Ruben out of the drug trade, and Ruben kept rationalizing that he was too far in to get out. But yes, they knew they were still brothers.

"I think I was in touch with Ruben more than anyone else was. I have written much about him—and many others like friends and family—in this journal. Are you sure you're ready to hear this?

"Abuelito," Elena said. "I'm almost eighteen. I'll be leaving for college soon. I'm ready to hear about Uncle Ruben. I don't care what he did for a living. I just feel I need to know."

Elena paused, thinking.

"I had no idea you had all this history until Papa recently told me. What you told me a few months ago about Uncle Hector's death was hard to accept. It keeps flashing through my mind. When I fought a girl in the *dojo* this morning, I knew she was thinking I was Mexican garbage, just like the Allen brothers regarded Uncle Hector. I've got to learn more about my family. I can handle it."

"You are angry, Elena. You take what happened to your brother, your Uncle Hector, and what other people say to you too far into your heart. You must make peace with yourself. You must go back to church!"

"I understand, Abuelito. But please tell me about Uncle Ruben. Papa won't, so you have to!"

Abuelito opened the journal again while continuing to look into Elena's eyes. He knew at that moment that her intense curiosity eclipsed her anger and confusion—at least for now. He turned to a certain page and began explaining.

"Your Uncle Ruben had two children, your cousins. As I said, one of them, Tito, is now in charge of the Brotherhood. His daughter, Fonseca, joined the Church and also lives in Culiacán. . . ."

* * * *

CULIACÁN, MEXICO
SEPTEMBER 1974

When Ruben returned to Mexico at age twenty-one, it was

not to Ensenada, from where his family had migrated just a few years before. He knew authorities from the United States had issued a warrant for his arrest and had most likely contacted the Mexican police in his hometown for murdering the Allen boys, so he headed for Culiacán in the state of Sinaloa, where he knew people like him could more easily avoid the law.

He had already had a brush with the authorities in Payette. He had stolen jewelry and pawned it for cash. He only eluded incarceration because the orchard foreman had intervened, paid his bail, and promised to take responsibility for him—mainly because Ruben was an excellent worker and because the foreman respected Ruben's parents.

After taking care of Hector's tormentors, he stole the orchard owner's truck and drove it to Las Vegas, where he traded it in for an older model motorcycle. He'd had no problem clearing the Mexican border and traveling down to Culiacán, which was located on the west coast.

The area was known, among other things, for its rich soil that yielded plentiful crops. A knowing smile appeared on Ruben's face. The kinds of crops people grew varied greatly—from wheat and beans to marijuana—and all could be harvested in huge quantities. Ruben knew that his criminal history would follow him to Culiacán and would facilitate his introduction to others who were living outside the law and thriving in that city's criminal element, an environment created by the illegal drug trafficking of marijuana and opium crops.

Ruben rode his motorcycle into the parking area of an old Catholic chapel he remembered from before.

Yes, I remember this place, he thought. *My friend Pepe and I visited here and talked to a lot of people about how easy it was to earn money!*

He smiled faintly at the little downtown chapel that housed the tomb of Jesus Malverde, the patron saint of drug smugglers. Located just across the street from the government palace, the chapel housed two busts of Malverde encased in glass and brick. As a young boy, he recalled hearing a string and horn band playing *corridos*, or ballad songs, glorifying Malverde's exploits as the thief who defied the dictator, Porfiriato Diaz, the same man who

27

disenfranchised so many families from Mexico's economic future. Malverde became the poor man's hero . . . the Mexican Robin Hood, stealing from the rich and giving to the poor until he was hung by the governor of Sinaloa, his body left dangling from the limb of a tree to rot.

Ruben sat on a dilapidated wooden bench to the side of the chapel. *I wish I could see Hector just one more time to apologize for not being there for him before the Allen boys got to him,* he thought.

In his mind's eye, Ruben saw his brother lying prostrate on the ground, face up, the side of his head covered with blood. He thought Hector was dead when he left in pursuit of the Allen boys. The ends of Ruben's lips curled into a grim smile as he recalled how desperate the Allens looked as he first ran over Ronnie with the tractor and then leaped onto Jimmy's back, thrusting his switchblade repeatedly into his fat neck. In his mind, he heard again Ronnie's terrified screams as Ruben chained the boy to the hitch of the tractor and dragged him over the stony ground outside of the orchard until the teenager's screams went silent.

I regret nothing, Ruben told himself. *I'm pleased. I gave them what they gave Hector.* But he knew he had crossed the line . . . and that it would not be so difficult for him to kill again.

The raucous arrival of a wedding party interrupted Ruben's reverie. The bride, wearing an elegant white dress, entered the sanctuary of the chapel and knelt before the shiny bust of Malverde, silently mouthed some words, and departed. She was followed by an elderly woman, short and graying, who had purchased three strings of "sacred" patron saint necklaces from a local vendor in a souvenir shop next to the shrine, and then bowed her head for a couple minutes, whispering quietly, as if in prayer, before leaving.

Ruben thought it strange that people did this. He himself wasn't religious, but he had distinct memories of his father always asking a blessing on their meals and of his mother taking him and his brothers to church each Easter and during the Christmas season in Ensenada to celebrate the "Day of the Virgin of Guadalupe."

From where he sat, Ruben observed through the large, open

doors, three young men get out of a fancy new pickup truck. They each wore glossy snakeskin boots and expensive cowboy hats and among them, they carried a big wreath of flowers, which they placed at the foot of Malverde's image. Ruben heard the tallest one exclaim in Spanish, as he knelt in front of Malverde's image, "Oh, great Jesus Malverde, thank you for the wonderful harvest of our successful run to the north."

Ruben noticed the young man's tribute was just one of many that had been given in recent days, noting that the walls of the chapel were plastered with the names of known drug traffickers or with pictures of other men and other shiny new pickups, all paying tribute for the successes of their "journeys" north.

The taller young man, the one who had placed the wreath, noticed Ruben staring at him. The man was almost six feet tall, lanky, and had black, wavy hair, a dark complexion, and brown eyes. He appeared to be in his mid-twenties. He wore an orange shirt, open at the neck, which revealed a three-quarter-inch scar at the neckline. He was wearing blue jeans and a large silver belt buckle, which featured an ornate engraving of a crocodile.

The young man walked over and stood in front of Ruben. He looked him over for a few moments and then said loudly, "*Hola.* We're celebrating a trip north. Where'd you get that old bike?" He gestured with his head at Ruben's dilapidated old motorcycle. "You need to make some runs north and get you a real bike, like a new Harley."

As he discussed motorcycles with Ruben for a few minutes, it was obvious the Sinaloan was well informed regarding the expensive toys being produced by the American automakers. Ruben wasn't surprised by the man's outspoken nature, having previously observed how open everyone in the city of Culiacán seemed to be about worshipping drug saints and discussing their drug runs.

Ruben eventually said, "I've considered making a few runs myself, but I just got here. I'm the new boy on the block. Is there really anything to all this patron saint stuff?"

The Sinaloan laughed loudly before responding. "Here's how it is, *hermano*," he began. "Around here, people who want to get ahead in life take marijuana and heroin up north for the *gringo*s.

The police here don't care. No one cares. Smugglers come here to ask Malverde for protection before taking their load north. If all goes well, they return and pay the musicians to serenade the bandit, or they place plaques or flowers, like I just did, at the bottom of his bust for 'lighting the way.' *Comprende?*"

"But, when all is said and done, do you really believe Malverde is helping you?" Ruben asked.

"Let's put it this way, my friend. If you go to a regular church here in Culiacán, and you are hungry, and you ask for food, the priest will give you advice. If you come *here* hungry, and ask for food, you'll be given food. What else can I say?" the young man spoke earnestly and with great feeling. The significance of his last statement wasn't lost on Ruben.

The tall Sinaloan stuck out his hand. "My name is Jaime Diaz, but my friends call me *Flaco* because I'm so skinny. What's your name? What brings you to Culiacán?"

Returning the handshake, Ruben introduced himself. "Ruben Guzman. I've been working up north in a town called Payette, Idaho, but migrated there from Ensenada. I had some problems in Idaho. Just barely came into town." Ruben bit his lip, knowing he may have given up too much information. *It's all right*, he reasoned. *He's already admitted to being a drug smuggler. He won't care if I tell him I'm on the run.*

Ruben continued. "I hurt a couple people up there in the orchards and had to get out of there—quickly."

"Did you kill them?" the Sinaloan asked.

Ruben hesitated briefly. "Yes. I killed two guys that killed my little brother." There, it was out. He could think what he wanted.

"Hey, man, good for you! They had it coming. Are you looking for something to do?" Jaime asked.

"Yeah, I could use work."

"Meet me here in three days at ten in the morning, and I'll take you to see *El Crocodillo.* He'll check you out, and if he likes you, he'll line you up with a truck. And before long, you'll be buying your own." Jaime seemed pleased to have found a recruit.

Ruben answered, "I'll be here."

He left Malverde's chapel and found a cheap hotel room where a dinner of a few strips of chicken, beans, and rice were included in the price, along with a Mexican *cerveza*. He drank a few more beers that evening, trying to battle the recollection of the scenes in the orchard, with Hector lying on the ground with blood running down his face. He hated Americans and would never regret killing those first two.

* * * *

Three days later, Ruben arose late, about 9:30 A.M. with a hangover from sitting around doing nothing but drinking beers. He never drank that much around his family and was not used to the aftermath. He had also been visiting a woman. *Why not?* he thought.

I have no family to judge me here. He drank coffee and ate the freshly baked fruit *empanadas*. By the time he finished eating and checked out of the hotel, he barely had time to ride his motorcycle back to Malverde's chapel, where he pulled in just as Flaco drove up in his Ford pickup.

I know drug dealing pays well, but this is something else! Ruben thought as he waved excitedly at his new benefactor, greeting him enthusiastically. "Buenos días, *Paisano*."

"*Buenos días*, Ruben. Let's throw your motorcycle and suitcase in the back, and then we'll go see the Crocodile about putting you to work." As Flaco looked over his muscular new recruit and considered the report his organization had received back from the Payette area regarding Ruben's violent past, he was pleased with his catch. *This guy has got a future with us*, he thought. If Flaco was satisfied, Ruben was doubly gratified with the prospect of lucrative employment.

As Ruben tossed his dusty brown suitcase in the back of Flaco's pickup, he took note of the fine truck bed enclosed by highly polished wooden slats. He and Flaco picked up the dirt-covered motorcycle and heaved it inside. As Ruben climbed into the passenger side of the truck, he thought, *If I can drive one of these, I'll tell these people whatever they want to hear.*

"You like the pickup, *Paisano?* There are several more where this one came from . . . all imported from the United States. We got about five miles to go to the Crocodile's house. I can only drive about thirty in town, but when we get to the outskirts, I can get up to eighty miles per hour in this baby."

Ruben was enthralled with the pickup. The old truck he drove in Payette surely had to be one of the first of its kind ever invented. It topped out at sixty-five miles an hour, but he was more than happy to have it when he had to flee Idaho. It seemed like an eternity before he finally arrived in Las Vegas, where he traded the truck in for his motorcycle. He knew the orchard owner would be upset with his parents because he had stolen it. *Then again*, he thought, *I had no choice. I had to get away, and I needed the money to get the motorcycle. Besides, stealing a truck means nothing compared to murder.*

The ride through downtown Culiacán told the city's story. Hoards of people hauled produce on their backs down the dusty streets for sale in the open markets. In stark contrast, the city's richest citizens wore expensive suits and drove through crowds in their expensive cars. They bought marijuana and opium from the farmers at shamefully low prices and sold the drugs up north at nearly ten times what they paid.

Once Flaco and Ruben crossed over onto Rosales Street, where the open markets were set up, they headed toward a massive old church, which Flaco referred to as "the cathedral."

Flaco became a tour guide. "This church was built in the 1830s, *hermano*. They hold many masses there each day. The people here are very religious, especially the poor. The rich don't go much.

"Still, belief in Malverde has always been very strong, especially among Sinaloa's highland farmers because they are the ones who benefit from the drug crops. Most of the major dealers, like the Crocodile, come from the highlands. Nevertheless, the Crocodile says he will never set foot in any church, not even Malverde's. But he makes some of us take flowers down to Malverde's chapel once in a while. He says he does that just in case there is some truth to the superstitions."

As they wound through the city center, the streets became

increasingly narrower. For the first time, Ruben noticed the several bridges extending out over the Tamazula River.

Flaco carried the conversation. "Culiacán was founded in 1531 by a Spanish captain named Nuno Beltran de Guzman. A relative of yours, perhaps?" he asked with a grin.

"Only if he left me any money," Ruben kidded. "No, I don't have any ancestors in this part of the country, as far as I know. When I was here as a kid, someone told me the famous explorer, Francisco Coronado, left from here to discover all those places in the United States. Is that true?"

"I don't know, *Paisano*," Flaco responded. "But if he did, his expeditions north into Gringo Land weren't nearly as profitable as ours!" Both men laughed loudly. Ruben knew he was going to enjoy his newfound friend but not nearly as much as he anticipated enjoying his future circumstances.

"Why is it so easy for the *narcotraficantes* to operate out of Sinaloa?" Ruben asked casually. He was eager to learn why but didn't want to exhibit undue curiosity.

"It has a lot to with the land itself," replied Flaco. "There are many rivers that flow out of the foothills and through the long valleys and deposit such rich soil. We also have a very warm climate because we're so close to the coast, and this side of the mountains lends itself to a long growing season. Everything grows here—all kinds of fruits and vegetables. Our climate is also perfect for growing marijuana, and lots of it. We harvest it in the fall, bundle it, and store tons of it in sheds where we keep it to meet the *gringo* demand. We also produce a rich opium crop every year that we make into heroin. Marijuana and opium are what we Sinaloans commonly refer to as 'the fruits of the fields.'

"The *gringos* have always liked our marijuana, but they've recently developed a taste for our heroin as well. We are only a two-day drive from the US border, where we have contacts to help us cross without inconvenience. We just give the American *gringos* what they want, *hermano*." Again, Flaco flashed a smile, and Ruben responded in kind.

"Just that easy?" asked Ruben.

"What you must realize, *hermano*, is that drug smuggling in

Mexico began in Sinaloa. Here, smugglers are folk heroes. The narco culture has existed a long time. Malverde, the patron saint, may be the 'religious' side of it, but this new pickup you are sitting in is the real side."

"There is so much wealth around here," Ruben observed. "It looks like drug smuggling is all they do."

"Not true, *hermano*. We have the largest fishing fleet in Mexico and a lot of work in the resort town of Mazatlán down south on the coast. It's just that resort work and commercial fishing don't pay as well. Here, we fish *our* way, and we *always* reel in the big catch." Both men were laughing again as they pulled into a large *hacienda* ranch home on the outskirts of Sinaloa.

CHAPTER FOUR
THE CROCODILE

THE TWO DARK sedans that had followed Elena pulled in to the senior housing development within a couple blocks of the residence of Julio Guzman, Elena's grandfather. They were awaiting the blue van with the SWAT lettering that would be in place sometime that evening, if all went as planned.

* * * *

Jose Jimenez de Calderón was proud of his home. The beautiful stucco-covered house with a reddish-orange tiled roof was encircled by lavish gardens and an orchard with apples and pears that were ready to be harvested. Scores of tomato plants had been picked clean earlier in the summer. There was a stable behind the house with a half-dozen Arabian quarter horses inside and expensive saddles and tack hanging on wood frames. The lawns were immaculately manicured and the edges clipped to perfection. For early fall, the grass was still surprisingly a dark, plush green and obviously well-watered. The servants' quarters extended out from the house, in front of the stables. The corrals for riding and training the horses were ample and well-maintained.

Jimenez de Calderón—known to his subordinates, the law enforcement community, and narcotics peers as *El Crocodillo*—invited Flaco into his parlor. He was wary of the recently arrived "refugee" from up north who Flaco seemed to have recruited so abruptly. After all, different groups of drug traffickers in the area were always trying to infiltrate each others' organizations in an effort to get inside information that might give a fellow competitor an edge in the "market." The Crocodile had been burned before by an informant planted inside his organization and was determined not to let that happen again.

Outside, Rosa, the Crocodile's eighteen-year-old daughter, showed Ruben around the immaculately maintained orchard and the beautiful flower gardens. As they walked, Ruben took note of her trim figure, the long black hair that hung loosely down to her waist, and her fine complexion. He struggled to avoid staring at her, especially since another young male Sinaloan, who wore a large belt buckle with the image of a crocodile similar to Flaco's, kept his eyes glued to the two of them.

"So, Flaco, the young fellow wants work?" the Crocodile asked indifferently as he poured himself another shot of tequila. He always tried to employ at least a dozen traffickers to cover his responsibility for the marijuana shipments to the States. There were other subordinates in his organization who were responsible for the sale and export of the laudanum, heroin, and morphine. That business was currently much more profitable than the marijuana runs. Flaco's responsibility to move the marijuana was less profitable but still vital to the Crocodile's business.

Once Flaco and the Crocodile finished discussing the details regarding some forthcoming marijuana shipments to the States, and after they both consumed several shots of tequila, the conversation shifted again to Ruben, the new recruit.

It was Flaco who brought up Ruben first. "*Jefe*, this man was at the Malverde chapel with only a few pesos in his pocket. He will work hard, and he will work cheap. He's wanted in Idaho for killing two *gringos* who killed his brother. He rode almost all the way down here on that hunk of garbage he calls a motorcycle, and he's hungry for a job. He will not hesitate to do our kind of work in confidence."

The words "our work" struck a sharp note with the Crocodile. Killing and maiming were essentials in gaining power and respect in the community of *narcotraficantes* and were a prerequisite for "our work." The words also implied trust—absolute silence—regarding crimes committed and complete loyalty not only to the boss, but also to others in the organization to whom Ruben would be introduced and with whom he would become affiliated, providing he first proved himself on the street. The Crocodile reminded Flaco of the absolute oath of silence and commitment required of the members of the *Hermandad de Los Ancianos*—The Brotherhood of the Ancients—and that Flaco alone would be held strictly accountable for the performance of anyone he personally recruited into the organization, for whose recruitment the Crocodile would pay a handsome commission.

"*Sí, mi jefe*. I understand the requirements. Ruben Guzman will serve us well. I know you need twelve men, and we have only ten. We need him," Flaco reasoned. Flaco was anxious not only for his commission but also for the manifestation of trust that would be placed in him, upon Ruben's acceptance.

The Crocodile nodded in assent. "Then bring in the young man. We will meet together . . . the three of us."

When Flaco returned from the gardens with Ruben, the Crocodile was standing with three servings of tequila on an expensive silver tray in his hands. He addressed Ruben directly. "*Buenos días*, Ruben. I've heard good things about you."

The Crocodile extended the tequila, which Ruben readily accepted and began sipping. After the boss served Ruben the tequila, he motioned for him to sit down. In a sweeping glance, the Crocodile looked his guest over, noting Ruben was of average build, about five feet nine inches tall, and quite muscular. He had a hardened look, yet he appeared intelligent and inquisitive. Ruben inspired confidence, even with the well-worn and somewhat soiled clothing that made his poverty quite apparent.

Ruben felt swept off his feet by the opulent surroundings he found himself in. While strolling with Rosa outside, he had seen the neatly fenced pasture with the Arabian stallion and the three mares standing in tall grass. The servant's quarters were nicer than any place he had ever lived.

Even more impressive to Ruben was the Crocodile's

appearance. Everything about him spelled money. He wore a full carat diamond ring encased in a gold setting that matched the fillings in two of his teeth. His somewhat corpulent body filled out a silky turquoise shirt and neatly-pressed gabardine trousers, set off with a snakeskin belt bearing the image of a crocodile on a large silver buckle. His waxed mustache was creased upward toward his ears and complemented an ample beard, obviously dyed dark black, the same as his hair. A gold necklace adorned his neck and descended over his shirt, opened in the front, exposing a barrel-chested, hairy torso. His eyes were dark and menacing and seemed to search for some sign of strength or weakness in Ruben.

"So, Ruben, do you have family here?" the boss asked, glaring at the interviewee for an acceptable response.

"In Ensenada, sir. There are some uncles, aunts, and cousins there, but my parents and brother are still in the United States, working in the orchards." Ruben threw the ball back into the boss man's court.

The wealthy man studied the nervous recruit's face for a moment longer and then said, "Ruben, let's get down to business. This is a very lucrative endeavor with few hassles from the police, if we do it right. We take no chances. We tolerate few, if any, mistakes. I am the devil if I am crossed. I demand absolute loyalty, and I give the same to my superiors. Do you understand me, Ruben?" The Crocodile was no longer smiling.

Ruben was surprised with the Crocodile's statement that he had superiors. *This goes beyond him?* he wondered. *Where are the superiors? Who are they? Just how big is this organization? This powerful man has more than anyone I have ever met. Could someone actually own more than this?* Ruben knew instinctively now was not the time to inquire about the structure of the drug trafficking organization he was about to go to work for. No, that was something he might learn about later. For now, he would only listen.

"Yes, sir. I understand one needs discretion to work here. I have that discretion. I can keep confidences."

"What do you know about the drug business in Sinaloa, Ruben?" the big man asked.

"Only what Flaco has told me, sir. I know there is much money to be made in it. I know I must keep my mouth quiet. I know I must work hard. That's all I know, sir."

The Crocodile seemed pleased with Ruben's response and launched into a spiel on the history of drug dealing in Sinaloa. "I tell you, Ruben, Sinaloa is the rose in Mexico's garden! When it comes to the drug business, heroin, marijuana, and coca wine have always been acceptable here for medical treatment. But the *gringos* criminalize drug usage, which has made it even more desirable, which means they pay well for it . . . very well."

The Crocodile saw that Ruben was taking in everything he was saying with widening interest. He continued. "We have been growing our poppies for opium since 1886. As I said, we are the cradle of the biggest drug trafficking activity Mexico has ever known, and our biggest business now is in opium: the mother of heroin and morphine. However, we are also exporting more and more marijuana, another precious fruit of our fields that grows leaves of Yankee dollar bills. Almost all our products go up north to the Americans who thrive on them. We Mexicans don't have near the need the Americans have for the products, and if we did, we could get them from almost any store or shop with no hassle. The *gringos* love that which is illegal, and that's why our businesses flourish." A smile spread over the older man's face as he perceived that Ruben's countenance betrayed his lust for wealth.

The Crocodile continued. "The poor *campesinos*—farmers from the hills here—have made it big, growing and selling our drugs. They've gone from being no more than dirt under the feet of the rich to major figures in our business. Today, you see them wearing the marijuana leaf belts as they go to Jesus Malverde's chapel with their offerings for his assistance in making them rich. *Sí, mi hijo,* the opium and the marijuana have changed the face of our country."

"So that thing about Jesus Malverde is true then? He really is a patron saint?" Ruben asked.

"Of course. His real name was Jesus Juarez Mazo. He was a tailor who began his life as a fugitive after his parents died of hunger. One day a Catholic priest started criticizing our belief about Malverde and said no one becomes a saint by robbing and killing people, as Malverde did, and referred to him as no more than a *bandido*. He even said Malverde was an embarrassment to religion. That priest was found dead the next day in the church."

The Crocodile found great satisfaction in the nodding heads and apparent approval and adoration of Flaco, and he could see that Ruben too was in awe of him. He continued with renewed vigor.

"You'll be helping us run the marijuana crop. We'll furnish you with a nice truck, like Flaco's, where we have built conceal-ment chambers. But even those are really not necessary, since we have so many friends among the border authorities who sympa-thize with us."

Ruben took note of the Crocodile's deep chuckle and wide smile, broadcasting the extent to which he had bribed the border patrol.

Having satisfied himself of Ruben's potential, the big man brought out a beautiful leather binder with the words "Oath and Covenants of the Brotherhood of the Ancients" inscribed upon it and removed a one-page document, containing some ornate handwritten paragraphs with a place for Ruben's name and a line for him to sign near the bottom of the page.

"These are the conditions for employment in the Brotherhood of the Ancients, Ruben. Only if you can live by these conditions, follow them completely, and give us your absolute loyalty, will you come to work for the Crocodile clan of the Brotherhood."

For one brief moment, Ruben wondered if he was in over his head. He had never done anything or signed anything official in his life, except for a driving permit in Idaho. He sensed that what he would be doing for these drug dealers had to be much more than just driving loads of opium and marijuana up north. As he read, the Crocodile watched him intently for his reaction, looking for any expression that might betray fear or lack of commitment. Ruben carefully examined the paper thrust in front of him.

MY COMMITMENT TO
THE BROTHERHOOD OF THE ANCIENTS

I commit myself, without reservation, to the following oaths and covenants:

Upon seeing the word *covenant*, he asked the Crocodile, "What does covenant mean?"

"It is a promise," the older man answered.

Ruben continued reading.

I vow that I will never, under any circumstance, reveal the identity of any member of the Brotherhood to anyone outside of our organization and that I will protect all members in whatever adverse circumstances they find themselves, even if they have committed murder.

I vow that I will take every opportunity to enrich the Brotherhood any way that I can.

I will always turn the proceeds of my work over to the head of my clan, knowing I will be recompensed later.

I will report anyone within the clan who is stealing assets of the Brotherhood but will never speak of it outside the clan.

I will not hesitate to eliminate those who stand in the way of enriching the Brotherhood. I will consider murder, trafficking the fruits of our fields, theft of the assets of our competitors, and other actions deemed criminal by the outside world, merely tools of our trade.

I am willing to accept an official name for my business documents and an unofficial street name by which I will be known that are both different from my true name in order to obscure my identity and to protect the integrity of the Brotherhood.

I will recognize the importance and discretion of certain secret words and signs that I will be given in order to deflect curiosity and investigative interests from outside our organization.

I vow never to steal from the proceeds of the Brotherhood or to, in any way, convert those proceeds to my own use or to maliciously betray the interests of any member of our organization.

I understand that in the event I'm guilty of violating any of the aforementioned oaths and covenants, I will be tried by other members of the Brotherhood either in action or pronouncement and may face consequences of death.

Signed: _____

"What do you say, Ruben? Can I trust you?" The Crocodile waited for Ruben's response.

Feeling a rush of excitement at being invited to join such an enterprise, Ruben quickly answered, "Yes, sir. I will be loyal." He signed the paper and turned it back over to the Crocodile, who counter-signed it, dated it, and placed it back inside the leather brief with a grunt of satisfaction.

"You will start immediately," the boss exclaimed. "You will work with Flaco for two weeks. You do what he says. Then, after two weeks, if you do well, you will be loaned a pickup somewhat like Flaco's for your own use. Flaco, you'll need to take him to get some decent clothes. When we deliver our product, Ruben, we cannot look like tramps. The young man outside in the gardens, 'Negro' Flores, who is engaged to my daughter, Rosa, will issue you a handgun and instruct you on how to use it, just in case. You never know when you may need it. He'll also give you your document for driving to use in your travels, with your official name: Rosario Martinez."

Suddenly Ruben looked up, appearing jolted, thinking, *How can this man change my name and my identity at his will? He already knew I would take the job and do as he wished.* Then he laughed inwardly, realizing that for what he would surely be paid, it would all be worth it.

"And my code name?"

"You will be known to all of us in the Brotherhood as *El Martillo,* or, 'the Hammer.'" Ruben smiled, expressing his pleasure with the new nickname. *A hammer represents strength and power,* he thought. He was thinking again of the Allen brothers and the way he had successfully employed that power to avenge Hector's death.

"I understand, sir. I like it," Ruben answered without hesitation. "And the pay, sir?"

"One tenth of what you receive, upon delivery, and all your expenses."

Not knowing exactly how that might translate into pesos or dollars, Ruben was still astonished. He was used to thinking about money in terms of the pittance he had been able to earn in the orchards.

"*Gracias, señor.* I will please you." Ruben smiled at his new benefactor.

"Two more things, Ruben," the Crocodile said. "You will wear the silver buckle we all wear with the image of a crocodile, and you will stay away from Rosa. As I said before, she is spoken for and will one day marry Negro Flores."

Ruben was astonished at how well his new boss could read his mind. *He must have seen me staring at her outside during our walk,* he thought.

"That will never be a problem with me, *señor.* I promise you." Ruben had broken many promises in the past. Breaking another would not make a difference. He shook his new employer's hand and accompanied Flaco out of the Crocodile's mansion, smiling profusely.

* * * *

Abuelito looked at Elena again, knowing she was hanging on to his every word. "That's how Ruben got started into the drug business."

"What happened next, Abuelito?"

Abuelito continued . . .

* * * *

CULIACÁN, MEXICO
1979

By the Crocodile's sixtieth birthday, he was less and less involved in administering the affairs of the Brotherhood, having turned increasingly more responsibility over to Ruben.

In the five years since joining the Crocodile's clan, Ruben replaced Flaco Diaz as the primary recruiter and became the boss's main henchman and confidant. Ruben became more energized, especially with the encouragement of the Crocodile's daughter, Rosa, who became infatuated with him, even though she was promised to Negro Flores.

Flores was aware of the budding relationship and considered arranging an "accident" for Ruben but knew the Crocodile would surely figure it out. Since Ruben had worked his way into the boss man's confidence and trust, Negro knew if he reacted aggressively toward Ruben, his lucrative work with the Brotherhood would be over.

Flaco and Negro, feeling disenfranchised from their prior places of prominence in the Brotherhood, now conspired against Ruben, feeling assured they could somehow get revenge after he usurped their positions of confidence with the boss. They were equally wrought with anger toward the Crocodile and his organization. Indeed, they had developed a technique for skimming off the sales of marijuana and opium.

When the "transporters" they supervised turned over their receipts from trips north, the two men pocketed up to twenty percent of the profit from each trip and deposited it into a joint account they had opened in a bank in a neighboring city using false names. Their plan was to stockpile enough cash from their embezzling to eventually break off from the Brotherhood and start their own drug trafficking organization. The money would go toward purchasing pickups, providing border bribes, and hiring transporters to buy marijuana, cocaine, and opium plants from local farmers and run them north.

Eventually, Negro was caught keeping the receipts on a load of opium . . . a load never reported to the boss or to Ruben. He was eventually brought before five men from the Brotherhood, including Ruben and the Crocodile. He was ordered to sit down at the end of a splendid oak table in a fine leather upholstered chair. As he sat, he mentally recalled the words from a contract he had signed many years before, words that now seared his conscious like a hot knife.

I vow never to steal the proceeds of the Brotherhood or to, in any way, convert those proceeds to my own use or to maliciously betray the interests of any member of our organization.

Beads of sweat broke out on Negro's face when he noticed the Crocodile glaring at him . . . the same man who, just a few years before, had gladly agreed to give him the hand of his daughter.

The Crocodile presented the evidence against Negro. He then looked at him and stated contemptuously, "Negro, you have disappointed me. You had a good income . . . all you would ever need and more. I had even promised you my daughter's hand . . . and still you would steal from me!"

Negro's stomach surged up into his throat. It was as if he'd lost his voice. He could not utter one word in his own defense. Instead, his entire ability to think or speak was sucked away by the recollection of another devastating statement in the oath he had signed with the Brotherhood.

I understand that in the event I'm found guilty of violating any of the aforementioned oaths and covenants, I will be tried by other members of the Brotherhood either in action or pronouncement and may face consequences of death.

As the Crocodile asked the next question, still glowering menacingly at him, Negro was so gripped with fear that he felt his chest begin to tighten and knew he was about to vomit.

"How do you respond to this, Negro?" the Boss thundered. To the accused thief, the Crocodile's voice seemed to reverberate through a vacuum . . . echoing through his conscience, as if from some faraway place. Again, Negro could not begin to articulate a response.

Negro slightly discerned the Crocodile nodding at Ruben, who arose from his seat and disappeared. Again, he heard the boss man ask, "Will you not say anything in your defense?" Negro again felt his stomach tightening, as if it had been placed in a vice with some unknown power turning the handle, securing him in its grip.

Suddenly, he felt his feet lift off the floor. He thrust his hands upward to resist another sensation of tightening that eclipsed even the tightening he had felt in his stomach. Ruben tightened the leather cord around the guilty man's neck more and more, until, eyes bulging and mouth agape, Negro slumped to the floor, lifeless.

That evening, Flaco was advised by one of the men who had attended Negro's "trial" that Negro had been executed for skimming profits and that records he had kept were being reviewed by the Crocodile to determine exactly how much money had been stolen from him.

Flaco paled, knowing his name was in those records along with Negro's. He quickly packed up, withdrew the funds he and Negro had accumulated in the bank, and moved to a remote part of Sinaloa, where he assumed a false identity and hoped he could safely hide.

By settling the score with Negro Flores personally upon the Crocodile's request, Ruben had not only proven his complete loyalty to the boss and his willingness to execute upon demand, but he had also become first in line for Rosa's hand. The couple was married within a month of Negro's death. Following a sumptuous wedding feast hosted by the Crocodile and his wife, Marta, Ruben and Rosa honeymooned lavishly in Mazatlán.

****

Now Elena was even more frustrated that her father had never told her about her uncles, Ruben and Hector. Abuelito sensed this and broke into her train of thought.

"Don't feel badly toward your father, *mi hija*. He thought you had too much to worry about with the challenges you have had as a family. He didn't think it would help you to know that your uncle was a drug lord and that your other uncle committed suicide. I'm telling you all this in truth because you asked, and because I am too old to start lying."

Elena was about to learn even more regarding her Uncle Ruben's nemesis, El Gordo Diaz, as Abuelito continued the account from his journal . . .

****

The Crocodile learned of Flaco Diaz's involvement in the profit-skimming scheme within two days of Negro's execution, and he was still infuriated at Flaco Diaz's duplicity. He ordered an intense search for Flaco, hoping to handle his disloyalty as he had Negro Flores's, but Flaco couldn't be found. After six weeks of searching for the defector, the hunt was discontinued, though the matter was never far from the boss's mind.

As Flaco Diaz fled from one hiding place to another to avoid detection by the Crocodile's men, he never recovered from being ousted from prominence in the Brotherhood for stealing profits. When he discovered that it was Ruben Guzman who reported Flaco's stealing, Flaco vowed to even the score. *After all,* he reasoned, *I was the one who found poor Guzman on the street with a broken-down motorbike and less than ten pesos in his pocket. He had nothing! I was the one who introduced him to the Crocodile, got him a job, new clothes, and his own pickup. Then I make one little mistake and he reports me, and I have to run. All those years of loyalty to the boss mean nothing. Someday I'll get even. Some day!* Flaco was seething inside.

Flaco knew the drug business inside and out from working for the Crocodile. He had been the Brotherhood's major recruiter for five years before he met Ruben Guzman. He had connections. He knew who could be bribed at the border and who would buy the opium and marijuana. He knew how to avoid risks and who would distribute the product efficiently in the States.

I don't need the Brotherhood, Flaco thought. *I'll start my own organization, and I'll run the Brotherhood into the ground!* But he needed help, so he started recruiting drivers and transporters to distribute the drugs to the ever-present North American wholesalers.

In just a few months, Flaco had assembled a sufficient number of men to organize his new cartel. His minions hungered for fast wages, flashy clothes, and new pickups. They would go to any length to get them. Their goal was to capture the life style that Flaco lavishly flaunted in front of them. Soon Flaco had put together his own band of bloodthirsty drug traffickers who referred to themselves as the Vultures.

Eventually, the Vultures took a rare step forward that other drug traffickers had not dared to attempt. They recruited American street gangs in San Diego, Los Angeles, and several other border cities to distribute their drugs and collect money. The Vultures' use of American gangs to "enforce" their interests in the United States became a major step forward in importing Mexican violence over the border.

Flaco and his gang tried to compete with the Brotherhood for the marijuana trade but were always too shortsighted to overtake them in the profits arena. Whenever possible, Flaco recruited members of the Brotherhood, who revealed some of the secrets of his competitors, giving him an edge. Those opportunities, however, were rare, and his obsession and jealousy only increased. For Flaco and the members of his cartel, violence was always the clear remedy for satisfying their goals. They threatened those who didn't pay up for their drugs with physical intimidation, never hesitating to break arms and legs when certain parties needed to be "persuaded."

Flaco Diaz dropped dead from a heart attack while sport fishing out of Mazatlán, and his son, twenty-two-year-old Horacio Diaz, took over. Unlike his skinny father, Horacio was a gargantuan man known as El Gordo. He had a degree in business science from a college in Mexico City, where he had whiled away his time eating at fancy restaurants and indulging his lusts in the local brothels, all at his father's expense. Lethargic and sluggish in nature, he had no interest in physical pursuits that might require exerting himself, but he had a brilliant mind for accounting, investment, and finance. His ability to invest the profits from the Vultures' trips north enabled them to become stronger under his leadership and more competitive in the drug trade than the organization had been under his father.

Under El Gordo, through their ruthlessness, the Vultures had become one of the most profitable cartels in the Sinaloa province but were still surpassed by the Brotherhood.

The Vultures were not successful in overtaking the Brotherhood in the very competitive marijuana traffic but became highly successful in dealing methamphetamine. Meth was growing in popularity; addicts were willing to sacrifice even their physical appearance for the high this artificial narcotic could produce. El Gordo established a contact in China who could acquire ephedra, the primary precursor for meth, at a huge discount.

Once the profit from dealing meth began supplementing their more meager, but still ample, income from marijuana, the Vulture organization was on the fast track to immense wealth.

For El Gordo and his traffickers, supported by a cadre of American gangs including the "Mexican Mafia" and "MS-13," it was not uncommon to assassinate public officials who stood in their way or to murder and subsequently decapitate their competitors.

Their goal was always to leave a gory reminder to anyone who might resist them. Human life meant nothing to El Gordo and his men. Drug profits were their god and little else mattered.

* * * *

The Crocodile had been dead for three years—a victim of his lavish eating and drinking—and Ruben was now the undisputed new leader of the clan, still referred to as the Crocodile clan of the Brotherhood of the Ancients out of respect for its original leader. The clan was now by far the most powerful clan in the Brotherhood. They had taken over the marijuana traffic to the north from three of the other clans that failed because of inner strife and breaches of trust. The leader of the combined clans of the Brotherhood, Kishke Maldonado, designated Ruben as his chief confidant because of all the contacts Ruben had developed within the Mexican police, the Mexican army, and the border authorities.

Kishke introduced Ruben to the North American drug outlets, with whom Ruben had been unable to negotiate without Kishke's authority. But Kishke was sixty-five years old and spoke of retiring as the leader of the Brotherhood in order to enjoy his life of luxury and to spend more time with his grandchildren at the family horse ranch near Mazatlán. Ruben, with his control over more than half of the Brotherhood's business, was now the obvious choice to replace Kishke Maldonado as the head of the Brotherhood, which he did in 1994, when all the clans in the Brotherhood consolidated for extra power and protection under the leadership of Ruben Guzman, "the Hammer."

Ruben's business had grown immensely. He had become known as the most efficient of all the drug lords in Sinaloa and one of the most successful, if not the most successful, drug trafficker in Mexico. His wife, Rosa, was a socialite who involved herself in all the charities for raising funds for the poor and every other activity that would deflect any criticism from the community because of her husband's involvement in the drug trade. But this was Sinaloa, where everyone who was anyone would have nothing derogatory to say about the source of another's income.

Compared to his obscure beginnings, Ruben was indeed

CHAPTER FIVE
LIGHTNING STRIKES

SAN DIEGO
7:10 SATURDAY EVENING

AURELIO SOSA BURIED his face by reading a newspaper, occasionally peering over the top at the old man's front door. Federico Valdez sat in the passenger seat, training a pair of high-powered binoculars on the pretty young woman who had stood up in front of the gathering of youth earlier that afternoon. Now she set about preparing a simple meal for her grandfather. Federico questioned why someone like her would have to go through what he knew she would by the end of the day.

Federico Valdez's well-contoured frame and chiseled facial features seemed in conflict with his scraggly beard and the long unkempt hair hanging down to his shoulders. The leather jacket, black T-shirt, and well-worn faded Levis, although clean and well fitted, still didn't compensate for the bad hair—both front and back. Federico's status as a "snitch" could justify his dressing down to fit in more easily with the Vultures, but that had nothing to do with it. He didn't need justification. He just didn't like shaving and couldn't care less who took any issue with that.

For Federico, abducting a helpless girl was not his idea of shameless employment. Being an informant for the Brotherhood of the Ancients, a competitive cartel that had infiltrated the Vultures, had its drawbacks. It was work that offered limited choices of assignment. His task was to obtain useful information for the

Brotherhood and report back—nothing more, nothing less.

If he had been a reflective man, Federico might have looked back at his own personal train-wreck of a life. Reared in a dysfunctional family with parents who condoned using drugs in their home and brothers who preferred abusing that privilege, Federico had always come up short on self-esteem. Although he never personally felt the need or the desire for drugs and alcohol, he *had* experimented with them, but only once.

The one party Federico went to when he was seventeen provided lines of cocaine available for twenty dollars a hit. A friend had also bought him his first beers that night. With his thinking clouded by the alcohol, he forked up his half of the twenty dollars for the drug and shared it with his friend. That was when the police showed up.

With a drug arrest on his record by the age of twenty, combined with a lot of muscle packed onto a six-foot frame, Federico was easy pickings for recruitment into a street gang and subsequently a drug cartel. The Brotherhood had come calling. *Why not?* he thought. *I have a record anyway. Who else would want me?* But deep down, a life of crime was never what he really wanted.

As one committed to physical discipline, working out regularly, and eventually getting in some college, Federico knew there was more to life . . . a lot more. But the money the Brotherhood offered him tipped the scales in favor of abandoning his idealism, at least temporarily.

Federico sighed as he contemplated his own circumstances. His work provided a decent income with which he could maintain his own apartment and a life away from his two older brothers, both drug addicts who still lived at home, much to the chagrin of their parents, who were struggling to eke out a living from farming a small plot of ground outside of Culiacán.

Federico felt fortunate to be employed by the Brotherhood, who, for some reason unknown to him, were much less inclined toward intimidation, violence, and murder than most Mexican drug traffickers. Their *modus operandi* had changed from an organization whose members engaged in murder and mayhem under the leadership of two iron-fisted men known as the Crocodile and the Hammer, to an organization that had softened in temperament. Few of its members knew exactly what brought about that transformation. However, Federico had heard a story of a young man named Miguel who had visited the Hammer and his family as a missionary years before and left a book the cartel men referred to as "Miguel's Holy Book." He heard that book had left a deep and lasting impression on the Hammer's family and had marked a new era in the way the Brotherhood did business.

Federico's thoughts returned to the young woman who was about to be abducted. He needed to know more about her. "So why does the boss want this girl, Aurelio?" he asked the man behind the steering wheel.

"I can't say much," came the response from Aurelio Sosa. "It is touchy business. I can only say it's to help his sons, who are in jail in San Diego." Aurelio was resolute in his commitment to hedge on the motives for the forthcoming abduction. Aurelio's comment made Federico's ears perk up. The boss's sons were picked up and incarcerated in San Diego a few days before. However, this was the first information Federico had heard linking the girl's abduction with the boss's sons.

"So she will be a ransom hostage?" Federico asked.

"I have told you enough!" Aurelio responded angrily. Federico shut up. He knew he was pushing it and that asking more questions would jeopardize his role as a cartel operative. He felt bad for the girl; she was no more than a pawn in the boss's plan. He hoped since she would be used for ransom that she would not be mistreated, but knowing some of the men in the Vulture group, he knew it was likely a vain hope.

Federico Valdez learned earlier that morning from another Vulture operative that the girl's name was Elena and that she was the daughter of the Vultures' nemesis: Prosecutor Enrique Guzman. He was unaware, however, that the Vultures were going after her for ransom for the boss's sons. Planted inside as an informant, he was only given second-hand information on a limited basis. At least, now he knew why Elena Guzman was being abducted.

The Vultures trafficked marijuana and meth into the United

States, mainly through Tijuana and into the San Diego area. Federico knew that wresting away some of the marijuana business from the Brotherhood was high on the Vultures' priority list, primarily because of long-standing contentions between the leaders of the two cartels. The Brotherhood was aware the Vultures were trying to take over their marijuana distributorships in the United States, so whatever intelligence Federico Valdez could pass back to the Brotherhood regarding the activities of the Vultures was all the better.

Aurelio Sosa's cell phone rang, and he pressed the button on the steering wheel that automatically answered the call. "Hello, what do you want?"

"*Ay, hombre! Qué pasa?*" The voice seemed irritated and bored from a long wait.

Aurelio looked again at the old man's home. "We don't know. We've had our eye on the girl all day. Earlier she gave a speech at the church, and it looked like it she was in tears."

"*Caramba*, man! What you mean she was in tears? Did she see you guys? She saw you, didn't she, and she told everyone about you. Right?" The voice was malevolent and shrill.

"No, *jefe*. She wasn't the only one crying. Many stood up, and they all cried! Those *Mormones* are strange people. Why don't they just go to mass?"

"You keep your eyes on that girl, you hear? If you lose her, we lose our leverage, and El Gordo will not appreciate you. You understand?"

"No problem . . . We will not lose her . . . Take it easy, okay?" Aurelio looked at Federico with a panicked expression. "Benito says if we lose her, we're dead! You can see her clearly, right, Federico?"

"I see her," Federico responded, putting down his binoculars. "She is sitting down now. And they are praying over the meal." Federico was fascinated with this young woman. Being only twenty years old himself, he was not far removed in age from the girl he was spying on. *I wish that just once in my life, I could feel whatever it is that she felt this afternoon,* he thought. Deep down, Federico wanted something better. Although his choice of employer, namely, a drug cartel, would cast suspicion upon his own motives, there was something in him that made him detest the way he lived.

* * * *

Elena and Abuelito had just sprinkled lime juice over their food when the peaceful atmosphere was shattered by a loud thud and the sound of splintering wood as the front door was kicked in. A man with a greased face dressed in green camouflage and carrying a semi-automatic rifle burst into the house. His expression was menacing and unyielding.

Unseen by Elena or her grandfather, several other men with blackened faces piled out of the back of the SWAT van parked behind the two dark-colored vehicles. They ran toward Julio's front door along with five more men in camouflage, all armed with pistols and rifles. Shocked neighbors stared helplessly from their front yards.

Julio Guzman struggled to push himself up from the table and yelled "Elena. . . . run! Run fast!" He then turned to face the intruders and pled softly, "Please! Don't!" as Elena fled out the back door. He raised his cane in futile defense as bullets shredded his body. The old man fell back onto a side table, where his precious and now blood-spattered scriptures and leather-bound family history lay, before falling heavily to the floor.

As Elena ran back into the kitchen to escape through the back door, two uniformed men grabbed her and dragged her toward the van. Spanish expletives filled the air as they forced her inside the vehicle. Elena fought back, clawing one of the men's faces, until blood streamed down his left cheek. When Eduardo Ramirez realized he was bleeding, he swore loudly, stepped back, and wiped off the blood. Infuriated, he hit Elena in the face with his fist, knocking her unconscious. She fell down onto the floor of the van.

To the neighbors, nothing was more unexpected than the bursts of rifle fire emanating from the old man's house. When the neighbors observed a blue police van with the words San Diego Police Department and the initials SWAT on it, they went inside, locked their doors, and rolled down their blinds.

Had Julio Guzman, the old man whose home had been invaded by police, fooled everyone all these years? Had he been corroborating with terrorists? Or worse yet, had he been a pedophile or some other kind of derelict? The events of the evening made no sense at all to those who knew him.

Few people in this quiet retirement neighborhood really knew one another that well, but when gunfire was heard and a young girl observed being dragged out of the house and forced into the blue SWAT van, curious eyes peered through their blinds, assessing the situation from the safety net of their homes, while others dialed the authorities.

One of the abductors, Benjamin Soto, yelled at the man who struck the girl. "You fool, Eduardo! Wait until the boss hears that you have roughed her up. Her father will want pictures of her before he will ever meet our demands. Now she'll have a bruise and maybe a black eye."

Ramirez gingerly wiped at his bleeding cheek. "Why would you complain about violence, Benjamin? You, of all people! You were the one that insisted we shoot the old man!"

"*Estúpido,*" Benjamin yelled. "You know the boss doesn't care who we shoot. He just wanted the girl in one piece . . . *comprende?* That means without black eyes or missing teeth!"

Soto and Ramirez both had such a propensity for violence that normally neither would have given a second thought to shooting an unarmed old man or beating up a woman. But this was different. The girl was to provide a ransom for El Gordo's sons. Ramirez knew he was in trouble.

Federico and Aurelio watched as Elena was thrown in the back of the SWAT van. Upon entering the house, Federico was sickened by the sight of the elderly man lying in a pool of blood. Next to him on the floor were two books—one that looked like a Bible, and another that looked like a journal—covered with blood splatters.

Feeling ashamed, Federico resolved that he would never be like the cowards who killed an old man and abducted a helpless girl. He turned and walked back to the car, where Aurelio was on the phone with the boss. As they pulled away, Federico took note of the mailbox. The name immediately captured his attention: "Julio Guzman."

The six men in SWAT uniforms left in the van with Elena and followed the two dark-colored sedans to a warehouse several miles away, where they stashed all three vehicles. There they transferred Elena, who was still unconscious, to another nondescript sedan and headed toward the Mexican border, south on Interstate 5.

CHAPTER SIX
THE AFTERSHOCK

WITHIN TEN MINUTES of the abduction, the San Diego Police Department had responded to the emergency calls regarding the shooting at Julio Guzman's residence and immediately began interviewing the neighbors about what they witnessed. When the *real* police department arrived, the neighbors' shock and confusion doubled. The police cordoned off the area to protect evidence of the crime scene. The county coroner arrived and conducted an examination of Mr. Guzman's body while the police took photographs and collected brass from spent bullets.

The FBI also responded after receiving reports that a neighbor had observed Elena being dragged across the backyard, struck in the face, and thrown into the back of a van.

Mark Madden, the regional coordinator of Homeland Security for the area, arrived on the scene. Mark was Enrique Guzman's best friend and professional associate. Elena had always referred to Mark as "Uncle Mark" or "Uncle FBI," since he had previously been a special agent with the FBI.

Enrique Guzman and Mark Madden were trademark names in the Southern California law enforcement community. Prosecutor Guzman was a slight man with a full head of salt-and-pepper hair that framed a dark Hispanic face. His hawkish eyes conveyed an aggressive demeanor. He had retired from the United States

Attorney's Office in San Diego but had been asked to return temporarily because of his effectiveness, his reputation as a no-nonsense prosecutor, and his intimate knowledge of the cartels. Law enforcement authorities and politicians in Southern California, Texas, and Arizona were desperate to eliminate the increasing cartel threat operating along America's southern border.

After his retirement from the FBI, Mark Madden was also requested to return to duty to coordinate the efforts of Homeland Security with the FBI's ongoing efforts to subdue the cartels. In his sixties, Mark was a big man with an athletic build. He had fine, chiseled features topped with a white mane of hair.

As an active FBI agent, Mark had specialized in investigating violent crimes by the drug cartels. But because he had no idea that the leader of the Vultures had sons in the San Diego County Jail, he was finding it difficult to determine the motive for Julio's death and Elena's abduction.

Elena's parents were attending a conference, completely unaware of the tragedy waiting for them at home. Enrique spent the day advising a group of government officials regarding the imminent threat of border violence from drug traffickers in Southern California. Mark had attended the same seminar but had been called out early on a pressing matter. When he was notified of Julio Guzman's murder, Mark ordered his dispatcher to send someone to the conference center to notify Enrique of his father's murder and that Elena had been kidnapped.

The messenger found the Guzmans where they were meeting with Enrique's boss, Shad Bennington, the United States Attorney. Devastated by the news, the Guzmans arrived at the crime scene within an hour of being notified. Mark Madden was there waiting.

Enrique stood silently, watching the ambulance that pulled away, carrying the remains of his father's body. He felt Mark's arm grasp his shoulders as Belinda held his hand firmly. Spasms of audible moaning shook him. Mark searched for words of comfort but couldn't find the right ones.

Enrique and Mark both had always known their roles in fighting and prosecuting drug lords could potentially affect their families. Both men always hoped and prayed that neither they nor their families would ever have to deal with the consequences of their relentless war on drugs. But its evil had always managed to find a way into their lives.

When the police finished their investigation and gathered all potential evidence, the FBI conducted their own inventory. It appeared the assailants had left no fingerprints. They found no hair or fabric fibers. There were twelve brass casings of .223 caliber rounds, 5.56 millimeter in dimension, possibly fired from at least one Colt AR-15 rifle. The police coroner would later find several matching rounds in Julio Guzman's upper torso. The FBI obtained a blood sample near the driveway adjacent to the back door, which was preserved as DNA evidence.

Once Julio's blood-spattered scriptures and leather-bound family history had been photographed, Enrique personally assumed custody of his father's treasured volumes. Enrique recognized the journal as one that had previously belonged to his son Miguel, who had maintained it during his mission to Mexico. After Miguel was killed, Enrique had given it to his father, who was a devout record keeper. Julio chose to add the Guzman family history to Miguel's writings as a way of honoring Miguel subsequent to his death. Enrique reflected on the irony of his father adorning his life's most prized possessions with his own blood.

None of the witnesses had any idea where the kidnappers took Elena. The SWAT van had headed out of the neighborhood from Julio's cul-de-sac, followed by two dark sedans and a silver vehicle. Since the men were all speaking in Spanish, no one had understood anything being said. The witnesses had a hard time offering helpful physical descriptions since the men were all dressed alike and had similar appearances.

Police cars and FBI vehicles were dispatched in all directions from the residence with descriptions of the SWAT team impersonators and their vehicles, while dispatches went out to all police vehicles with the information gleaned from the crime scene. All FBI offices in Southern California were put on high alert.

Mark loved Enrique and Belinda and asked himself how these good friends were able to endure their trials. Losing their son,

Miguel and his wife three years before was ultra-traumatic and now, this. Mark knew that his friends' faith and conviction in the principle of eternal families was the only thing holding them together just then.

Mark had never been at such a loss for words. He was a leader in the Church and had presided over many funerals and subsequently counseled the grieving. As a career FBI man, he had seen a vast amount of human suffering and pain. But this was different. Enrique and Belinda were almost like his own flesh and blood.

Words simply wouldn't cut it.

Mark's wife, Katie, drove up, ran from her car, and joined the three gathered in front of Julio's house. She hugged Belinda and cried with her. Over the years, as a result of their husbands' involvement in the cartel wars along the borders in Southern California, Katie and Belinda had become the best of friends. They had often comforted each other when anonymous threats arrived on their phones and in their mailboxes. Sometimes they found inflammatory messages tacked on their front doors. Messages from the cartels were always the same: "Back off, or else!"

In his capacity as an FBI agent, before becoming involved with Homeland Security, Mark received numerous threats, but unlike Enrique's family, the threats had never materialized.

Finally at midnight, after all the investigators departed the crime scene, the Maddens accompanied Enrique and Belinda back into the house, and the two couples knelt together in prayer, as they had done so many times before when their children had special challenges or when the two men embarked on dangerous assignments. They prayed for comfort and understanding and for the inspiration to find Elena safe. Then they hugged each other again and parted ways.

Meanwhile, kidnappers drove Elena, bound and gagged, further and further south, deep into the heart of Mexico.

CHAPTER SEVEN
THE MADDEN/GUZMAN CONNECTION

SAN DIEGO
1:15 SUNDAY MORNING, SEPTEMBER 26, 2010

"BELINDA, DEAR, PLEASE come to bed," Enrique pled. "It's past one in the morning." His wife stood motionless, staring out the window, a look of resignation and despair clouding her face.

"Please, dear," he continued. "You've just taken your sedative. Go to sleep and try to rest. Come on now." Enrique guided Belinda to the bed, helped her lie down, and covered her with blankets.

"We've lost her, haven't we, Enrique? We've lost her just like we did our Miguel. And now they've killed Papa Julio! They want to destroy us all, don't they?" Enrique could see that Belinda was on the verge of surrendering to hysteria.

"No, Belinda. We haven't lost Elena. We've prayed for her. Tomorrow, I'll meet with the strike force, and we'll find her. As for Papa, well, my father was eighty-eight years old. He lived a long and wonderful life. He didn't have to suffer a prolonged illness. He's back with Mama. So, everything is okay, my love. Just rest for now, Belinda. Please!"

Enrique sat on the bed at Belinda's side until he noticed her eyelids drooping. Tears forming under his glasses, he kissed his wife softly on the forehead, turned off the bedside lamp, and walked into the living room. There, exhausted and emotionally drained, he slumped down on the couch. Unable to even consider sleep, he opened his father's leather-bound family history, and, in an effort to escape the storm of sorrow sweeping over him, he began thumbing through it.

As he read, his thoughts wandered. *I've always known that going after the cartels could result in something like this, yet I was so aggressive. The same thing happened with our son and his wife . . . all because of my involvement with the strike force!* Enrique continued questioning himself, doubting the merits of his commitment to stop the cartels. *Would Elena still be here if I had slowed down? Would my father still be alive?*

Elena's pleading face, crying for help, kept flashing in Enrique's mind. He knew she was depending on him and on "Uncle Mark" to come for her. He turned again to his father's journal. Reading it would perhaps help him circumvent the agony. As he fought off sleep and read about how he and Mark's families had come together, he felt slightly comforted. Mark was the one friend he knew he could count on.

As Enrique read, he discovered the brief account of a chance meeting between Julio and Harley Madden, Mark's father, in Idaho's Sawtooth Mountains many years before. On an elk-hunting trip, both men had simultaneously shot at a big six-point bull from opposite directions, unaware of each other's presence. Rather than argue about who got it, Julio and Harley had cleaned and skinned it together, split it in half, and spent that evening feasting on elk steaks and swapping hunting stories. The men became best friends and from that point on, their families were like one.

Harley Madden was a lean, leather-faced man who looked much older than the years he had lived. Since he was seventeen years old, he had made a living by dinging out fenders and painting cars. Meeting Julio Guzman at the site of the elk kill when they were in their late forties was still one of the major highlights of his life.

Harley worked on Julio's vehicles when they needed it. In return, Julio helped plant, prune, and harvest fruit trees for Harley. They and their families had both ended up in the Clairemont

Mesa area of San Diego, California. Their sons, Enrique and Mark, even went to the same college. Enrique's father, Julio, was a skinny, but agile Hispanic man who had been a laborer all his life and devoted all his energy and resources to his family. Since migrating from Mexico to Payette, Idaho, to work in the orchards, then to San Diego, he had become fluent enough in English. He loved maintaining his journal.

The two men, Julio and Harley, were both hardcore baseball fans. As a younger man, Harley had broken several knuckles playing pick-up baseball games wherever he could find them. Enrique remembered coming home from school and hearing them argue good-naturedly about which team was best: the St. Louis Cardinals or the New York Yankees.

"I'll tell you, Harley, it won't be as easy for the Cards this year, no matter what you may want to think!" Julio went on. "They say the Yankees have signed a couple of heavy hitters that turned out this spring. Not only can they hit the ball, but the talk is that they can really scoot around the bases too." Julio was impassioned in his reasoning, but he knew Harley wasn't convinced.

"You know, Julio," Harley retorted, "you Hispanics have a rare quality of stretching your imagination. They say the same thing about those Yanks every year and what does it get them? They're overpaid and overrated. It's what happens at the end of the season that counts. So don't get carried away!"

Harley was okay with Julio and his wife being Mormons. The young missionaries had come to his door several times, and he always let them in and even fed them a couple times. Though he was impressed by their zeal and sincerity, their unusual beliefs just never quite took hold—not to mention he didn't want to give up his pipe and coffee. *But if Julio chooses to believe that, then more power to him,* Harley often thought.

As Enrique searched for consolation, he ran across another memory in the journal of a camping trip he and Mark had been on with Harley Madden.

**** **

"Harley the Hunter" stories ran rampant in the family. To

young men like Mark and Enrique, Harley was comparable to Daniel Boone or Davy Crockett. The young admirers knew Harley had probably spent more nights sleeping under the stars than under a roof. They also knew he had shot more deer and elk than they had seen in their lifetimes. The best part about Harley the Hunter was that he always invited Mark and his friends to camp with him, even when they were older.

The year before he died, Harley took Mark and Enrique, who were then in their thirties, on a fishing trip to the town of his birth, Ketchum, Idaho. They drove a few miles up the Wood River, just north of town. After the three men rigged their fishing rods with treble-hooked wedding ring spinners with night crawlers hanging from them, the rainbow trout went wild. Harley and the younger men caught their limits by dusk.

Enrique built a camp fire while Mark pitched the tent and Harley prepared dinner. Before long, Harley was dipping trout filets in his special "Madden's Batter," a mixture of flour laced with his trademark seasoning, and dropping them into a wide frying pan with a half cube of butter sizzling in it. The trout filets, browned perfectly on both sides, captivated everyone's taste buds. If that weren't enough, Harley added some Idaho spud hash browns fried up with just enough green onions for extra flavor. It was a meal that in Harley's words, "was enough to make your tongue slap your brains out!"

Harley fed the two younger men until they were ready to burst and then announced it was time for dessert. Fitting a heavy leather glove onto his right hand, he carefully scraped the coals off the lid of a Dutch oven he had buried in the camp fire. When he removed the lid, the aroma of a well-browned apple cobbler, smothered with a walnut-cinnamon glaze, permeated the crisp mountain air, filling the camp with the tantalizing aroma of a bakery.

Next, Harley shuffled over to his old station wagon, opened the rear door, and removed a cooler. Inside, the wooden bucket Harley used for churning vanilla ice cream was packed with dry ice.

"Dad, you've outdone yourself," Mark said. "It smells amazing!"

"Well, come on over here," Harley said, "and you can do more than smell it."

As the older man ladled out the heavenly, creamy white treat into bowls of warm apple cobbler, the three of them were all convinced that they had died and gone to heaven.

"Well, whaddaya think, fellas? Was that some real fishin' or what?" Harley was grinning wide. Mark and Enrique agreed enthusiastically.

Harley went on. "And how about those eats? Was that enough to keep body and soul together?"

Enrique asked, "Mr. Madden, do those trout always bite like that?" Out of respect, Enrique still referred to Harley as "Mr. Madden."

"Of course not, Enrique! They only take the hook if the worm agrees to it. And I have a way of persuading them to do that," Harley said, his face stone-faced serious.

Both Enrique and Mark looked at Harley wide-eyed. Finally, Mark broke the silence. "Sure, Dad."

"Fellas, it all boils down to knowing your way around the outdoors. You just pick up certain things, like knowing how to bugle a five-point bull elk down off a high ridge with a flute-a-phone—you know, the kind you learn music with in the fourth grade—or how to make really good flapjacks, like the ones I'll make you in the morning." He waited for a response.

"What are flapjacks, Mr. Madden?" Enrique asked, still frustrated at hearing an English word he was unfamiliar with.

"Hotcakes. You know, pancakes. There's a certain way to cook them so they taste just right. It comes down to waiting till there's twenty-six bubbles before you turn them. Then you slip them off that griddle thirty seconds later. You just learn things like that, fellas, but it takes a man a little time." Harley began coughing from deep down in his chest where the ever-present pain was.

"Are you okay, Dad?" Mark asked.

"Oh, sure," he wheezed. "It just comes with age. Anyway, that's the story on the flapjacks."

"Mr. Madden, we need to do this a lot more often," Enrique said.

"Well, that's something we need to talk about a little, fellas. There won't be a whole lot left for you to do with me, me havin' this chest pain and all. But I sure hope you'll keep up the tradition. A man should spend sufficient time in the woods to keep his mind clear. Huntin' and fishin' seem to be the right medicine for most things that ail you. Did you know that before I was married, I used to spend lots of time in the mountains near here prospecting?"

"That's the same as mining, like for gold and silver, right, Mr. Madden?" asked Enrique. Although Enrique had lived in the United States since he was eighteen, some words still needed explanation.

"Right. I had a claim up Warm Springs Creek, just this side of the Dollar Hide Summit, about twenty-five miles from Ketchum. And I want to tell you a little about that. I had tunneled into a mountain, digging for lead and silver ore. I was in about seventy-five feet, where I had reinforced the mineshaft with Hemlock wood posts every so many feet. I figured it was pretty secure." Harley went quiet suddenly as a lump formed in his throat. He even seemed a little teary-eyed.

Mark asked, "What's wrong, Dad?"

"Nothing, fellas. Nothing really. I was just remembering this feeling I had . . . like nothing I had ever felt before."

"What kind of feeling?" Mark asked.

"It was a feeling that I needed to get out of there. But it was more than that. I felt like something was grasping me by the shoulder, leading me right out of that tunnel. It wasn't a strong push—it was pretty gentle—but it was there, and I just had to follow what I felt."

"What happened?" both Mark and Enrique asked simultaneously.

"Well, no sooner had I got out than the whole tunnel caved in!"

Mark had never heard his father tell that story, and he and Enrique listened intently, wide-eyed.

"Yeah, I was saved by something, or someone. I've thought about it ever since. Why? Why me? All I know is there was a reason I had to live, and I have felt it must have something to do with my family. Like I had to live so my family could be here on the earth. Now, you both know I've never been a churchgoer, but I have gone some to different churches. Some say there are people who only go to church on three occasions in their lives—when they are 'hatched,' 'matched,' and 'dispatched.' I've done a little better than that. Doris and I used to go to the Mormons' church sometimes. Occasionally, when I was in their church, I felt the same thing I felt that day in the tunnel. I'm glad you boys joined up with them when you were in college."

Mark and Enrique looked at each other, no doubt pondering their own conversions."

"Well," Harley said, pulling them away from their thoughts, "let's see who can eat the most of this cobbler and ice cream."

That was one of Harley Madden's last outings. The strong heart that had taken him through so many decades of tracking deer and elk in the Sawtooth Mountains finally gave out at the age of sixty-six.

And now, just two years later, Julio Guzman was dead. Prior to their passing, the two men always joked about there being baseball in heaven. They found evidence of that in the first verse of the Bible, where, according to them, it says, "In the *big inning* . . . " The only part they couldn't agree on was whether there would be more Cardinal or Yankee uniforms up there.

CHAPTER EIGHT
SOUTH INTO MEXICO

SOMEWHERE IN MEXICO
2:00 SUNDAY MORNING

AS THE DARK sedan came to a sudden halt, Elena's head was thrown forward, causing it to hang down over the backseat, where she lay on her back with bent knees. Nausea swept over her from deep down. Suddenly, she was awake, feeling the need to vomit. She had no idea where she was or who she was with.

Elena's captors had transported her from San Diego through the San Ysidro, California, border checkpoint and into a huge warehouse just north of Tijuana on the US side of the border. There they met the gatekeeper of the cartel controlling the Tijuana Plaza and paid him the going rate for use of their tunnel, which was one thousand dollars total for the four vehicles in the motorcade. Elena's captors had passed through before repeatedly with guns and drugs, paying the obligatory fee of $500 per arms shipment or the $10,000-per-million value of illegal drugs. The Vulture operatives didn't consider for one moment trying to evade paying the gatekeeper, realizing he was second in authority only to the cartel leader.

The tunnel was an unbelievable engineering accomplishment, traversing one-quarter mile underground into Tijuana, Mexico. It went seventy-five feet underground, was eight feet high, and had a concrete floor. There were lighting and ventilation systems and drainage capacity built in. It was this tunnel and forty more similar to it that made the newly constructed fence between Tijuana and the United States irrelevant.

After entering into Mexico at about 8:30 the night before, the group had traveled several hours into Mexico, first heading east then south toward the Sinaloa Province. Elena remained medicated and unconscious, unaware of her circumstances. Eventually the sedan she was in pulled up in front of a safe house.

A burst of cool air swept in as the back door of the vehicle was swung open by a large Hispanic man wearing an ominous expression. The drugs had a hallucinatory effect on Elena, and as two Mexican women approached her, their blurry figures appeared more ghostly than human, and to Elena, they made sounds that were barely audible and indiscernible.

Forcing herself to sit up in the back seat, Elena struggled to focus her vision, trying to comprehend what she was seeing. On the street there were two little cars, toy cars, with little miniature drivers, racing down the street next to her. They drove in front of a house that was spinning around on its foundation. The silhouettes entering the house were also spinning . . . in a direction out from the house.

Next, Elena noticed other silhouettes leaving another car parked next to the one she was in, a green one. It too was spinning and was connected to the house by a line of figures moving from the house to the car. Another little car, a red toy car, came into view as it headed toward her.

Now the kaleidoscopic images of the ghost silhouettes and toy cars appeared as a giant caterpillar coming out of the center hub of the house, spinning even faster. More cars were pulling up with more silhouettes, and even more caterpillars radiated out from the hub of the house.

Elena was fascinated with the toy cars and got out of the car on the street side to pick up the little red one coming toward her. As she reached out to cradle it in the palm of her hand, a big man's arm clutched her by the elbow and yanked her back into the car, cursing her in Spanish, calling her a crazy *gringa,* and telling everyone how he had saved her from being run over.

With no idea where she was or who was with her, Elena was

steadied by the two Mexican women, as she wobbled into the small stucco house. She plopped down onto a sofa and was given two tablets and a glass of water. Parched for lack of fluid, she drank deeply and swallowed the medication. The woman who gave her the water placed a plate in front of her with rice, beans, and fried fish. Elena ate ravenously. Whatever drug she had been given had triggered overwhelming hunger and thirst within her. She ate until she was full and then dozed off on the sofa.

When Elena awoke, it was 3:00 A.M., and she could see and think more clearly. The room was occupied by the two Mexican women—one in her forties and the other a teenager, possibly fifteen or sixteen years old. Both stared at her curiously. There was also a kindly looking middle-aged man who Elena assumed was the husband and father. Elena's first impulse was to scream as the events surrounding her grandfather's death and her abduction cascaded back into her memory. She tried to ask the occupants of the house where she was, but couldn't speak due to her swollen tongue.

Two men opened the door and walked into the living area where everyone was seated. She remembered her kidnappers calling one of the men Eduardo. He had hit her . . . hard! Her lips creased into a snarl as she glared at her attacker.

"It's time! We've got a long ways to go," said Ramirez. "Is she ready?"

"No!" answered the older woman. "We still haven't injected her. She just woke up. It would be dangerous to make her travel again without more rest . . . especially after her concussion and the heavy drugs you gave her."

The man accompanying Ramirez, Benjamin Soto, chimed in. "See, *estúpido,* I told you! You messed her up! If the nurse," signaling toward the older female, "hadn't been around to dress her head wound and feed her and demand we let her rest, she might be dead. You're lucky El Gordo is at the bar eating and drinking and didn't see her when she was swollen and bleeding."

"So did you tell him who hit her, *idiota?*" Ramirez asked. "Did the little bird sing?" Ramirez was always chiding Soto about being short.

Suddenly, a cool breeze blew into the house as a gargantuan

fat man lurched through the front door. Well over three hundred pounds, El Gordo stood in the doorway with sweat running down over his puffy, inebriated face. "Let's go! Pay the people and get her out of here," he growled without looking directly at Elena. Ramirez breathed a sigh of relief when he realized El Gordo had not taken note of Elena's swollen face.

El Gordo staggered toward the door and took one last glance over his shoulder, yelling, "I said *now!*" As his jowls quivered with anger, he added, "I've already heard about you, Ramirez, and I'll deal with you later! You better pray the little *gringa* survives the trip!" Then the boss stumbled out the door.

Still extremely weak, Elena took a mental photo of the huge man while looking directly into his puffy, reddened eyes. She knew she would never forget his face.

As the nurse injected her with a long needle, Elena had no strength to resist. She faded slowly away into another long slumber. Minutes later, she was dozing in the back seat of the same dark sedan . . . heading ever south.

★★★★

Three hours had passed since Elena was medicated for the second time. It was now light outside, and she wanted to sit up and figure out where she was, but she was afraid if her captors noticed she was awake, they would drug her again. Whatever she'd been injected with, the drugs had not had the same effect. There was no nausea, no sensation of spinning, and no confusing motion. The nurse at the safe house knew just how much medication she needed, unlike the abductors who had so recklessly injected her before.

By the substance of the conversation between the driver and the big man in the passenger seat, Elena knew she was deep into Mexico, headed toward some kind of training camp or staging area. She soon learned that the two men were involved in drug trafficking as well. They spoke freely, unaware that Elena was awake and that she understood Spanish. Elena still struggled to understand why they needed her.

Elena noticed the sedan was ascending into a hilly area and

eventually observed some terrain covered with green trees that resembled pine. Negative thoughts permeated her thinking. *I'm too far away! How will anyone ever find me?* Tears began pooling in her eyes. Fear was taking over.

Elena was softening. She knew now, more than ever, how much she valued her parents' nurturing and their care giving that she had always considered too restrictive. She regretted resenting her father and his work as a prosecutor. She understood it wasn't fair that she had rebelled against him for going after the low-lives like those who had taken her. She had blamed her father for her brother's death. The image of Miguel's car bursting into flames flashed in again. *I have to put this away! I just have to!* Elena thought. *It wasn't Papa's fault.*

The tears flowed freely, but she continued listening intently to the two men.

"How long have El Gordo's sons been in jail?" the driver asked.

"Eight days, they say," replied the man in the passenger seat. "And they say there will be no bail until after the preliminary hearing because they are a flight risk. With El Gordo's wealth, they are afraid he will put up the bond, and his sons will leave San Diego and hide in Mexico."

The driver responded, "The boss—he has some stupid sons, eh?"

Both men chuckled as they continued down the road.

When the sedan eventually came to a stop many miles later, Elena realized the car had pulled into a gas station. As the driver got out to fuel the vehicle, she heard him complain to the attendant that the pumps were not activated. She also noticed another dark blue sedan pull up at an adjacent pump. A young man with an athletic build got out and glanced over toward her. She heard the other man in the passenger seat of their car call him "Federico." She was not impressed with Federico's shaggy appearance.

The attendant, who had just arrived and had barely unlocked the front door, advised the men that the owner had the keys to activate the pumps, but would not arrive until 6:30 A.M.—twenty minutes later. Elena heard two other cars drive up, and by the animated conversation that followed, she realized they were all part of the same group.

Suddenly she heard the voice of the boss, the man they called El Gordo.

"Okay, *hombre,* open up the pumps and give us gas!" El Gordo yelled. "Now, you hear? Quickly! We have a long ways to go and we are hungry and tired!" The boss was adamant.

"But, *Señor,*" responded the nervous attendant, an elderly man, dressed poorly, but smiling humbly, "You see, the *dueño* is not here yet, but he will be in just a few minutes."

The fat man seemed insulted. "Didn't you hear me, *Paisano?* I know you have a way to do it. Give us gas! Now!"

"But, *Señor,*" came the pleading response, "I would not lie to you. I have no keys to the pumps. My boss, the owner, he will be here any minute. I promise you!" The old man had taken on a frightened countenance.

The next words terrified Elena.

"No, *Señor.* Please! No! Please, *Señor!*"

A shot rang out. Elena heard the attendant gasp before his body hit the ground. Next came the boss's voice, barking out with chilling effect, "That is the only bullet I will waste on this one. Take the gas!"

A second shot was heard. The lock had been breached and the pumps activated. As she lay with her head down on the backseat and her eyes closed, Elena heard the stolen gas gurgling down into the tank.

As they pulled away, Elena envisioned the scene behind her with the elderly man lying dead on the ground, next to the gas pumps. She was terrified. She now knew more than ever the nature of the men she was dealing with—especially the fat one. As she remained silent and still in the backseat, she silently petitioned the Lord to help her.

****

7:30 SUNDAY MORNING

As Federico and Aurelio drove down the highway following

the sedan that Elena was in, Federico pondered the name Julio Guzman.

Federico looked over at Aurelio. "Hey, *hombre*. Tell me something. The name on the old man's mailbox was Julio Guzman. The chief strike force prosecutor is a Guzman . . . Enrique Guzman, right?"

"Right," responded Aurelio, somewhat reluctantly.

"So if this girl was staying with the old man, she would be some kind of relative, like a niece or granddaughter, right?"

Aurelio refused to answer.

Federico continued. "So this girl is being held as ransom for the boss's sons, right?

"You are far too nosey for your own good, Federico!" came Aurelio's response. "And don't tell anyone I said that."

Federico had seen how Elena was staggering and stumbling as she was whisked into the nurse's home. He knew she had been sedated far too heavily by men who knew nothing about administering medication. He had witnessed her almost being run over by a red car.

Federico also saw El Gordo gun down the elderly gas attendant. The Vulture boss's total disregard for human life sickened him. There was nothing about the fat man that Federico could respect.

He knew he needed to sneak off to a phone at the next gas stop. He had much to report to Tito Guzman, leader of the Brotherhood. Federico was sure Tito knew of Elena. He'd be angry that she had fallen into the hands of the Vultures. Federico determined to keep a close eye on the girl in the coming days.

Even in her subdued and distraught condition, there was something about the young woman that charmed Federico. She knew little, if anything, about what was happening around her, and this fear of the unknown must have stripped her of any pretense by now. The one time he had seen her on her feet, she held her head high even while staggering.

The bloodstains on Elena's white blouse served as another brutal reminder of the Vultures' nature. There was no discipline, no temperance. They indulged themselves in whatever atrocities pleased them. They had no moral compass and no parameters when it came to violence and physical gratification. *It all starts with their boss,* he thought. *It all starts with* El Gordo.

Federico looked over at Aurelio again, who still insisted on driving, even though his head was drooping over the wheel.

"What makes this business so easy?" Federico asked. "I mean, in just a few weeks, fourteen- to sixteen-year-old kids have made almost a dozen drug runs up north into *gringo* Land, and next thing you know, they own the pickup, have all the spending money they want, and walk around with a swagger like grown men, acting like they own the place."

"The *gringo*s up north make it easy for them, Federico. They want what we deliver. They love the fruits of the fields: the marijuana, the opium, and the cocaine. The US border is like Swiss cheese—there are holes everywhere. We have contacts with the border people who gladly accept bribe money. Sure, some get caught and we lose a few loads, but that is just a business expense. The boss doesn't care what happens to those kids. They are expendable. There are always many more waiting, anxious to make the big money."

Federico responded. "I know the loads I have taken were very easy. At first I thought the bribe money was such a huge amount, but it's nothing compared to what the Americans pay for the drugs. And now that their government has moved so many agents from the southern border, it's even easier to move our products. Why do you think they're doing that?"

"I have heard it is for political reasons," responded Aurelio. "Apparently the American leaders want more of our people across their borders—thousands, even tens of thousands more—so they can get all the Mexican votes possible. They would even make them legal citizens to get the votes. I have heard the people in power now think that the Mexican vote will keep them in power forever. That's what I hear, anyway."

"Strange people, those *Americanos,*" replied Federico. "Don't they realize that our people who cross over without papers are helping us distribute our products up there?"

"They don't care," Aurelio said. "The *estúpidos* think that all the illegal people are doing is going after jobs that the *gringos* don't want anyway—you know, like picking fruit and working in hotels. So many American employers like paying them low wages. Farmers and ranchers pay our people less than half what they pay Americans for the same jobs. It's all the better for them."

Federico marveled once again that the way he made his living, like so many of his people, was dependent upon the insatiable appetites of the Americans.

CHAPTER NINE
ENRIQUE'S SOUL SEARCHING

SAN DIEGO
7:15 SUNDAY MORNING

THE PHONE ON the end table next to Enrique rang. It was Mark Madden.

"Hey, I was just thinking about you, friend!" Enrique half whispered into the phone.

"Enrique, how are you doing, brother? Get any sleep?" Mark asked.

"I didn't sleep at all. I was reading our family history." Enrique awaited Mark's response.

"*Our* family history, Enrique?"

"You need to see it, brother. My father wrote our histories—yours and mine—like it was one big story, like we were all one family. He added it all to Miguel's missionary journal. And he wrote a lot. With Elena gone, that was all I had to hang on to during the night. Belinda is still knocked out. I dread watching her wake up only to realize that our daughter is still missing." Enrique fell silent.

Mark responded, feeling the hurt for his best friend. "We have nothing so far on Elena. The lieutenant at the police department wants us to meet over there with the strike force at ten o'clock. Is that okay with you?"

"Absolutely," Enrique responded. "I'll plan on being there most of the day."

"See you at ten, Enrique. Hang tough, okay?"

"Right, Mark. Thanks."

Enrique checked on Belinda and saw she was still sound asleep from the medication. He went to the kitchen and poured himself a glass of milk, spread jam over some wheat toast, and sat back down next to the end table where he had placed the Guzman journal. As he ate his toast, he continued reading, this time reflecting back on his own life . . .

★★★★

SAN DIEGO
1972

After two years in Idaho, the Guzmans moved to San Diego, where Julio had been promised work as a foreman in the orchards. Harley Madden had purchased part interest in a paint and body shop there and had converted the Guzmans to the idea of joining them in the sunny country.

After two years at the University of Idaho, Enrique went home to San Diego for spring break. It was then that he and his parents met a pair of Mormon missionaries. Six weeks later, they joined The Church of Jesus Christ of Latter-day Saints. Enrique and his best friend, Mark Madden, transferred to Brigham Young University, where Enrique eventually attended law school.

At the end of his first year at BYU, Enrique submitted his papers to serve a mission and was called to the Church's Bolivia La Paz Mission.

Not only did he have a successful mission, but while in Bolivia, Enrique gained a conviction of the need to stop the drug lords, who were capitalizing on the production of coca leaves. He witnessed the brazen, overt nature of the cocaine production in that country, with poor farmers being paid twenty times as much for producing a bushel of coca leaves as they were for growing a bushel of corn. The coca leaves were sent to Colombia to make paste that would be processed into cocaine. His experience as a missionary not only provided Enrique with a firm foundation for his testimony and eventually Church leadership, but it also cemented his conviction to join in the war against drugs one day.

When Enrique returned from his mission, he completed his undergraduate work at Brigham Young University, where he met his future bride, Belinda Hernandez, from Quito, Ecuador.

Enrique graduated near the top of his class from law school. When he was thirty-five, he applied for and received an appointment as an Assistant United States Attorney in San Diego. His boss, US Attorney Shad Bennington had a reputation for being a hard-nosed prosecutor willing to go out on a limb when it came to the identification and prosecution of drug cartels. He was delighted to have a new bilingual assistant who wanted to join his drug interdiction campaign.

For years, Enrique hammered the cartels mercilessly, while Mark Madden did the same with the FBI in San Diego.

In 2008, the roof caved in on Enrique and Belinda Guzman for the first time when his twenty-two-year-old son, Miguel, and his wife were murdered by the Vultures.

Enrique was near retirement at the time and had been receiving an unusually high number of death threats from the Vultures, telling him to back off. Drug cartels had just started hiring members of street gangs in Los Angeles and San Diego to enforce payments and monitor and protect distribution sites on the US-side of the border. Over the course of his career as a narcotics prosecutor, Enrique had put so many of them away that the cartels weren't so much at war with the United States Attorney's Office as they were with Enrique Guzman himself. Enrique was a threat, and he had to be stopped.

After Mark Madden's squad of FBI narcotics investigators successfully identified the assailants who killed Miguel and his wife, they eventually found them in Mexico with the aid of their legal attaché office in Mexico City. Arrangements were made for their extradition to the United States, where Shad Bennington personally prosecuted them for drug trafficking. They were sentenced to prison for twenty years. He subsequently assisted the San Diego County Attorney in convicting the men with homicide. They received life sentences to run consecutively with the federal sentences.

Still, Enrique anxiously awaited the day when the warrant would be issued for the arrest of the man responsible for killing his son . . . El Gordo Diaz, head of the Vulture cartel.

Enrique accepted any case from any agency that arrested suspects affiliated with any of the cartels and their drug-trafficking activities. If the case had any merit at all, Enrique or his assistants would prosecute it. His name was known in every province of Mexico and among the membership of every drug cartel. He sent trafficker after trafficker to prison and made the drug lords pay heavily for their crimes. Enrique Guzman was a constant irritation and threat to them.

When Enrique reached retirement age, he was granted a special extension due to his preeminence as a prosecutor. Now he was fifty-seven, and he still worked ten to twelve hours a day tucking drug traffickers away into all kinds of jail cells.

Glancing at the clock, Enrique realized it was time to get ready for his meeting with Mark and the other officers at the San Diego Police Department. As he closed the journal a note fell out. The blood drained from Enrique's face as he read the words written in Spanish.

> *We have your daughter at a place in Mexico where she is safe and where she will be treated well, as long as you cooperate.*
>
> *Within the past months, you have put all your energy into pursuing and prosecuting us. You have singled our organization out from all the others. You are encouraging your FBI and DEA to pay informants within our organization in an attempt to turn against us, which is in strict violation of sacred oaths and covenants of loyalty we have made to one another.*
>
> *You are holding six of our people in the San Diego County Jail who were arrested last week and who are awaiting arraignment in your federal courts.*
>
> *You have one week to free them and deliver them to us. They names are Pedro and Lorenzo Diaz, Emilio Blanco, Pedro Huerta, Jaime Cruz, and Francisco Gonzalez.*
>
> *You will bring them in a San Diego County van to the San*

Ysidro checkpoint at midnight next Wednesday. Only your driver will accompany them. We guarantee him safe passage. The driver will cross two miles into Mexico along the Interstate, where we will have a dark brown van waiting. There we will exchange your daughter, unharmed, for the six men. If other vehicles or aircraft follow, we will kill your daughter.

Do not underestimate our determination.

—The Vultures

Enrique swallowed hard and dropped the note in his briefcase. He dressed, kissed Belinda good-bye, and headed to his meeting. Determination outlasted his desperation. Enrique Guzman had lost a son and a father to this riff-raff. He would die before losing his daughter too.

En route to the strike force meeting, Enrique picked up his cell phone and punched in a number in Culiacán, Mexico, that he had rarely called since his brother, Ruben, had died a year before.

CHAPTER TEN
THE MISSIONARY

SAN DIEGO
7:45 SUNDAY MORNING

AT TWENTY-NINE years old, Tito Guzman was the youngest drug lord to ever lead the Brotherhood, but there was no doubt he was the most prepared of all his predecessors. His father, Ruben, had made sure he received a higher education, which included a law degree from Stanford University.

When Tito received a frantic telephone call from his faraway uncle, he assured Enrique he would do everything in his power to locate Elena. Ending the call, Tito put down the phone and remembered the circumstances that first brought him and his cousin Miguel together . . .

* * * *

SAN DIEGO
JUNE 2004

The Spirit of God like a fire is burning!
The latter-day glory begins to come forth;
The visions and blessings of old are returning,
And angels are coming to visit the earth.
We'll sing and we'll shout with the armies of heaven,
Hosanna, hosanna to God and the Lamb!
Let glory to them in the highest be given,
Henceforth and forever, Amen and Amen!

The congregation sang the hymn with commitment and zeal. Enrique and Belinda Guzman had anticipated their son Miguel's mission farewell for years. They always hoped their son could serve a mission to Mexico and contact some of their relatives. Miguel's fluency in Spanish and unshakable faith would serve him well.

"I'm proud to be able to take the message of the gospel back to Mexico, the land of my ancestors," Miguel testified sincerely. He looked directly at his friends from many other faiths who were present. "It is my great desire that all of you here may know as I know that this church is true and that the message I'm taking to Mexico is not just for Mexicans."

Miguel was soon on the streets of Mexico, preaching the gospel.

In the fall of 2005, Miguel conducted the baptismal interview of an elderly man who operated a motel near the old Jesus Malverde chapel. The old gentleman, Jose Quintaro, now in his sixties, had listened to the missionaries, obtained a testimony of the Book of Mormon, and was seeking membership.

After the interview with Elder Guzman, Jose stared at him intensely and remarked, "Elder, you bear a remarkable resemblance to a young fellow who came here many years ago." He looked off into the distance, past Elder Guzman and his companion. "He was riding an old motorcycle. I think his name was Guzman as well, but I can't remember for sure. He said he had come all the way from Idaho, where he had worked in the orchards." The wrinkled man paused, trying to collect his thoughts before continuing. "He had to leave Idaho quickly . . . something serious had happened to his younger brother. He only stayed here a couple nights and then got a job with a group of drug runners . . . The Brotherhood. You . . . you look very much like him."

Miguel was excited. "Brother Quintaro, I have an uncle I have never met. He returned to Mexico after my other uncle took his own life. He never contacted my father, probably because he was in serious trouble with the authorities and didn't want to be tracked. My father lost contact him. Have you seen him since?" Elder Guzman asked.

"Not really, but I have heard of him. Many people in his

situation find themselves working with the *narcotraficantes*. So," he said in an attempt to bring humor to the conversation, "he may be a drug dealer, but he's probably very, very rich." The old man flashed a toothless grin.

Elder Guzman completed the interview, wished Brother Quintaro well, and left.

The next morning, before returning to Mexico City, Elder Guzman and his companion went to the local police department and inquired after the location for Ruben Guzman without success. The police had no record of anyone in the clan. The two missionaries thanked the officer and departed.

Shortly thereafter, one of the Crocodile clan's contacts at the police department called Ruben, advising him that a Mormon by the name of Miguel Guzman, the son of an Enrique Guzman who had lived in Payette, Idaho, had come to the police asking questions about the location of his uncle—a man named Ruben Guzman.

Ruben ordered that Miguel and his companion be tailed back to Mexico City and his address verified.

★ ★ ★ ★

One week later a chauffeur-driven automobile pulled into the mission headquarters of The Church of Jesus Christ of Latter-day Saints in Mexico City. The driver remained in the vehicle as Ruben Guzman, dressed in a blue blazer, yellow silk shirt open at the neck, sporting ample amounts of gold jewelry, and wearing expensive sun glasses, stepped out, brushed off his coat, and entered the office.

The elderly mission secretary stood and walked up to the counter. "May I help you?" she asked the visitor, who was gazing curiously at the pictures of Jesus Christ on one side of the office and the Quorum of Twelve Apostles on the other, which hung next to the picture of an elderly, distinguished-looking man.

"Who is this man?" Ruben asked.

"His name is President Gordon B. Hinckley. He is the president and prophet of our church," came the response.

"Prophet? What is a prophet?"

"He is the leader of our church, who receives the word of God for us, just as the prophets Jeremiah or Isaiah in the Bible."

Ruben recalled his parents reading something about a man named Isaiah to him and his brothers when they were little. *Oh,* he thought, *so this is what my nephew does. He talks about prophets!*

"Is there something I can do for you?" the lady asked.

"Yes, I've come to visit with an Elder Guzman. Is he available?"

"He's actually meeting with our mission president. I'll tell him you are here. May I have your name?" she asked.

"Ruben Guzman," he answered. Ruben realized that was the first time he had used his true name in public for some time. It felt good—much better than using the name Rosario Martinez to sign documents and letters in the drug trade.

"Excellent, Mr. Guzman. Please have a seat. He'll be with you very shortly." Ruben sat down and picked up a copy of a strange looking magazine written in Spanish, entitled *Liahona.* As he skimmed through the pages, he was impressed with the many pictures of Jesus and of a building labeled the "Salt Lake Temple." He wondered how this strange American religion could have such a foothold in Mexico. He had observed a few Mormon missionaries as he had traveled throughout Mexico, but he could not figure out how this young man, who was being referred to as "Elder Guzman," who was probably his own nephew, could have become a missionary, nor could he understand how he could be called "elder" at such a young age. His interest was truly piqued, and he had to know how all this had come about. Even more than that, he needed to establish some contact with his family after more than a quarter of a century.

Suddenly, an office door opened, and a slight but handsome young man wearing a pair of suit pants and a white shirt and tie walked out. At first, Ruben thought he was seeing a shadow of the young man that he had been several decades before. Another young man about the same age followed his nephew out of the office. His name tag read "Elder Jones." He was taller and stockier than Elder Guzman. Ruben rose, stepped toward Miguel, and offered his hand, which Miguel took and began shaking vigorously. Elder

Guzman spoke first. "I'm pretty sure that I'm your nephew, Uncle Ruben, at least according to an old man who rented you a room years and years ago."

Ruben extended his arms and exclaimed excitedly "What a pleasure! My own flesh and blood." He hugged Miguel tightly. "Let me look at you. You have something of your father, yes, but you look more like your uncle." Ruben was smiling contentedly.

"But the police had no record of you, Uncle! Brother Quintaro told me you'd gone into business with the drug industry. I know in Sinaloa it is an acceptable way to make a living for many people. I don't condone it, but I don't condemn you for it either. I hope you understand." Miguel was eager to know he hadn't offended his newly-found relative.

"Nephew, everyone in Culiacán knows what I do. I have good friends in the police department who know what I do. In fact, they helped me find you. I'm a very wealthy man who, like many others, have made their fortunes with the fruits of the field. No one interferes with my business. I give many people employment, and I bring much wealth into the community of Culiacán. You have not given me offense. I'm glad that you are bold and that you say what you mean. Your father, Enrique, my older brother, was always like that." Ruben seemed sincere.

Elder Jones, Miguel's companion, was blown away. *Drug business? Fruits of the field? Friends in the police department?* His mind went through question after question as he sat in the mission office. He decided this was the most interesting conversation he had witnessed in his whole life. He watched in amazement as his companion spoke with one of the most powerful drug lords in Mexico.

Ruben continued. "Your father, is he well? Your Uncle Hector and I were always so proud of him for wanting to go to college. Did he become an attorney like he'd hoped to?"

Miguel could tell that his uncle was intensely interested in his family. That pleased him. Although he knew his uncle had the blood of those two boys in Idaho on his hands and that he had probably committed additional crimes since then, Miguel resolved to withhold judgment.

"Yes, Uncle. He is a practicing attorney in San Diego. He makes a good living, but he is not really wealthy. He is known as an excellent prosecutor who is dedicated to protecting the people. My parents both joined The Church of Jesus Christ of Latter-day Saints—"

"Wait," interrupted Ruben, "I thought you were with the Mormons."

"Mormon is a nickname, Uncle. We get that name from the Book of Mormon, a sacred scripture that we have. We go by both names, but The Church of Jesus Christ of Latter-day Saints is our official name. My parents have loved this church from the day they heard about it from the missionaries, and they conveyed that love to me. That's why I'm here in Mexico, to tell others about it." Ruben could tell by Miguel's expression that he was sincere.

"Do you go to college in America, Miguel?"

"I finished my first year. When I get back, I'll finish." Miguel answered.

"They must pay you well to miss college for those years you are away. How much do they pay you?" Ruben asked.

"They pay me nothing, Uncle. I volunteer my time, and Father pays my expenses here in Mexico."

Ruben's jaw dropped. Could his nephew be stupid? *No one works for free*, he thought. *I have always been paid. For every row I picked in the orchard. For every tractor load of fruit I ever hauled. For every trip up north with the fruits of the field. For every trafficker I have recruited, I am paid a profit. No one works without profit! No one!* He stared at Miguel in disbelief.

"Uncle, what's wrong?" Miguel asked. "You seem surprised."

"You mean you . . . you just . . . you just work . . . for nothing? Surely your father never taught you to work for nothing, Miguel!"

"I volunteer as well, sir," Elder Jones said. "It's a sacrifice we are willing to make to spread the restored gospel. It's okay. We only do it for two years." He smiled at Ruben with the satisfaction of one who had just borne his testimony to a pagan drug trafficker. *Boy, could I write home about this!* Elder Jones thought. *No.*

On second thought, I couldn't! My mom would fly down here and make me come back home.

Ruben was lost in his own thoughts. *Restored gospel? Restoring something . . . doesn't that have to do with furniture and paintings? And what is this gospel? Matthew and Luke. Those are the gospels. Right? But "restored gospel?" What are these boys talking about?* he asked himself.

"Listen, Nephew, I don't understand much about what you're doing here, but I'm sure it's good. But still, you should come and work for me. In five or six hours a day, you will make as much as your father makes in a week. What do you say?" Ruben expected his nephew, who had but one year of college, would accept his offer enthusiastically.

Elder Jones rolled his eyes. He couldn't believe what he was hearing. The most powerful drug lord in Mexico just offered his companion a job dealing drugs. He knew if Miguel went to work for his uncle, he would probably make more money the last four months of his mission than Elder Jones would make the first ten years after he returned to the States. He was ready to pinch himself.

"You know I wouldn't be interested in that line of work, Uncle. I don't believe in it. I think drugs are harmful. But I do appreciate you thinking of me. Before I leave for the States, I have one more interview that I have to conduct with a young man who wants to be baptized in Culiacán. Can I meet with you one more time then? Do I have any cousins who I could meet?" More than anything, Miguel wanted to meet his uncle's family.

"Indeed you do, my boy. Tito, my oldest son, is now twenty-six, and Fonseca, my daughter, is twenty-one. When you're next in Culiacán, stop by that same motel that your Brother Quintaro owns. I'll leave word with him that you'll be calling on me, and he will give you the directions to my residence. Please, tell your father you've seen me and that one day I'll be in touch with him." Ruben got up to leave, and Miguel embraced him.

"Be careful, Uncle Ruben. I'll see you soon. Please, tell Aunt . . ." Miguel laughed, realizing he didn't know his own aunt's name.

"Rosa," Miguel said with a smile. "Your Aunt Rosa."

"Please tell Aunt Rosa and my cousins that I look forward to meeting them."

The uncle and nephew embraced again. Ruben shook Elder Jones's hand and departed. Elder Jones still seemed stunned as he watched Ruben enter his chauffeur-driven vehicle.

Three and a half months later, Elders Guzman and Jones travelled back to Culiacán and conducted their baptismal interview in the spacious old home that was used for a meetinghouse for the growing number of members there. In spite of the drug traffic, the people whom the missionaries had met from that city seemed to have a humble and welcoming spirit about them.

As Ruben had promised, Brother Quintaro gave the missionaries directions to his home, which one of Ruben's men had left for them. The directions indicated the best time of day to come and instructed them to ask for Rosario Martinez, not Ruben Guzman. That request had Elder Jones's interest on high alert.

As they pulled into the parking area of the Crocodile's beautiful old mansion, which he had left to Ruben when he died, both missionaries were astonished at the opulence manifested in every corner of the estate.

Elder Jones was first to speak. "Elder Guzman, pinch me and tell me if this is really happening. You and I are just two missionaries, right? How is it that we got invited to dinner at a mansion belonging to one of the major drug lords of Mexico, who happens to be your uncle and who's killed a bunch of people? Do you think he'll have another job offer for you? What do you think the odds are of us both getting a job that doesn't require us to kill anyone, but pays us just as well? Whaddaya think, Elder?"

"Elder Jones, don't worry about it! Let's go eat!" Elder Guzman opened the car door for his companion, who got out very warily, looked around for a few seconds, and then followed Elder Guzman up to the front door.

When the door was opened by a tall, sinister-looking guard holding a shotgun, Elder Guzman glanced at Elder Jones and was quite sure, by the ashen expression on his companion's face, that he was going to pass out. Elder Guzman spoke to the guard in

Spanish, announcing their identity, and the guard waved the two boys in. Elder Jones couldn't take his eyes off the shotgun, craning his neck to the rear as they walked into the parlor.

"*Buenas tardes,* nephew." Ruben came around the corner with his son and daughter. "Tito and Fonseca, meet your long-lost cousin, Miguel. And the young man with him is his *compañero,* Elder. . . . Elder . . . "

"E-Elder J-Jones . . . from A-Arizona . . . i-in the United States," stammered Miguel's companion.

Both Tito and Fonseca came forward and greeted the missionaries by kissing them on the cheek according to the local custom. "I didn't know I had Mormon cousins," Tito exclaimed as he stared at the unusual ring on his missionary cousin's finger that bore the letters "CTR."

"Yes, you do!" Elder Guzman explained. "And in the city of San Diego, California, you have an Uncle Enrique, my father, who is a lawyer, and his wife, your Aunt Belinda."

"Couldn't we go see them, Papa?" asked Fonseca.

"You know it's difficult for me to go to the United States, Fonseca. I have too many people depending on my work here." Ruben cringed a little, realizing that he would always have to lie to his children about why he could not return to the United States. He never wanted them to know he was wanted for murder. He was sufficiently embarrassed that Miguel knew of his past.

Ruben changed the subject. "Let's have dinner and you will meet my *señora,* the beautiful Rosa."

Now they were talking food, which happened to be Elder Jones's first language. Excited at the prospect of a delicious meal, he followed everyone into the dining room while looking admiringly at Fonseca.

As they entered the dining room, they were greeted by the enticing aromas of roast pork marinated in locally grown herbs and spices and wild rice. The table was immaculate. A maid was setting dishes of stuffed potatoes and black beans on both sides of the meat, along with side dishes of sea bass and shellfish delicacies. A large pitcher of iced *horchata,* a popular traditional sweet drink made from rice, was placed near the center of the table.

Rosa, a pleasant-looking woman with long black hair and pretty Romanesque facial features, entered the room. She immediately recognized her nephew from Ruben's description and kissed him on the cheek.

"Miguel, we've looked forward to this day since the moment my husband returned from his visit with you in Mexico City. Our house is your house." She curtsied gracefully before Elder Guzman and shook hands with Elder Jones, also welcoming him warmly.

After a few minutes of conversation aimed at getting better acquainted with one another, Rosa announced, "Dinner is now ready. Please be seated. Miguel, please . . . sit here at the head of the table with your uncle. You have a special place of honor tonight. Your companion can sit by me."

Ruben began filling his plate, the signal for the others to eat, when Elder Guzman asked, "Uncle, could we have a blessing on the food before we eat? We have that custom, and we would like to ask a blessing on this house."

Ruben was a little taken back. It had been over thirty years since he had heard the food blessed. "Of course" he responded. "Would you like to do that, Nephew?"

Elder Guzman thanked the Lord for the food, asked a blessing on those who provided and prepared it, and prayed for a special blessing on his uncle's household—that they would be protected and comforted through life's struggles, that they would always be grateful for all their blessings, and that they would someday experience the blessings of the gospel. Fonseca looked up at Elder Guzman and Elder Jones and noticed a brilliance about them. She felt a ray of warmth shoot through her that she had never before experienced. It was something she would never forget. When Miguel asked a special request for the hungry and needy, Rosa's eyes filled with tears. When he closed the blessing in the name of Jesus Christ, there was a prolonged silence as all at the table paused, realizing they had experienced something new and different.

As the family ate the delicious meal, they shared pleasant conversation. Miguel and his uncle's family took turns trading news of both families, while Elder Jones devoured plate after plate of the succulent pork. The meal was followed with large servings of mouth-watering *tres leches* cake, a Mexican favorite that originated in Sinaloa.

All through the meal, Tito had been fascinated with the CTR ring on Miguel's finger. "Cousin Miguel," Tito asked, "what is the meaning of that ring? What do those three letters stand for?"

"The letters in English stand for 'Choose the Right.' They are a reminder to me of the importance of following a true course for living as God wants me to live. As long as I wear the ring each day, I will remember to do only those things that are proper and to avoid evil."

Tito was amazed that someone would put such a premium on living high standards. He would never forget it.

Ruben spoke in detail about the history of Culiacán, the same history he learned from Flaco, so many years ago. "You know, Miguel, before the Spaniards arrived here from Europe, this city was just a small Indian village. Then, in the year 1531, a Spanish army captain, Nuno Beltran de Guzman—another famous Guzman . . . we're all famous, you know—anyway, this Captain Guzman named the village San Miguel de Culiacán. The famous Spanish explorer Francisco Vasquez de Coronado set out from here to explore the southwestern part of the United States."

Finally, the subject came around to how Ruben had made his fortune in his adopted state of Sinaloa. Ruben spoke unapologetically, and it was obvious he wanted Miguel to report back to his family somewhat favorably regarding his livelihood.

"Eventually, Culiacán became the center of the import and export of our products," Ruben concluded. "We operate openly here in Culiacán and throughout the province of Sinaloa because nobody here feels it is a crime to sell customers what they already want." Throughout the remainder of the evening, nothing more was mentioned about the drug trade.

Finally, the missionaries announced they had to leave for Mexico City for another appointment. Elder Guzman embraced his newfound family, left his address with them, and obtained their promise to stay in touch. Elder Jones, who was so full he could barely move, lumbered from one person to another, shaking hands. Then, after personally escorting the missionaries to their car, Ruben walked back inside the *hacienda*, picked up the Book of Mormon his nephew had given his family, and placed it on a shelf in his library.

Once the missionaries had departed, Fonseca retired to her room and pondered the incredible feeling she had experienced when her cousin had asked the blessing upon the food. She couldn't forget the glow she had observed on the two young men's faces. She knew she had to learn more about the Mormons. A short while later, with her parents' permission, she found the Mormon elders in Culiacán and asked to be taught about the Church. She was baptized two months later.

* * * *

Tito recalled that first meeting with pleasure, as well as the subsequent contacts both he and his father had with Miguel as his father helped Miguel financially through law school. He recalled the great sadness each of them had felt a couple years ago, when they had received word that Miguel and his wife had been murdered by drug traffickers. He bristled with anger in recalling that the Vultures were probably involved not only in Miguel's death but also in the murder of his grandfather, Julio, and in the abduction of his cousin, Elena.

Tito paused again to consider the effect both Miguel and Fonseca had upon his father. He vividly recalled what happened the night Fonseca called their father to be present during her blessing.

* * * *

Fonseca had been pregnant twice before and had lost both babies in miscarriages. With this third child, she had gone eight months before experiencing the same kind of unusual, frightening contractions and internal movements she had with the first two. This time she decided to call the elders of her church for a blessing.

The phone rang in Ruben's study. "*Hola!* Who is it?" he asked.

"Papa, it's me, Fonseca. I have a favor to ask you."

"Of course, precious girl. What is it?"

"The men from my church are coming tonight at seven to bless me and my baby. I want you here, Papa! I just feel I need you."

"But, Fonseca, my dear, you know I don't do these religious things. I don't have your faith. I would only hinder. Please understand."

"No, Papa! No! This is your grandchild. You must come, Papa . . . you must!" Ruben could hear his daughter weeping.

"All right, my love. I'll be there. I'll bring Tito too."

"*Gracias*, Papa! Thank you!"

Ruben had never felt so uncomfortable. He hated pretense and knew if word got out that he was patronizing *Los Mormones*, those who knew him, who *really* knew him, would accuse him of hypocrisy. But then he thought, *This is my daughter! The grandchild is my own flesh and blood. I will do this. I must! Let them think what they wish!*

At 6:45 P.M., Ruben's driver left him at Fonseca's home and was ordered to pick him up promptly in thirty minutes.

Ruben knocked and was immediately greeted by Fonseca's husband, who kissed him on the cheek, shook Tito's hand, and ushered them into the couple's bedroom where Fonseca was lying quietly on her bed. She smiled at her father and brother while wiping away the beads of sweat dripping down over her forehead. Ruben embraced his daughter tenderly and kissed her repeatedly on both cheeks. Ruben was stunned to see his daughter in so much pain.

What kind of father am I? Ruben asked himself. *I haven't even inquired sufficiently to know what she is going through!* As he continued to embrace his daughter, he uttered. "Sweet angel, I'm sorry! What can I do?" Fonseca said nothing but held her father's hand tightly, as he kissed her again on the cheek and placed the dozen roses he had brought next to her bed.

"*Gracias*, Papa. Thank you so much for coming. I needed you here."

A tear appeared on Ruben's cheek. Then he moved slowly over to an empty chair and sat down next to his wife, Rosa, who had spent the last two days with their daughter.

There was a knock at the door. Rosa went to the door and

greeted two men in their fifties who came in and introduced themselves as *Obispo* Perez and *Hermano* Blanco. After shaking hands and introducing themselves to Rosa, Tito, and Ruben, Bishop Perez produced a vial of oil from a pocket in his jacket and advised it was for blessing the sick.

"Brother Guzman, it's wonderful to see you here," said Bishop Perez. Directing his remark to Ruben, he smiled at him and Tito enthusiastically, again taking his hand and shaking it vigorously.

Ruben smiled back as he thought, *Brother Guzman? How could he think I'm his brother? Does he even know about me? About what I do? And this other man . . . this "counselor." I wonder if he has heard about me.*

For the first time in many years, Ruben felt he was in an environment that he couldn't control, with people he couldn't influence. He grew more and more uncomfortable. It was unnerving, and yet in a strange way, refreshing. *I don't have to make anything happen here,* he thought. *This isn't business. I can support what these men are doing. They are here to help my daughter.*

"Brothers and sisters, first we will anoint Sister Fonseca with consecrated oil. Then we will bless her," the bishop explained. Ruben was mesmerized by what he was seeing and hearing. He had seen magic before but had never experienced a manifestation of faith. *Consecrated oil?* he asked himself. Ruben felt so out of place.

As Brother Blanco anointed Fonseca and Bishop Perez sealed the blessing, Ruben noticed something in his daughter's countenance that he had seen only once before. He recalled a similar glow on the two missionaries' faces when his nephew, Miguel asked the blessing upon the food and upon his family. He was completely absorbed by his daughter's demeanor as the bishop pronounced the blessing.

Ruben was amazed when he heard Bishop Perez promise his daughter she would have a healthy baby and that she would make it safely through her delivery. Ruben also vowed at that moment that if the promise wasn't fulfilled, he or one of his men would "look up" that bishop.

Fonseca lovingly embraced her father and brother and thanked them for coming before the driver rapped on the door and they departed. "Oh, Papa! You will never know how much your presence meant to me today! I felt your strength."

Ruben smiled at Fonseca and kissed her again on the cheek. Both he and Tito shook hands with the "brothers," Bishop Perez and Brother Blanco, and kissed Rosa good-bye.

As the driver pulled out onto the street, Ruben turned to Tito and said, "Very interesting, these Mormon blessings. . . . We'll follow up to see that the bishop was telling the truth about Fonseca and the baby making it through. He better be right!"

Ruben recalled Fonseca's statement: "I felt your strength, Papa!"

My strength? he asked himself. *These hands have shed blood and broken bones!*

Three days later, Fonseca's baby girl was born, premature, but healthy. Fonseca's entire demeanor changed. She gained color in her cheeks and was out of bed and caring for the infant within a week.

A flame had been ignited in Ruben Guzman. Not a flame that would draw him into any religion but a flame of curiosity that would change the way the Brotherhood did business—a curiosity that would cause him to look inward and begin to ask himself where he stood with God.

* * * *

From the recollection of Fonseca's blessing, Tito's mind raced forward in time again. This time to his father's death bed . . .

* * * *

CULIACÁN, MEXICO
2008

Beads of sweat formed on Ruben's brow and cascaded over his pallid countenance. He woke abruptly, noting it was 4:30 in the morning. Even with the regular administration of morphine by the physician who attended him around the clock, the pain from the bone cancer had become excruciating. His constant fever would not recede.

Ironically, the first prayers he had ever uttered were pleas for death . . . but it wouldn't come. The faces of his victims flashed before him like neon lights: the Allen brothers, Negro Flores, and many others. He wished he had never read those pages in the book of scripture Miguel had given him four years before, especially the ones about his mortal life being the day of his probation and all that was said about judgment. He cringed at the thought of missing out on the promise of eternal joy and happiness that he had read about. He sighed heavily, realizing those promises were only for the righteous. He knew that even though he had enjoyed every possession an earthly life could offer, his luxuries would mean little, considering his huge accountability. He hoped the book was wrong! He wanted to die and experience nothing in the aftermath. No pain, no judgment, no accountability . . . nothing. Deep down, something told him that would not be the case.

Finally, Ruben's fever broke a little. His thoughts were not quite as clouded as he pondered the Maya and the oaths and signs passed down to him from the old Indian, the same oaths and signs that had made the lying, the deceit, and the murders so easy. *I should have stopped after the Allen boys,* he thought. *That was just payback for Hector. The other killing was business. What's my excuse for that? I just want to disappear!*

Ruben's physician administered another shot of morphine, and his pain receded just enough to usher in the memories of the Maya, along with the poison of the oaths and signs . . .

CHAPTER ELEVEN
THE CURSE OF ZAKE-VAL

A YEAR PRIOR to his own death, the Crocodile had invited Ruben into his private quarters and offered him tequila.

"How are my grandchildren? I haven't seen them yet today," the older man said as they sat down together. Since their marriage ten years before, Rosa had borne Ruben two children, a boy Tito, now nine, and Fonseca, age six.

"They are well, sir. Rosa took them to visit her sister."

"*Mi hijo,*" the Crocodile said, "we need to travel to the Yucatan and have you meet 'the Maya.' I am nearly seventy, and my health is failing. You need to become acquainted with the other clans in the Brotherhood, and you must meet the Maya before I am gone."

The Crocodile was adamant, but Ruben was unsure what this meeting entailed. Did the Crocodile intend for Ruben to take over as the head of the clan? That in itself had its own implications. He knew he would be wealthy beyond his wildest imagination if such were the case. It helped that he was already married to Rosa, the boss's very beautiful daughter.

"But, *mi patron,* what are you saying?" Ruben pretended to be disconsolate and saddened by the Crocodile's indication he would soon be dead. "You will always be the boss man. Let's not talk of your leaving us."

Although Ruben was excited for untold wealth and power,

he had grown attached to the Crocodile, and for the first time in many years, Ruben felt his heart soften as he realized the Crocodile was serious about his time on earth being limited.

The Crocodile continued. "We must be realistic, my son. The only reason you have not met the other clan leaders before is that the code of the Brotherhood of the Ancients dictates that only the leaders of each clan are permitted to know one another's identities. That way if the authorities recruit informants from any clan in the Brotherhood, they'll be unable to share information on the other clans. The only men who can attend the annual meeting with the Maya are the clan leaders and those designated to take over the clan when the leader passes on. I need to designate you as the new leader before I am too feeble to do so."

"The Maya . . . " Ruben said. "Who is he?" Ruben didn't recall his boss mentioning the name before, and he found himself overcome with curiosity. *What would someone with that name who lived in the Yucatan have to do with the Brotherhood of the Ancients?"*

The Crocodile responded eagerly. "The Maya is an old man, an Indian, who is almost eighty years old now. His son, the Red Maya, will succeed him when he is gone. Many years ago, when opium was initially grown for sale, a Sinaloan man by the name of Don Diego de Maldonado traveled throughout the Yucatan seeking wisdom of the Occult he had heard was found in the Maya's tribe. Legend maintained that this wisdom enabled the Mayans to prevail over other tribes, eliminate anyone who resisted their aggression, and steal vast quantities of wealth from the surrounding tribes. Rumors of the success of the Maya's tribe had spread throughout Mexico, but they would not share their secrets with anyone. That is, not until Don Diego entered into an agreement with the Maya that would make both of them perpetually rich in return for his 'secrets.' "

Ruben was at a loss; he had no idea where his father-in-law was headed with all of this talk about an old Indian.

"After making that pact, Don Diego died a wealthy man in the drug trade. His son, Horacio Maldonado, who goes by the code name 'Kishke,' became *el encargado* of the Brotherhood. He knows all of our places of residence and has much information about each of us, but none of us, who are the leaders of the clans in the Brotherhood, have the same information on him.

Ruben looked at the older man, perplexed.

"There is much enmity in our organization and much jealousy. Kishke didn't want anyone in the Brotherhood, who, for whatever reason thought they were cheated or otherwise taken advantage of, to be able to find him if they became a threat to him.

"I see him only once a year at the annual *conferencia* in the Yucatan. The meeting is held the first day of summer, July 21, when the poppy and marijuana crops are blessed by Malverde, our patron saint. You will come with me this year, and you will meet Kishke, the Maya, and the Red Maya. You will be taught much."

Ruben's curiosity was still unsatisfied. "How do Kishke and the Maya benefit from all this?" he asked.

"Each clan leader, including me, sends copies of the receipts from our profits to Kishke's accountant in Mexico City with two personal checks: one to him and one to the Maya for five percent each from our earnings."

"But why? What do you pay them for?" It was obvious that Ruben was disturbed by this new information.

"Kishke has contacts with the central police, military, and border authorities that Don Diego, his father, cultivated and passed on. That is how we pass through the American borders without a problem. It's how we operate out in the open without fear of being arrested. Kishke also maintains our organization's clients in the United States and talks with many politicians in our government and theirs that benefit indirectly in bribes and payoffs. We could not function without Kishke."

"And the Maya? He is probably nothing but an old toothless Indian from the wastes of the Yucatan," Ruben said derisively.

The Crocodile seized the younger man by the shoulder tightly. With a scornful frown, he warned, "You better never be heard talking like that again about the Maya. If others in the Brotherhood heard you, you would die! You are lucky we are related in marriage and that you have my confidence."

The Crocodile loosened his clutch on Ruben's shoulder and went on: "The Maya has delivered the perfect plan for our success that he refers to as 'the secret combinations of the ancients.' These secrets are the very foundation of our wealth and advantage in today's unwary and trusting world. You will discover the Maya's value for yourself. As I mentioned, he is very old. When his teachings are perpetuated by his son after his death, you will meet annually with him. We will leave in one month for the Yucatan."

****

It was hot—very hot—in the small Mayan Indian village of Zake-Val, located in the interior of the Yucatan between the ancient ruins of Tulum and Chichen Itza. In spite of the discomfort during the trip to the Yucatan, Ruben was caught up in the glamour and luxury of the journey. They stayed in fancy hotels whenever they were available and ate superb meals.

What topped it off was riding in the Crocodile's sleek, air-conditioned, chauffeur-driven Peugot. He was impressed with its stunning opulence: the mid-size four-cylinder vehicle was painted a light beige with black trim, with three tinted windows on each side and a fancy luggage trunk in the back. The vehicle was equipped with a bar stocked with the finest tequila and food. The bar was nearly emptied by the time they arrived at their destination in Zake-Val.

When they finally arrived at Zake-Val, Ruben was struck with the exotic beauty of the town's richly designed homes and well-watered gardens and vineyards. Ruben was surprised at the town of such wealth located in the middle of nowhere.

Their chauffeur pulled up and parked in front of an elegant hotel, obviously designed for well-heeled spenders. It was completely different from the other lodging facilities in the towns they had passed through, which often displayed little or no luxury at all. The two men noticed a half-dozen fancy vehicles parked outside, none more than a year old. Many other cars, just as new and luxurious, were scattered all throughout the little town of Zake-Val.

As Ruben recalled the Crocodile's accounts of the Maya's town and how its inhabitants had become so wealthy and powerful through their utilization of what his boss had referred to as "secret methods," he became convinced that the Maya stood for much more than he had ever imagined.

Upon entering the hotel, he observed several Mexican men drinking *cervezas* and chatting while seated in swanky, upholstered leather chairs. It was apparent to Ruben that his boss was well-known to all the men there who were in their late forties to seventies. He was introduced to each of the other six clan heads.

At the appointed hour, the men present were summoned into a suite on the second floor, which was home to the Maya. Ruben took note of the elegant setting. The room was furnished with lush rugs and beautiful hardwood floors. He even noticed some gold inlay throughout the walls and on the ceiling and some paintings with unique desert landscapes. A Mayan sun dial calendar, also with inlaid gold, was displayed in one corner on a metal tripod.

As Ruben and his father-in-law entered the living room, Ruben noticed paintings of several older Indian men and asked the Crocodile, "Who are those Indian guys?"

The Crocodile responded reverently, "Those are paintings of some ancient Mayan chieftains. The Maya has always kept a history of his ancestors and likes to talk about some of their exploits, especially in war. I think he likes to think this is what they looked like.

The men seated themselves in turn-of-the-century leather chairs that reclined. Coffee tables were topped with trays of *tortas* and *galletas con queso*. House servants poured out bottles of well-aged wine.

The Maya had seen the many fancy vehicles drive up and park near his residence and heard the men enter the living room area of his suite. As he recalled how he had initially been introduced to the Crocodile by Don Diego de Maldonado many years before and had subsequently become the benefactor of the Crocodile Clan and the other several clans of the Brotherhood of the Ancients, the Maya's lips turned up into a slight smile. He thought of the millions of *pesos* that had filled his pockets as a result of their collaboration. He actually considered the Mexican men rather gullible. They so readily accepted his counsels and instruction. The oaths, signs, covenants, and combinations he advocated and instructed them in had been passed down through generations of ancestors who lived first in the area of Guatemala and subsequently migrated into the far reaches of the Yucatan in Mexico.

How easy it is to take the Mexican pesos when all they want is to feel the spirit of the Serpent and learn how to kill in secret, the Maya thought. *All the better that I never revealed to them that they could have the same knowledge without having to pay me if they just turned their spirits over to the Underworld.* He smiled again at his own cunning and superior thinking.

The Maya glanced across the room at his son, the Red Maya, who was playing solitaire. His son loved cards and gambling, even though the Maya considered it a waste of time. *Soon I will die,* the Maya thought. *Soon I will return to the Underworld. It is good that I will never have to see the end result of this unenlightened young man who only lusts after the things of the world.*

The old man looked at his wristwatch, motioned for his son to follow, and knocked on the door of the adjacent room occupied by Kishke Maldonado.

The three men entered the living area: Kishke Maldonado first, then the old host with white hair flowing down to his shoulders, and finally the younger man with reddish hair, whose arm the Maya was holding onto. As the Maya hobbled slowly along, he stopped to greet each of the eight men individually.

When the three men stopped to greet the Crocodile, Ruben observed his boss kiss Kishke on the cheek. Kishke pointed at Ruben and whispered something into the Maya's ear.

Kishke was the first to speak to Ruben. "Señor Rosario Martinez, I have heard much about you over the years from your father-in-law here. He has always been very complimentary toward you and tells us you will become the next representative and leader of the Crocodile clan upon his passing. We will be pleased to work with you." It became clear to Ruben at that moment that the standard of the Brotherhood was to use the official names assigned by each clan at these annual meetings. The only exceptions were the clan leaders, who were permitted to maintain their true names. He strained to recall Kishke's name. *Horacio . . . Horacio Maldonado. . . . yes, that was it,* he recalled. *And his father was Don Diego Maldonado. Right!*

"Thank you very much, Señor Maldonado. It has been my good fortune to have been not only employed by Señor Jimenez de Calderón, but to also have the honor of being married to his daughter, Rosa." It all seemed much too polite and cordial for a group of men who murdered and committed mayhem for a living. But if such was what it took for appearances to facilitate what would one day fall into his hands, he was willing to play along.

Ruben studied Kishke's face as Kishke smiled at him. The man had a hardened appearance. *Is this hardness a mirror to his past?* Ruben wondered. Surely the man had made many adverse pro-nouncements and issued numerous death sentences. The gold he wore around his neck and on his wrists bespoke power and con-trol as did his perfectly trimmed hair and fingernails.

Ruben had heard rumors that Kishke had undergone surgery to alter his appearance in order to escape the attention of certain police authorities bent on harassing him in spite of the numerous bribes he had offered them. The surgery had left the skin of his face taut and somewhat youthful. However, that potential youth-fulness was betrayed by a black toupee that didn't quite match his eyebrows. His slender, six-foot frame was buried in a green silk dress shirt left open at the neck. He wore a two-piece gabardine suit that was overly ample and hung loosely from his shoulders. A black patch over his left eye almost completely covered a knife scar that deprived him of half his vision but earned him a reputation as a fierce street fighter in his early years.

Once the Maya was finished speaking with the Crocodile, he sauntered over to Ruben and extended a leathery, age-worn hand. Ruben slowly accepted his hand and shook it as he looked into the Maya's eyes. He almost jumped back. The man's coun-tenance unnerved Ruben. The Maya's old eyes were a piercing black, almost void of light, with just a hint of pink invading his pupils, shutting out his vision. Where Ruben had expected an exchange of smiles, there was only a suspicious scowl as the old man's gaze bored into the younger man's eyes. *What is he hoping to find?* Ruben wondered. *A hint of weakness? A lack of commitment?*

As the Maya grasped Ruben's hand even tighter, the leathery surface of his aged hands grated like sandpaper against Ruben's palms. To Ruben, it was as if the Maya were trying to force a confession out of him—anything that would satisfy his suspicions about him as a newcomer. Ruben did not flinch but maintained his gaze into the old man's eyes. He had come too far to lose his future now. In return, he strengthened his grip on the blotched hand in his. The old man seemed to respect that gesture, slackened his grip on Ruben's hand, and shook it, as a smile formed on his weathered face.

"Are you ready, Rosario Martinez?" he asked Ruben. "Can you meet the challenges you may soon inherit?" The Maya's Spanish was adequate, but he spoke it with the staccato nasality typical of the Mayan dialect.

"Yes, *señor.* I can, and I will. Each year I meet with you or your son, I'll honor you with favorable reports. I look forward to being strengthened by the traditions of the ancients. I will venture ahead where others have turned back."

A half-smile appeared. The Maya was pleased. He signaled toward the man at his side and said, "Meet my son, *El Maya Rojo.* Upon this arm that now supports me in my old age will rest the future of the Brotherhood of the Ancients. It will be he who will call up the blessings of the Serpent, and it will be he who will renew the oaths and covenants from the Underworld. He will be the one to intermediate on your behalf with the founder of the secret combinations. He'll trace the power of those works throughout history and will guarantee the Serpent's support for the Brotherhood of the Ancients. Yes, my boy, my years are numbered, but the Red Maya, my son, will be with you always."

The Red Maya was forty-two. Unlike his father, he was much lighter complexioned. He was only five foot six inches tall and was slight of build. The distinct features that set him apart from the people in the small community of Zake-Val were his reddish hair and eyebrows and his soft, brown eyes. It was common knowledge that the Maya had many wives and children, but this son from a white woman, probably of Spanish descent, had become the Maya's favorite. Both of the Mayan men spoke Spanish and a Mayan dialect.

The Maya spoke again. "My son is the shaman for the people of our village, but he is seldom used because we have modern doctors from Mexico City whom we pay very well. However, it is an honorable title that will serve him well when he takes over for me."

The old man looked out at all those present. "I am now ready to address the gathering." He glanced at Ruben once more. "I wish you well, young man. The Brotherhood will expect much from you." The Red Maya smiled at Ruben but kept his distance. He followed his father to the front of the room and sat down next to him as the elderly man began speaking. The Maya extended his right arm directly out from his shoulder with his fist clenched and stated the words, "Peace from the Serpent." Immediately, all the other clan leaders stood up, extended their right arms in the same gesture, and responded, reverently, "Peace to the Maya." Ruben followed the other men in this formal greeting.

The Maya continued, "Please be seated. I will first grant your leader, Kishke Maldonado, time to cover the pressing affairs of your business, before delivering the will of the Serpent and administering to you his blessing." Ruben thought, *What is this "Serpent" business? I still can't believe that old man is worth five percent. Are these men crazy?*

Kishke Maldonado stood before the ten men and greeted them with the same extended arm and clenched fist that Ruben later learned was one of the secret signs used for reinforcing "unity in silence." He also learned that the greeting the Maya had used, "Peace from the Serpent" and the greeting returned to the Maya, "Peace to the Maya," were also code words used to generate energy and enthusiasm. As time passed with the Brotherhood, Ruben would learn a number of secret words and signs that would support the oaths administered by the Maya on behalf of the Brotherhood—secret words and signs that could not be revealed under any circumstances outside of their organization and that could be used to obscure intent and to confuse outsiders and authorities that might be interested in monitoring their activities.

When all eyes were on Kishke, he began a report on the net receipts of the Brotherhood for the past year. He also reported the monthly amounts that had been earned by each of the seven clans, five of which transported cocaine and opium and the other two, including the Crocodile Clan, that transported marijuana. He asked each clan leader to approve his findings. They all did.

Next, Kiske brought everyone up to date on the "cooperation" the Brotherhood continued to receive from the local and national police, the Mexican army, the politicians running the country, and authorities on both sides of the border. He went through the contacts in the United States who cooperated in the receipt and distribution of the Brotherhood's drugs and detailed any notable incidents that had occurred within the past year. It appeared they had all been resolved, always in favor of the Brotherhood. Last, reports were discussed that had been disseminated to Kishke from informants both in and outside of their organization that had presented new issues that needed to be resolved—including a couple of transporters in one of the clans that had broken their oaths and covenants of secrecy and had betrayed the Brotherhood. The untimely deaths of those two people were emphasized . . . obviously, for the warning effect. The floor was then opened for questions, but none were asked. Everyone present seemed anxious to hear from the Maya.

Kishke concluded, "Brethren of the Ancients, it is now my pleasure to relinquish the remainder of the time to our host and our benefactor, the Maya." Again, each man present extended his arm in a closed fist salute and chanted the phrase, "Peace to the Maya."

The elderly Maya slowly rose to his feet, extended his arm in the same sign, and exclaimed again, "Peace from the Serpent." He then continued, as he lifted his right arm, pointing out the window, in the direction of some surrounding hills. "I have consulted with you, the Brotherhood since Kishke's father, Don Diego Maldonado, asked me to share the secrets of our wealth and prosperity with him. Don Diego had begun a new venture with the opium and marijuana in Sinaloa, which he referred to as 'the fruits of the field.' " Ruben recognized that expression now. It was one he heard with more frequency from the people associated with the Brotherhood.

The elderly Maya continued. "This was many years ago, decades ago, when he and I were both much younger men. Don Diego, like many others in Mexico, had heard how we had gleaned wealth unheard of in this town and throughout the surrounding area. However, Don Diego was the first and only man to enter into an oath and covenant with me. I fasted for three days in the hills as I pondered his request. Through my fast, I had prepared well before I consented to provide him our secrets for wealth. His offer to pay my tribe the twentieth part of all his profits seemed good business for us. It was, as you can see, how we have prospered, when others in the surrounding communities have nothing. Because of our prosperity, our tribe does not find it necessary to utilize the ancient combinations with as much frequency. However, when necessary, we still have authority from the Underworld to use the ways and means the Serpent has provided."

Ruben questioned himself as to why the Crocodile had never talked about this aspect of their business before. *And what power does this old Indian hold over all these clans, that he gets five percent?* he asked himself once more. *I can understand why Kishke gets five percent for setting everything up with our clients in the United States and securing our passage through the border . . . but five percent to this old goat?*

The Maya's face took on an expression of condescension and solemnity as he instructed the group to arise. The Maya then continued, "Now I will repeat the commitment that each member of your clans has accepted. As I repeat these, you will ratify them with the appropriate sign.

"I vow that I will never, under any circumstance, reveal the identity of any member of the Brotherhood to anyone outside of our organization and that I will protect all members in whatever adverse circumstances they find themselves, even if they have committed murder."

Every man present, including Ruben, made a strange, sweeping gesture with the introduction of each oath and repeated in unison what the Maya had said, word for word.

"I vow that I will take every opportunity to enrich the Brotherhood any way that I can.

"I will always turn the proceeds of my work over to the head of my clan, knowing I will be recompensed later.

"I will report anyone within the clan who is stealing assets of the Brotherhood but will never speak of it outside the clan.

"I will not hesitate to eliminate those who stand in the way of enriching the Brotherhood. I will consider murder, trafficking the fruits of our fields, theft of the assets of our competitors, and other actions deemed criminal by the outside world, merely tools of our trade."

As the Maya continued administering the oath of the Brotherhood, Ruben noticed an unusual rustling in the surrounding tree branches. A strange, eerie spirit seemed to fill the room.

"I am willing to accept an official name for my business documents and an unofficial street name I will be known by which are both different from my true name in order to obscure my identity and to protect the integrity of the Brotherhood.

"I will recognize the importance and discretion of certain secret words and signs that I will be given in order to deflect curiosity and investigative interests from outside our organization."

Ruben noticed the other men in the room swaying slightly from side to side, as if in a drunken stupor. The strange spirit turned into a dark and oppressive feeling, almost material, yet still invisible. The rustling noise in the trees increased in volume.

"I vow never to steal from the proceeds of the Brotherhood or to, in any way, convert those proceeds to my own use or to maliciously betray the interests of any member of our organization."

The rustling sound grew more pronounced, as if a wind were entering the room. Though the room was well lit with lamps, the room grew steadily darker, as though a heavy, dank atmosphere were smothering the light.

Seeing the men around him immersed in a kind of trance, swaying from side to side, oblivious to those around them, Ruben became increasingly uncomfortable, even fearful. He looked directly into the eyes of the Crocodile, but the older man's eyes were void of recognition toward him. *Are they all crazy?* he thought. *Or is it me? Who or what has gained control of the room and everyone in it?*

Ruben fought the instinct to flee as the curtains now flapped out from the walls, even though the windows were opened only a couple inches, and the rustling sound was now a rapping sound at the doors, sounding as if sticks and stones were being hurled at them. As the bedlam increased, Ruben glanced about desperately. Everyone else in the room had a look of frenzied euphoria on their faces.

The Maya continued to intone the oath as the head clansmen repeated it back:

"I understand that in the event I'm found guilty of violating any of the aforementioned oaths and covenants, I will be tried by other members of the Brotherhood either in action or pronouncement and may face consequences of death."

Suddenly, as the Maya concluded the oath, the noise and the wind abated, but the old man's eyes were a glowing red, as though a fire had been built in them. His countenance had darkened, and a strange reddish glow surrounded his head. After a moment, he spoke.

"The Serpent is in our presence, although invisible, and has accepted your oaths. The powers of the Underworld, our benefactors, have again manifested themselves. They are pleased with our work and are anxious to inspire us in their methods . . . the same methods Cain used in the fields to destroy his condescending brother, Abel . . . the same methods that were given by the Serpent so that Cain's works should not be known unto the world . . . the same methods used by two of our great forbears, Kishkumen and Gadianton, to bring about the destruction of an entire evil, white nation who have always opposed us and our people—yes, a white nation of false worshippers who have placed their god and their so-called redeemer above all of our wise forbears, even a nation that deceived our ancestors and tricked them out of their inheritances."

Ruben liked the way the Maya spoke so contemptuously of white people. He hated white people, especially Americans, for what they had done to Hector. Yes, he felt very comfortable with the Maya's anti-white sentiments.

The Maya continued: "Yes, these are the same methods used by some of our other forbears, Akish and Heth, to murder unrighteous rulers who wished to discredit them, even the methods that all of you have used so successfully in gaining great wealth and advantage. Our oaths of silence, our secret words and signs, are our protection and our future—the basis of our lasting wealth and advantage in deception. Treasure and preserve these methods, and you will continue to succeed. Disregard them, and you will fail.

"Let us never forget the purposes of our oaths. The Serpent himself first administered these oaths to keep the people in darkness, leaving them at your disposal. The oaths are to help those who seek power to obtain power. They permit you to murder when you must, to steal from your competitors when necessary, and to commit all manner of iniquity with impunity when you know that these actions are justified by your quests."

Every man in the room seemed both inebriated and exhilarated by the flow of energy from the Maya and his gesticulations. The old man's son sat at his side adoringly, anticipating with excitement his future role of prestige and enhanced financial status in ministering to the Brotherhood. Ruben felt something powerful, yet sinister, that he had never felt before—a sensation even more gratifying than the pleasure he had experienced in murdering the Allen brothers and Negro Flores. He now understood the value of the Maya. He knew the clan leaders would return to their work emboldened, supervising the clans and perpetuating their murders, thievery, and whatever else was necessary to further the narcotics trade . . . the source of their wealth and power. He knew that the signs, secret words, oaths and covenants, and power of the Serpent, whoever he was, were vital to his success.

The Maya was finishing his discourse: "Now, brethren, return to your work with my blessing." He lifted a beautifully varnished wooden staff above his head, grasping each end with his hands and bowing his head. "O Great Serpent, today, in conclusion, I present your workers. Empower them!"

The rustling returned, and the wind blew in a fury inside

the room. This time, Ruben heard something else: a low wailing sound and a groan.

"Bless us, O Great Serpent!" the Maya finished, and the room suddenly became silent. The clan leaders once again extended their clenched fists toward the Maya, bowing their heads and awaiting his individual blessing. The Maya sauntered slowly toward the men in front of him, placing his raspy hands briefly on each of their heads as he came to them. When he reached Ruben, who was at the end of the line next to the Crocodile, he again frowned, searching Ruben's face for any sign of weakness . . . then the old man smiled, placed his hand on Ruben's head, and pronounced his blessing. Once finished, he left the room with his son. After the two Mayans were gone, the clan leaders started drinking in earnest.

The Crocodile turned to Ruben, smiled, and said, "There. You had to see it. I could never have explained it even if I was allowed to!"

CHAPTER TWELVE
CHANGING OF THE GUARD

TITO DIDN'T LIKE re-experiencing the chill he felt from the contacts with the Maya and the Red Maya when he accompanied his father to the annual meetings in Zake-Val. He recalled the explanation his father had given him, which he had heard from the Crocodile regarding the origin of the power of the Maya and his son.

★ ★ ★ ★

Subsequent to the meeting in Zake-Val, as the two men set out for home, seated in the backseat of the Peugot and out of earshot of the chauffeur, the Crocodile asked Ruben, "Do you have any idea why Kishke Maldonado is called Kishke? It doesn't sound like any Spanish name you have ever heard, does it?"

"No, it doesn't," Ruben said, trying unsuccessfully to conceal his curiosity.

"Kishke comes from the name Kishkumen, whom you will recall the Maya mentioned as one of the great forbears of the Mayan people. Kishkumen and a man called Gadianton were two of the ancient principles who perpetuated the secret oaths and combinations that empowered them and facilitated their victory over the white nation. These two men were successful in bringing to pass the pollution of the morality of the white nation, which eventually destroyed them."

"But what has that to do with Kishke's name?" Ruben asked.

"The Maya always emphasized that the leader of the Brotherhood of the Ancients would be guaranteed success if he adopted a portion of the name of one of the great ones from the past. The leader of the Brotherhood could adopt part of the Great One's name, but part only, since it would be offensive and presumptuous to take on the Ancient's full identity. That is why Horacio Maldonado is known among the Brotherhood as Kishke Maldonado."

At that moment, Ruben made another commitment to himself. First, when the Crocodile was gone, he would discontinue his five percent contribution. Second, he, personally, would never take upon himself another name and couldn't care less if anyone else did.

"What is it about this white nation that seems to spur so much hate in the Maya?" Ruben asked.

"Throughout almost a thousand years of history, the Maya's ancestors and the white nation warred with each other. There were many intervals of peace between the two nations, but the Maya's people adhered to the tradition that their birthright had been stolen by the white nation. Both groups claimed to have descended from the same parents who brought their family over to Central America from Jerusalem about six hundred years before Christ, but that is about all they had in common. The Maya's descendants were warlike and lived off the land. The white nation built cities and churches and constantly tried to proselytize the Maya's ancestors to their faith. Great resentments built up and eventually blood spilled over, with the Maya's people, being much more numerous and warlike, completely destroying the white nation. But they were only able to do that because they had what we have now. I refer, you understand, to those special powers that you witnessed today." The Crocodile spoke almost reverently as he referred to what they had both heard and felt inside the Maya's hospitality house.

Ruben thought of the murmurings and rustling noises he had heard and recalled the dark and chilling atmosphere in the conference room. Ruben shook his head and said, "I have never . . . felt that way," he said. "Never!"

The Crocodile responded. "It was the Serpent manifesting

himself, my son. I have felt it many times and have been strengthened by it and inspired to carry on our work through it. We are in league with the Underworld and are in its debt. Never forget that."

****

As Tito continued reflecting on his past experience with his father, his thinking centered again in the last hour he had spent with him . . .

****

With the bone cancer now consuming all his energy, Ruben knew his time was short and he felt pressed to pass on some confidences to Tito, who was to lead the Brotherhood. After embracing Rosa and Fonseca one last time, he asked them to leave the room, requesting that Tito remain. In obvious pain, he asked Tito to come close to his bedside.

"Tito, you're a good son. You've made me proud. You've obtained a law degree, you married well, and you brought me a grandson." Ruben struggled to utter each word. "Tito, this organization we have run for so long is very . . . dark. You know that as well as I do, don't you?"

"Yes, Father. I've been with you when we visited the Maya at Zake-Val. I felt and heard the powers of the Underworld, rumbling through the trees, shaking the leaves. I sensed the deep chill. I've always known it wasn't good that the oaths were directed to the Serpent as the signs were made." Tito seemed embarrassed and saddened for his father, as he finally divulged what they had both known but hadn't previously brought to the surface.

Ruben continued. "It has been our living, son, our existence, the thing that has put bread in our mouths and fine linen on our tables. But with the blood shed to market the fruits of the field to the Americans, the deceit and the bribes, I am sure there will be a price to pay." A look of regret and apprehension clouded Ruben's face.

"Fonseca, in her religion with the Mormons, has almost convinced me of a hereafter . . . . a place of accountability. She has tried to convert me to her way of thinking, as I'm sure she has you, and she almost succeeded. It all sounded so refreshing . . . like drinking cold water in a fiery desert. But I couldn't just turn away from all that we have here—our mansions, our new automobiles, our living. She always told me it was possible for a person to own the world yet lose his soul. I don't know where I go from here, son, but I think she's right. You should probably listen to her."

"After your cousin, Miguel, returned to the States from his mission to Mexico and until his death, I made several trips to San Diego while doing business for the Brotherhood and visited Miguel while he was attending college." Ruben's speech was fraught with mounting pain. "Miguel always tried to convince me that I shouldn't be involved in the drug business. He tried very hard to get me to believe in his church and in the Book of Mormon. I was hard-headed and kept telling him he should just come to work for me and forget religion. I tried to convince him that he would be much better off."

Tito looked surprised. "You never told me you were meeting with Miguel, Father."

"I had two good reasons for keeping these visits quiet," Ruben explained. "First of all, can you imagine the disrespect I would have received from the Brotherhood if they knew I was listening to Miguel about religion? And second, if Fonseca knew I was listening to Miguel, she would have given me no rest until she had me baptized in the Church!"

"Did Miguel ever give up on you?" Tito asked.

"No. In fact, he and his wife, Judy, kept telling me they were praying for me to leave my 'ways' and some day go with them and their faith. Miguel kept notes of the things we talked about and the things we did in a leather-bound journal. He said that's how he would remember me and that he kept a record of all the things of importance in his life."

"A journal?" Tito asked. "Why?"

"Miguel said all the information that I gave him was important . . . that it was part of what he called our 'family history.' He had already written in the details of his mission and the occasion when he first met me in the mission home in Mexico City. Then he wrote everything down that I told him about what I did to the two boys in Idaho who caused my brother, Hector, to end his life. He had also written what I told him about how I got started in the drug business in Culiacán with the Crocodile, how they referred to me as the Hammer, and how I came to be in charge of the Brotherhood. He promised he would never let this information go outside of our family.

"Just before his death, he turned the journal over to your grandfather, Julio. He asked Julio to record his experiences in it. Since Miguel and his wife were murdered soon thereafter, Julio kept the journal and added to it the history of his friendship with the Madden family. My brother Enrique, Miguel's father, always said that although one family was from Mexico and the other from Idaho, they were inseparable."

Tito looked at his father curiously. This was the first he had ever heard of this leather-bound history and the first he had heard of the Maddens.

Tito's eyes brightened with understanding. "So this is it, Father? This is why you have surprised everyone with such a change of heart these last few years? Miguel got to you, didn't he, along with Fonseca? This is why the Brotherhood has distanced themselves from acts of violence over the years"

Ruben flinched with pain as he responded, "I never believed I could escape the consequences of the blood on my hands. But I hoped to point you in a better direction . . . and others who I care about."

Ruben then gestured to a small desk a few feet away from his bed. "Bring me that metal box, son." Tito brought him the box engraved with the words "Miguel's Holy Book." Ruben glanced one last time at the book in the box and handed it back to his son.

"Do you remember when Miguel left us this Book of Mormon?"

"Yes, Father, I do." Tito replied. "He came with Elder Jones, the missionary who ate almost everything we had in the house." Both men smiled as they recalled Elder Jones and his capacity for food.

"That's right, son," Ruben said in a weakened voice. "Miguel left that book." Tito took it out of the box and held it up, examining it.

Ruben continued. "I never felt comfortable reading it, probably because of my lifestyle, but I read a few parts, and some I have marked. After reading a promise toward the end of the book, which was also marked, I almost prayed to know if it was true. Although I never said such a prayer, deep down I had a good feeling about it. I went to the Mormon Church with Fonseca twice. I felt warm inside when I was there with her. Since then, I have compared that warmth with the cold, overpowering influence of the Maya when he presents the signs, oaths, and covenants of the Serpent. What a difference! Someday I'd like you to take a look at this book of Miguel's and maybe read some of it to your children. It would make your sister, Fonseca, very happy."

Tito seemed surprised, even confused by that request, especially coming from his father but nodded affirmatively. "Yes, Father."

Ruben continued, intent that Tito understand the importance of what he was saying. "After making those trips to Zake-Val to meet with the Maya, I learned that he passed on his authority to his son. The first thing the Red Maya wanted was to raise his percentage of the drug profits from five percent to ten percent, and for what? For repeatedly calling forth the power of the Underworld so that we could have the strength and support of evil permeating our lives and our actions? The Red Maya insisted lying for one another and employing all the power of deceit was the *only* way to get that power. Now, I sense those were not the principles we should have implemented in the Brotherhood."

Ruben had more to say. "When it was obvious that the Red Maya was so interested in personal profit, I thought twice about our relationship with him and whether we really needed him. I had even become reluctant about paying him."

Tito carefully studied his father's demeanor, realizing in advance the conclusions he was arriving at. He sensed that his father felt betrayed by the two Mayan men who his organization had been putting their faith and trust in for decades.

Tito asked, "Is that why we stopped going to Zake-Val, Father?"

"That was part of the reason. I heard the Red Maya was meeting with other groups at Zake-Val, including the Vultures, when, as far as I know, his father had met only with us. When I discovered the Red Maya was peddling the signs, oaths, and covenants to other drug cartels and street and prison gangs on both sides of the border, I wondered if what we got from him wasn't obtainable from other sources."

Now Tito was truly perplexed, as he stared at his father. " 'Other sources,' Father? I don't understand."

"Sources like us. You and I. The Maya and his son never passed on anything tangible, anything they owned. They used signs, oaths, and covenants that had been passed down through centuries . . . many centuries . . . from their ancestors." Tito was puzzled at the direction his father was going.

Ruben continued. "After I stopped going to Zake-Val, I went into my office one day, locked the door, and made the sign of the Serpent that the Maya had shown me. I recited the oath of the Brotherhood. That same surge of overwhelming dark influence entered my being and empowered me. It was the same kind of confidence that I had received from the Maya all those years at Zake-Val."

Tito could hardly believe what his father was telling him.

Ruben sounded almost apologetic as he went on. "The concepts of murder, mayhem, deception, and secrecy were suddenly even more ingrained in my way of thinking than at Zake-Val. Some invisible force started programming these avenues into my mind and soul by some invisible power as sure roads to success in our business. I was compelled to believe these acts were not only important but absolutely necessary in carrying out our work."

Tito was amazed that his father had been able to invoke the power of the Underworld without the intervention of the Mayan men.

Ruben's face clouded with a look of stress and apprehension. "I even heard the same loud, rustling sounds, like tree limbs shaking in a fierce wind. Do you remember? The rustling of the leaves, the groaning sounds coming out of the storm, the wind blowing through the window shutters while the windows were closed—all those same things. It was all there and maybe even more. I understood then and there that the evil powers of the Underworld are so anxious to manifest themselves to and through human beings that they don't need to be conjured up by any one person. Anyone can submit themselves to the powers of evil without all the drama we'd experienced with the Maya. Those powers enter the hearts of men when men give room to them by letting down their guard and craving that which is not right, as I have done!"

Tito didn't know what to say. He just continued to observe his father carefully, wondering if his father could possibly be speaking rationally in his sickness.

Ruben was intent on getting his message through to Tito. "It's a diabolical form of inspiration, son. Over the years, the Brotherhood has needlessly paid millions to the Maya for something that we believed we needed to excel in this business."

Ruben's voice grew quiet. His strength was waning. Tito leaned over his father as he listened intently. "I learned an important lesson," Ruben whispered. "We never needed the Maya or his son. We only thought we did. The powers of the Serpent are so intent and anxious to burst out into humanity that they will come forth to support anyone involved in the work of evil. Miguel's Book of Mormon refers to that serpent as Satan, or the devil."

Tito's eyes opened wide. "We've been supported by the devil, haven't we, Father? That's why we're so rich, isn't it?"

"I believe so, son. That's why we've been so successful, as have our competitors. It has nothing to do with any patron saint of drugs, as many would have you believe. We kill someone, nobody says anything. We rob from another gang, so what? That's how it's done. We lie to get ahead. If we don't, we get behind. We gain our advantage dishonestly. Then we just look at it as survival."

Tito was frustrated and confused. For years, he had known that what the Brotherhood was involved in was dishonest and immoral. He just hadn't thought of it as satanic—as something that could propel him toward damnation. Up to that point, he personally had never spilled blood nor ordered such an act. At that moment, sitting at his father's deathbed, Tito vowed he never would.

Ruben continued. "When I read a certain page in Miguel's book, I found out all about the being the Maya had always referred to as the Serpent. It's in a part of the book called the book of Helaman. I've marked the place. Please, read it to me, son."

Tito found the section his father referred to. He had indeed marked it heavily with red ink. Tito began reading the sixth chapter of Helaman, verse twenty-one.

" 'But behold, Satan did stir up the hearts of the more part of the Nephites' . . . Father, who are the Nephites?" Tito asked.

"Miguel said they were the white-skinned people who lived near here about twenty-five hundred years ago. At first they were a good people, but they grew evil. That's all I know, son. Keep reading . . . please."

Tito continued.

" '. . . Insomuch that they did unite with those bands of robbers, and did enter into their covenants and their oaths.' Those are the same words the Maya and the Red Maya used. Covenants, oaths . . . this is incredible!" Tito kept reading, " 'That they would protect and preserve one another in whatsoever difficult circumstances they should be placed, that they should not suffer for their murders, and their plunderings, and their stealing—' "

Ruben interrupted. "Remember the contract we make each of our people sign, Tito, before they can go to work for us? The Maya gave me those contracts. I always wondered where he had come up with those commitments. I always thought they were his own idea."

Tito's voice rose a little. "Father, what have we gotten ourselves into?"

"Just keep reading, son."

Tito continued on verse twenty-two. " 'And it came to pass that they did have their signs, yea, their secret signs, and their secret words; and this that they might distinguish a brother who had entered into the covenant, that whatsoever wickedness his brother should do he should not be injured by his brother, nor by those who did belong to his band, who had taken this covenant.'

" 'And thus they might murder, and plunder, and steal, and commit whoredoms and all manner of wickedness, contrary to the laws of their country and also the laws of their God.' "

Tito felt lightheaded as he closed the book and reached slowly to place it on the table next to his father's bed. He looked at the ailing man straight in the eye. "This is us! It describes us perfectly. Us and the Vultures and all the other people working the fruits of the field like we are. This is how we survive. This is how we succeed.

"How can we change anything? This is all we know how to do! We're too far into it now to just walk away. We have established our place in society and our place in the community."

"I know, son, I know. I've struggled with this dilemma for years. I've made my choice. I chose to continue harvesting the fruits of the field—the marijuana, the opium, the cocaine—and now I fear the consequences of my choice, but I had to be forthright with you because I'll be gone soon. Then the choices for the Brotherhood will be yours to make."

Ruben pointed to the book still in Ruben's hands. "There is one more part in Miguel's book that sometimes haunts me, Tito. It is in Alma. I have marked it. Please read it."

Again, Tito read for his father from the thirty-fifth verse of the thirty-fourth chapter.

" 'For behold, if you have procrastinated the day of your repentance even until death, behold, ye have become subjected to the spirit of the devil, and he doth seal you his; therefore, the Spirit of the Lord hath withdrawn from you, and hath no place in you, and the devil hath all power over you; and this is the final state of the wicked.' "

With a saddened and somewhat frightened expression rolling over his countenance, Ruben looked solemnly into his son's eyes and said, "Tito, I fear I have fallen into this category. I implore you, don't make the same mistake!"

Tito honestly feared not only for his father but for the direction his own life had taken. "I won't, Father. I will remember what you have said."

Ruben pulled his son close to him and whispered in a rapidly waning voice, "Look after your sister and your cousins as much as you can. I love you, Tito."

For the first time in many years, Tito felt a tear working its way down the side of his face. "I love you too, Papa." It was the first time either of them had uttered those words to each other.

Tito embraced his father, kissed his forehead, and left the room, cradling in his arms the metal case with the Miguel's book inside. It was the last time he saw his father alive.

During Ruben's funeral and subsequent burial, Tito pondered all that Ruben had told him from his deathbed. He reviewed the pages in Miguel's book that his father had marked, and as he read them, Tito experienced a strange, cleansing feeling that he could not quite understand.

CHAPTER THIRTEEN
THE PHONE CALL

CULIACÁN, MEXICO
9:00 SUNDAY MORNING

FEDERICO'S CELL PHONE vibrated in his pocket as he rode in the passenger seat of a sedan following the car taking Elena further into Mexico. Federico asked Aurelio to pull over for a bathroom stop.

Once Federico was alone in the bathroom, he punched in a number. "Yeah, boss, it's Federico."

"*Hola,* Federico. We've got something urgent." Tito's tone was serious. Federico, like the rest of Tito's men, held the boss in high respect. When the boss called like this, in the wee hours of the morning, advising something was "urgent," Federico listened intently. He figured it had something to do with Elena.

Tito continued, "Remember when our other sources advised that El Gordo was considering a 'hit' on my uncle? Enrique Guzman, the prosecutor?"

Federico knew what was coming. "Right, boss. It was about a week ago."

"The Vultures have his daughter, Elena. They have declared war on my family." Tito's voice was dead serious.

Federico sucked in a deep breath and said excitedly, "I'm already on it, boss!"

"You're what?" Tito demanded.

"I was with the Vultures yesterday afternoon when they grabbed her at her grandfather's house in Clairemont Mesa. They killed the old man in cold blood. Then they snatched her."

"Where are you?" asked Tito with heightened interest, sickened by the news of his grandfather's murder and his cousin's abduction by the Vultures.

"We're a few hours south into Mexico via the San Ysidro check point, heading toward some training camp the Vultures have outside of Culiacán. I tried to call you before from some hilly country but I couldn't get service. I think they're going to hold her at the training compound as ransom for the release of El Gordo's sons, who are being held at the San Diego County Jail on drug charges.

Tito asked, "How is Elena?"

"One of the men hit her in the face, and then they gave her too much medication to calm her down." Federico related how he had observed Elena almost stumble into the path of an oncoming vehicle as she reached out for it. "She has been treated by a nurse since then, who seemed to know what she was doing. The girl seems a little better. I've kept an eye on her."

"Anything else?" Tito asked.

"One more thing," Federico added. "She saw El Gordo kill an old man at a gas station, just to get gas in a hurry. She's been pretty well shocked."

"Federico, I'm putting this into your hands." Federico had never heard Tito so serious. "Keep her safe until I can work something out to get her out of there. And remember, Federico, this girl is my cousin . . . my own flesh and blood!" Tito couldn't have been clearer.

Federico felt a little chill inside, realizing that failure in this matter was not an option as far as his boss was concerned. He knew that assuring the Guzman girl's safety was a "life or death" situation for him as well as for her.

"Federico," Tito added. "You haven't been with the Brotherhood that long, but you haven't let us down yet. I know you won't now, will you?"

As Federico felt the sting of that remark, he knew the comment was more of a warning than a question. He knew the boss could be nice, real nice, but Tito was not one to tolerate failure either. Federico was well aware that there could be life-ending ramifications for failure.

"I'll be all over this, boss. You have my word. I'll keep you posted."

"*Gracias*, Federico. *Muchísimas gracias!*"

Once Tito had ended the call, Federico walked out of the bathroom and back to the car.

"I thought you'd died in there!" yelled Aurelio.

"It was the jalapenos, my friend," Federico replied, grinning.

CHAPTER FOURTEEN
POLITICS, RELIGION, AND ICE CREAM

SAN DIEGO
9:35 SUNDAY MORNING

DUE TO HIS advanced emphysema, seventy-five-year-old Erwin Granger, the stake patriarch, was becoming more and more limited in his ability to present his Sunday School lessons.

Before retiring at age sixty-eight, Brother Granger had found time to serve as a bishop twice, a counselor in a stake presidency, and as a mission president for three years in Bolivia, where Elder Mark Madden was one of his missionaries.

It was Erwin Granger who had given Elena her patriarchal blessing a year before—a blessing to guide her throughout her life. When Brother Granger was notified earlier that morning about Elena's abduction, he and other local Church members began a special fast for her. At first, he agonized for Elena. But as the impressions he received while giving Elena her blessing returned to his memory, he was comforted in his concerns for her. Somehow, he knew she would be rescued and would eventually live to become a mother.

Erwin Granger was one of countless ward members who admired Elena for the kindness she demonstrated to elderly people, especially her poor grandfather, although she remained somewhat indifferent toward Church activity.

The doorbell rang. It was Jim Taylor, a neighbor and fellow widower with whom Erwin visited regularly.

"Hello, Jim!" Erwin motioned for his friend to come into the living room, where they sat down on either end of the couch.

"So, Erwin, how's the emphysema?" Jim asked.

"About the same, really. I'm still hacking away . . . about like a chainsaw."

A smile creased Jim's lips. He admired the way his old friend was able to joke about his ailment. He tried to conjure up a little humor of his own: "Maybe a little lubricant would help . . . a squirt of WD-40 or something along that line." Both men chuckled. Their friendship went back many years, and they were totally comfortable with each other.

"The truth of the matter is, Jim, I'm beginning to realize my time on earth is very limited now, and that's okay. I'll be more than happy to be back with my Helen. The problem is, I've still got a couple of really important messages to get out to my Sunday School class before I croak. One of them is this afternoon."

Jim was saddened at the thought of losing his old friend and didn't want to talk about it. "What's the lesson about?"

"It's sensitive, Jim. Quite sensitive. But people need to hear it straight, instead of all this beating around the bush."

Jim's eyebrows lifted slightly. "What do you mean, Erwin?"

The old patriarch's face reddened as he removed a handkerchief from his pocket, covered his mouth, and began hacking away.

"Erwin, can I get you a glass of water?" Jim asked.

Erwin raised his hand, shaking his head, stopped coughing, and stuffed the handkerchief back into his pocket. "No, Jim. I'm okay. Anyway, I know it's not considered 'politically correct' to mix politics and religion. In today's world, we're supposed to walk on eggshells as we mask important details about our religion and political beliefs because we don't want to offend anyone." Jim knew that his old friend was deeply opposed to society's status quo.

"How do we change that?" Jim asked.

"As I approach my Sunday School lesson today, I know there's a real stigma in expressing how I feel, especially if it goes against the grain of socially acceptable views—even those of some Church members."

"You're right, Erwin. It's a real problem!" Jim answered. "A man just can't say what he really feels anymore. I've loved this country all my life, but in this liberal political environment, I feel like I have to skate around any issue that appears debatable or the least bit controversial just to avoid confrontation. I know, just like you do, that Elena Guzman wouldn't have been taken if we didn't have such porous borders, but you say anything about illegal immigration, and you're instantly branded a troublemaking radical!"

"I know, Jim," Erwin said. "But at this stage of my life, with one foot in the grave and the other on a banana peel, I just want to tell it like it is. Like so many of our neighbors here in Southern California, I'm more concerned than ever about the skyrocketing number of violent deaths along the border. But with all this talk about a fence and about beefing up our border security, nothing is really happening to prevent what happened to Elena. In fact, they're talking about taking two hundred and eighty officers off the border and reassigning them.

"Someone needs to confront the drug cartels and prevent them from doing business in the United States. And I'm not just referring to the drug trafficking violence between the cartels but the number of innocent bystanders being hewn down by stray bullets on both sides of the border. I'm referring to people like Elena Guzman and her grandfather." Erwin knew deep down that if society's indifference continued, especially regarding the border, abductions and kidnappings such as Elena Guzman's would become the norm. All these concerns had haunted him over the last several months, even before he had received word of Elena's disappearance.

"It's a rolling snowball," Jim lamented, "and I don't know how we stop it. We're living in a changing society where the government has taken over Wall Street, the banks, the auto industry, and now wants to control our health care. They want to pull out all the stops in order to promote socialism. Leaving the borders open for political advantage, hoping all the illegals will vote a liberal ticket when they're given amnesty is part of the plan. Of course, that just leaves the borders open for terrorists and cartel thugs to come and go at their leisure. You know how I feel? I feel like I'm on the outside looking in, without being a part of the country anymore."

Erwin looked directly into his old friend's eyes. *He's right,* Erwin thought. *America's values are becoming increasingly challenged and headed for extinction. I've got to be forthright. I've got to tell it how it is—starting with my class today!*

"You know, Jim, I'm going to be honest with you. Things just aren't the same without Helen. Besides, since I've stopped mincing words, I've noticed people are becoming less and less comfortable around me. I don't want to be a thorn in anyone's side."

"I'll always be your friend," Jim assured Erwin as he flashed a smile and placed a hand on his friend's shoulder. "Especially as long as you keep making breakfast over here on Sunday mornings."

"I will, Jim, as long as you're still backward enough to want to eat it!" Both men broke into subdued laughter.

"I know what you're saying," Jim continued. "Believe me. With my conservative views, I'm painted as an extremist. You know my attitude about liberal government and how I feel toward our trend toward socialism. People tell me not to worry . . . that it'll all be over in a few years. But who knows for sure? And how do you repair all the damage?"

"That's just it. You can't diminish standards of morality and responsibility and then masquerade them in terms like 'change' and 'progress.' "

The two men moved into the kitchen, where Erwin pulled a carton out of the freezer and asked, "How about ice cream for breakfast again this week, my friend? Would you like your regular . . . chocolate syrup without the nuts?"

Jim grinned at Erwin's audacity. "You never cease to amaze me, Erwin! You've got a real flair for making those sundaes . . . and even remembering my *gustos!*"

Once the friends were seated at the kitchen table, Erwin

admitted, "I'm only feeding you so you'll have the energy to answer my next question, old friend. It's the same question I'm going to ask the members of my class today."

"Okay, I'm ready," Jim answered as he downed a spoonful of ice cream.

"All right," Erwin said. "We're members of The Church of Jesus Christ of Latter-day Saints. As members of that faith, we accept the twelfth article of faith, which states: 'We believe in being subject to kings, presidents, rulers, and magistrates, in obeying, honoring, and sustaining the law.' Now, how do we balance our support of that belief with our need to be courageous and active in taking a stand in defending our country's standards when its foundation is being shaken by our own leaders?"

Jim was silent. He looked perplexed as he struggled to articulate a response.

Erwin continued. "Think about it, Jim. The exemplary standards that have set us apart for so long as the last bastion of enduring freedom and morality are clearly being challenged from within."

Jim's silence was not unexpected. *Few Church members are able to answer that question,* Erwin thought. But it was a question that needed a response. *How do we really support the substance of the twelfth article of faith when we can't, in good faith, agree with the direction our government is going?*

Jim finally came around. "I'm glad *you're* teaching that class, Erwin, and not me!"

The men finished off their ice cream and put their dishes in the sink.

Erwin thought of the occasions when he had been criticized by people who stated almost in blissful ignorance, "You just can't mix church and politics, Brother Granger!" He feared deep down that if people didn't take a stand soon, they would be lulled away until they found themselves part of a socialistic society that looked to the government—instead of themselves—for their answers.

As Jim was leaving, he hugged his old friend and said, "Erwin, don't hold back today in your class. I'll have your back!"

"So you like it down there in the lions' den too, Jim?" Erwin said with a laugh. "See you in a few hours."

Before putting on his suit coat later that afternoon, Erwin knelt at his bedside and prayed that the members of his class would receive his message in the spirit in which it was intended. He prayed with great energy for Elena especially and then walked out the door toward the chapel just two blocks away.

CHAPTER FIFTEEN
THE SUNDAY SCHOOL CLASS

THE PRESIDENT OF the Gospel Doctrine class reminded everyone of the special fast for Elena, and the brother who offered the opening prayer asked for her well-being and for a blessing of peace and comfort for her family.

Brother Granger then arose, excited about his lesson. He fought through a bout of emphysemic hacking, but after drinking from a bottle of water, he regained his composure and looked out at his class.

"In the year 1847, when the Church was gathered at Winter Quarters in Council Bluffs, Iowa, the Lord revealed to Brigham Young what is now Section 136 of the Doctrine and Covenants— a revelation that we need to endure great challenges if we are to be worthy of returning to live with God. Verse 31 reads as follows:

" 'My people must be tried in all things, that they may be prepared to receive the glory that I have for them, even the glory of Zion; and he that will not bear chastisement is not worthy of my kingdom.'

"This relates indirectly to Elena Guzman's abduction. When we speak of enduring and suffering, we often think of physical trials . . . such as passing through the freezing snows of Wyoming in handcarts in the 1860s or protecting ourselves against wild Indians. I submit that with all the early pioneers had to suffer, they would still not trade their trials for the more subtle, spiritually challenging trials of today. We have heard that when we meet those pioneers in the hereafter, they will say, 'Wow, you endured the trials of the twenty-first century! You guys were gutsy! How'd you ever do it?' "

Brother Granger surveyed the class, evaluating their response, before continuing.

"Currently, brothers and sisters, we are enduring the frustration and the despair of experiencing a transition in our society that has indirectly opened the doors for Elena Guzman's abduction. Our government has softened its stance on illegal immigration, allowing the borders to become more porous for lack of action. I believe the kind of suffering the Guzmans are suffering are part of what President Young was alluding to.

"Here is the question: What are the limits to *your* endurance and longsuffering? The Guzmans have lost a son, a daughter-in-law, a grandfather, and now, temporarily, a daughter. This has to do, in large part, with our government not adequately securing our borders with Mexico. Put yourself in the Guzmans' shoes. They obviously have not turned to vigilantism, nor have they denounced the President or his administration. Haven't they proven through Enrique Guzman's dedication to public office that they believe in 'being subject to kings, presidents, rulers and magistrates, and in honoring, obeying and sustaining the law,' one of the basic tenets of our faith? Of course, they have. The Prophet Joseph Smith was arrested numerous times for crimes he never committed, yet he still submitted to the laws of his country and never denounced the government leaders.

"What about us? How can we continue to sustain and be subject to our leaders even though we might be extremely uncomfortable and fearful of the direction our country and our society are going?"

Brother Granger realized he had hit some "hot buttons" when he noticed several class members with raised eyebrows and others fidgeting in their seats.

"But," he continued, "the other side of the coin is this: if the Spirit within you tells you there will be more abductions like Elena's because we're soft on our borders, if you truly feel embracing abortion and weakening our military and taking over our banking systems and health care are directions that will morally bankrupt us and internally weaken us, then you have a huge challenge. How do you balance being true to your conscience and other spiritual principles with living the twelfth article of faith?"

The room was silent. No one seemed willing to answer, but deep down, Erwin Granger somehow understood that somehow everyone present knew they had to find a way to deal with the current situation. Some idle chatter erupted toward the back of the classroom regarding an incident that had occurred about the same time Elena was abducted. An innocent American bystander had died in a crossfire of rival drug traffickers in one of the parks in San Ysidro.

John Farnsworth spoke up and was adamant in his views. "I don't have the answer to that question, Brother Granger, but like everyone else here who lives near the border, I'm way past being just frustrated. Apparently, there's no end in sight to all this killing, more and more of which is happening on US soil. We are now the victims."

Another class member, Tom Kline, interjected his thoughts. "What can we expect from such loose border security? Drug traffickers are even starting to grow their marijuana over here. Then you hear a member of Congress stand up and tell the illegals they're the hope of America, that they're the real patriots, and that immigration raids in our country are un-American!"

These remarks were of particular concern to Mark Madden, who was present with his wife, Katie, and who was riding a fine line in his positions as regional coordinator of Homeland Security and stake president. He wasn't happy with political diatribe being enacted in a Church setting like this. Nevertheless, he was sympathetic to the concerns being expressed by members of his stake who were becoming increasingly alarmed over the rising violence sweeping across their borders.

Brother Granger met the issues head on. "I appreciate both

your concerns, brethren, but rather than dwell on sad events we're witnessing, it would be wiser to learn the reasons for our dilemma and become aware of how we, as Church members, can understand the problem and never become part of it. In light of recent events, I've decided to present a special lesson today on what I believe is at the core of all this. I've heard several of you voice your concerns both in and out of the Church regarding the organizational capacity of the drug cartels, how much more effective they seem to be than the Mexican police and military, how they can penetrate even armored vehicles with their sophisticated weaponry, how within five years, the cartels could be in charge of Mexico, and how Mexico could become a 'failed state.' "

Mark Madden's eyebrows turned up a little as he wondered where his old mission president was going with all this.

Brother Granger then looked out over his class almost pleadingly. "May I offer my humble opinion regarding what I believe is the reason these evil organizations have so much power? And then could we consider together what we, as families, can do to counteract their influence? What we can do as members of the Church?"

Silence fell over the class. Brothers Farnsworth and Kline, the two more outspoken class members, were just about ready to expand on more of their opinions, but when they noticed the steely, serious demeanor in Brother Granger's countenance as he struggled to hold back another coughing spasm, they bit their lips and listened intently.

"The Book of Mormon teaches us that 'the blood of the saints,' which I say could also apply to the innocent victims in these border wars, 'shall cry unto the Lord because of secret combinations and the work of darkness.' I strongly believe that those secret combinations—the same ones that eventually destroyed the Nephite nation, are at the core of the bloodshed along the border today."

Brother Granger's statement struck a chord somewhere deep down in President Madden's soul. *He's right!* he thought. *This is what I have always believed.*

Mark could tell that some class members were a little taken

back. He could imagine their thoughts: *What does old Brother Granger really know about all this? He's not really speaking under the influence of the Holy Ghost, is he?*

"The reason the Gadianton robbers and others affiliated with them were successful in destroying their society is found in Helaman 6:21. Will someone read that for us?"

One of the class members said, "I've got it," and began to read:

" 'But behold, Satan did stir up the hearts of the more part of the Nephites, insomuch that they did unite with those bands of robbers, and did enter into their covenants and their oaths, that they would protect and preserve one another in whatsoever difficult circumstances they should be placed, that they should not suffer for their murders, and their plunderings, and their stealings.' "

Brother Granger said, "Thank you. Please read verse 21 as well":

" 'And it came to pass that they did have their signs, yea, their secret signs, and their secret words; and this that they might distinguish a brother who had entered into the covenant, that whatsoever wickedness his brother should do he should not be injured by his brother, nor by those who did belong to his band, who had taken this covenant.' "

"So, brothers and sisters," explained the elderly teacher, "in my opinion, this is why the drug traffickers, and many like them in other evil enterprises throughout the world, are so successful. Let's read on. Who has verse 23?"

A sister began to read:

" 'And thus they might murder, and plunder, and steal, and commit whoredoms and all manner of wickedness, contrary to the laws of their country and also the laws of their God.' "

Brother Granger once again covered his mouth with a handkerchief, coughed a few seconds before going on in a raspy voice.

"Satan figured out all the angles with these secret combinations. He even inspired them to punish any informants among them. Listen to verse 24:

'And whosoever of those who belonged to their band should reveal unto the world of their wickedness and their abominations, should be tried, not according to the laws of their country, but according to the laws of their wickedness, which had been given by Gadianton and Kishkumen.' "

As he turned the pages excitedly, Brother Granger asked the class to consider the meaning of Ether 8:22:

" 'And whatsoever nation shall uphold such secret combinations, to get power and gain, until they shall spread over the nation, behold, they shall be destroyed.' "

"Brothers and sisters, are there evidences of that today?" he asked.

Brother John Cloverly, a high-school history teacher, responded, "Yes, I believe there are. I would consider Iraq under Saddam Hussein an example. Another would be Germany under Adolph Hitler."

"Good!" Brother Granger declared. "What are some examples closer to the text we are considering? In the Book of Mormon, John?"

Brother Cloverly responded, "The Lamanite groups, interspersed with evil Nephites that joined them, and the Gadianton robbers, which we read about toward the end of the Book of Mormon; these people wiped out the few remaining righteous Nephites, and what was the result? Look at the ruins in Central America: Tikal in Guatemala, Palenque in Mexico, Copan in Honduras . . . beautiful palaces, government buildings, and temples were suddenly abandoned and subsequently deteriorated. I believe many evil individuals among those nations may have been in possession of the same secret combinations you referred us to in the scriptures. And I believe those combinations led to their eventual destruction."

Brother Granger smiled. He had found someone who really got it! "We're on the same frequency, John. I believe these warring cartels who are destroying Mexico and endangering the United States will eventually be destroyed, but much will depend on our righteousness as a nation and as families, to see that come to pass."

Erwin Granger could see that people were finally beginning to understand as they listened attentively. "As Christ's followers, we need to seriously ponder how we can avoid evil so that we don't become like those who followed Gadianton and Kishku-men, the leaders of the robbers. We don't need to become part of the problem. Let's read earlier in Helaman, chapter 6 about how the people became susceptible. Who has that?" A young, preg-nant woman held up her hand. "Yes, Sister Gates. If you will.

Sister Gates read:

" 'For behold, the Lord had blessed them so long with the riches of the world that they had not been stirred up to anger, to wars, nor to bloodshed; therefore they began to set their hearts upon their riches; yea, they began to seek to get gain that they might be lifted up one above another; therefore they began to commit secret murders, and to rob and plunder, that they might get gain.' "

Looking out over the class, Brother Granger asked, "In what ways do we lift ourselves up above one another?"

Myrna Haycock answered. "I think we try to minimize one another's accomplishments, especially if we haven't achieved them ourselves. We have a tendency sometimes to want others down on our level so we can more easily climb up to theirs. Sometimes we try to lift ourselves up by wearing expensive clothing and driving expensive cars that we can't really afford. We do this in an effort to elevate ourselves to a point where we can look down on others."

"Good point, Sister Haycock," Brother Granger said. "In addition, those who live by evil oaths and covenants will never be governed by enlightened leaders, nor will they listen to the teach-ings of a prophet. Read with me in the book of Ether 11:22:

" 'And they did reject all the words of the prophets, because of their secret society and wicked abominations.' "

Brother Farnsworth raised his hand. "Brother Granger, if this is the case, then why haven't the general authorities of our church come out and told us what you have?"

Brother Granger looked Brother Farnsworth straight in the eyes, and said, "But they have!"

Brother Farnsworth was left with a puzzled expression.

The aged patriarch continued. "Our church leaders have been exhorting us for decades to study the scriptures. The prophets have discussed major issues of morality and sin and the effects of both for a long time. They have given us volumes of information and revelation, in addition to the standard works, to quicken and facilitate our understanding. We are told that we should not be commanded in all things. We are told instead to be prayerful and studious and then draw our own conclusions, based on what we know and feel.

"Our Church leaders can't come out publicly and identify certain elements of our society and say, 'It's them! Go get 'em!' or 'That group or organization is evil.' That would create chaos for—and possibly even violence against—the Church. Instead, our leaders enlighten us so we can understand the scriptures and the important issues of our day. Then they hope we will draw fair and accurate conclusions. As I said at the beginning of this class, these are conclusions that I have drawn, based upon my light and knowledge. My own conclusions are that Mexican drug cartels, along with other bloodthirsty, sinister organizations throughout the world who strive only for power, material gain, and unrighteous influence, are sustained by secret oaths, words, actions, and combinations."

President Madden was impressed by Brother Erwin's confidence and commitment to what he believed.

Erwin Granger continued. "The first murder ever, when Cain slew Abel, is when the secret combinations surfaced for the first time. We read about that in Helaman 6:27.

" 'Yea, that same being who did plot with Cain, that if he would murder his brother Abel it should not be known unto the world. And he did plot with Cain and his followers from that time forth.'

"So much of the damage we are seeing today came down from the time of Cain's assault on Abel."

The members of the class thoughtfully pondered Brother Granger's statement.

Tom Kline was ready with another question. "Where the heck are these secret oaths and combinations documented? How do the bad guys find access to them, anyway?"

Brother Granger referred Brother Kline to Helaman 6:26 and asked him to read it.

" 'Now behold, those secret oaths and covenants did not come forth unto Gadianton from the records which were delivered unto Helaman; but behold, they were put into the heart of Gadianton by that same being who did entice our first parents to partake of the forbidden fruit.' "

"That answers that," responded Brother Kline. "Apparently the secret oaths and covenants weren't recorded anywhere. They must have been passed down orally and inspired by the devil."

The questions really started flying.

"So, if you're right about this secret combination thing," one sister near the back began, "what you're saying is that Satan is behind it. How do we know that for certain? Couldn't these cartels and other evil organizations have conjured up those ideas on their own?"

Brother Granger was ready. "Read in 2 Nephi 26:22. What does it say?"

" 'And there are also secret combinations, even as in times of old, according to the combinations of the devil, for he is the founder of all these things; yea, the founder of murder, and works of darkness.' "

The class members were silent, obviously reading and rereading the verses for more understanding as Brother Granger stood there smiling, realizing he was getting through to his class.

Brother Granger went on. "The prophet Alma knew what would happen to the people of our day who had this secret evil at the core of their operations. In Helaman 6:25, it states:

" 'Now behold, it is these secret oaths and covenants which Alma commanded his son should not go forth unto the world, lest they should be a means of bringing down the people unto destruction.'

"We need to understand what it is that can move us and other Christians from Point A, where we are keeping the commandments and are righteous, to Point Z where we will enter into an evil society, as so many of the Nephites did. When the Nephites joined in with the Gadianton robbers and other evildoers, they eventually brought about the destruction of the righteous part of the Nephite nation. In Helaman, we are told specifically that

Gadianton and his followers, with their secret combinations, did prove the overthrow and entire destruction of the Nephites."

Tom Kline's hand shot up again. "Okay, Brother Granger. We know the Nephites were wiped out. But that's where it stopped, didn't it? I mean, how do you know those combinations, or whatever they are, are still around?" Brother Kline had that "I gotcha now" look on his face.

Brother Granger asked "Who'd like to read Helaman 6:30?"

A sister raised her hand and began reading: " 'And behold, it is he who is the author of all sin. And behold, he doth carry on his works of darkness and secret murder, and doth hand down their plots, and their oaths, and their covenants, and their plans of awful wickedness, from generation to generation according as he can get hold upon the hearts of the children of men.' "

"I believe that's your answer, Tom." Brother Granger was grateful to have those scriptures right at his fingertips on the day he needed inspiration. "Those evil oaths, covenants, and combinations come down from generation to generation, and it's my own opinion that they are still here today. Furthermore, I believe the end result of that fact is the blood being spilled today along our borders by those who seek to get gain."

Many in the class nodded their heads in support of the patriarch's conviction.

Brother Granger continued, "The Lord has a plan for those individuals in league with Satan. We know the Lord is, and always will be, in control. In 2 Nephi 10:15, it says:

" 'Wherefore, for this cause, that my covenants may be fulfilled which I have made unto the children of men, that I will do unto them while they are in the flesh, I must needs destroy the secret works of darkness, and of murders, and of abominations.'

"In other words, with all their wealth, their high-powered weaponry, their sneaky ways, and their evil intents, they'll live like fat cats today, but tomorrow they'll be in a world of hurt." Again, people nodded in agreement.

Ray Dalton spoke up. "Brother Granger, you mentioned that you believe several other evil organizations in the world today may have those secret combinations. I suppose there could be a lot of them, besides the drug cartels. There are the prison gangs, certain motorcycle gangs, some street gangs like the Bloods and the Crips. Then there's Al Qaeda, the Taliban . . . . Couldn't the list just go on and on?"

"It could," agreed Brother Granger. "Where there is murder, plunder, deception, mayhem, and other forms of abomination at the foundation of an organization, we would be correct in believing that it is evil, and we need not hesitate to believe that Satan is the source of evil, and that the same Satan who whispered into the ears of Cain, Gadianton, Kishkumen, and other evil men we read about in the scriptures can also whisper into the ears of evil men today."

Brother Farnsworth was ready with another question. "You've mentioned the oaths quite frequently. How can an oath be powerful enough to motivate individuals to commit the kind of mayhem we are seeing take place on our borders?"

"I don't know exactly how that works, John," answered the patriarch. "I only know it does. In Ether 8:16, you can read about that."

Mark Madden noticed a change in Erwin Granger. He perceived a brightness surrounding the aged patriarch as his coughing and wheezing abated. His brightened countenance seemed increasingly refreshed and invigorated as he cited scripture after scripture without hesitation to each question posed and to each inquiry brought up. He thought to himself, *I wonder if everyone else here is seeing Erwin as I am right now?*

The stake president had been particularly pleased with his old mission president's comments but was even more impressed with his near angelic countenance and the Spirit that was beginning to pour forth over the class. Mark and others in the classroom felt an awesome sense of appreciation for the fine man in front of him. Mark raised his hand and said, "I'll read that one, Brother Granger. That's Ether 8:16, right?"

"Right, President Madden. Thank you. Go ahead, please."

Mark read:

" 'And they were kept up by the power of the devil to administer these oaths unto the people, to keep them in darkness, to help such as sought power to gain power, and to murder, and to plunder, and to lie, and to commit all manner of wickedness and whoredoms.' "

Mark removed his reading glasses, pondered for a moment what he had read, and then added, "So, brothers and sisters, this indicates that if these oaths, covenants, and secret combinations can keep people in darkness and help evil people gain power, murder, and plunder, then these oaths just might be powerful enough to bring to pass what's happening today on our borders."

There was a long, thoughtful pause. Brother Granger knew the timing was right for his next question. "How do these problems brought about by secret combinations affect our own country?"

An answer came from the class. "The same way they are affecting Mexico."

"Can you be more specific?" the aged teacher asked.

The majority of the class was now scrambling through their scriptures to document an intelligent response. It was obvious that this class had really come alive, as they too witnessed the renewed vitality in their teacher and the change in his countenance. Sister Haycock was first to offer an answer. She stated excitedly, "In 3 Nephi 7:6–7, it reads:

" 'And the regulations of the government were destroyed, because of the secret combinations of the friends and kindreds of those who murdered the prophets. And they did cause a great contention in the land, insomuch that the more righteous part of the people had nearly all become wicked; yea, there were but few righteous men among them.' "

Even Tom Kline was eager to contribute. "Just before that scripture, there's another in 3 Nephi 6:27–30 that states in essence that the friends of wicked judges entered into covenants against righteousness. We all know what a bad judge can do."

Bristling from that remark, Brother Chris Heppner, a county superior court judge, cleared his throat a little nervously.

Brother Granger again took over. "In closing, brothers and sisters, I hope you can now appreciate why it is that I believe these references in the Book of Mormon and other scriptures that we have covered this afternoon correlate with the current problems we are facing, particularly the strife and tribulation along our borders and the Satanically inspired calamities happening in other parts of the world and even in many of the governments throughout the world. Most relevant, of course, is what has recently happened with our dear Elena.

"I would close with this last scripture from Ether 8:20:

" 'And now I, Moroni, do not write the manner of their oaths and combinations, for it hath been made known unto me that they are had among all people . . . ' "

"In summary, it is my fervent belief and conviction that these oaths and covenants were never put away, but that they are running rampant at the foundation of evil in the world today. I believe, however, that the organizations that have those same oaths and covenants at the core of their strength will be destroyed by the Lord in his due time, and that perhaps, we, through righteous living, can hasten that time.

"Regarding Elena Guzman, even though I consider her disappearance a great concern, I do not share the same apprehension of uncertainty that most of you do. I assure you now, as I have assured her parents, that when I gave her a patriarchal blessing at the age of sixteen, the Spirit inspired me to make certain promises to her, based on her faithfulness, regarding her future and her posterity. I promise you all, as I promised her parents, in the name of the Lord, that Elena will weather this storm." As Brother Granger said these words, his countenance continued to exude an unusual brilliance.

He continued. "I mentioned before that we must identify what it is that causes people to transgress from Point 'A' to Point 'Z,' where they become as evil as those we have discussed. We'll cover that more in detail in another lesson. I hope you'll all be there." The patriarch bore his testimony, closed in the name of Jesus Christ, and sat down.

Erwin Granger was never able to present that lesson. He passed away the following Wednesday.

CHAPTER SIXTEEN
THE TRAINING COMPOUND

TWENTY-FIVE MILES OUTSIDE OF CULIACÁN, MEXICO
1:30 MONDAY AFTERNOON, SEPTEMBER 27, 2010

AS THE FOUR sedans drove up to an isolated location in the Mexican landscape covered with the leftovers from an abandoned military training facility, several half-cylinder shaped rusted metal huts and a dozen rustic log cabins came into view. This is where the Vultures had set up their training compound where, twice each year during the spring and fall, they would come to retrain their veteran operatives and conduct initial training to identify and qualify recruits. All their men were afforded training in firearms and defensive tactics, surveillance, counter-surveillance strategies, and weapon and drug concealment methods—all of which were highly valuable techniques for drug traffickers.

Among the many rough dwellings was a more elegant home, apparently the past residence of a military commander where El Gordo resided off and on during the two-week period. He usually stayed five to six days total to ensure the training was moving along to his liking and subsequently creating headaches for all his underlings. It was an opportunity to spend time away from his family in Culiacán and to indulge his lusts in the company of other Mexican women who were willing to cook for him and otherwise accommodate his personal agenda.

Although it was early in the afternoon and several hours had passed since she had been medicated, and even though the past fifty miles had consisted mostly of bumpy and dusty dirty roads, Elena was still sleeping soundly upon the motorcade's arrival at the training camp. Federico and Aurelio carried the girl to one of the cabins and laid her down on a dusty army cot. Before leaving, Federico placed an old army blanket over her and a sweat-stained pillow under her head. When they left, Elena was still asleep. Federico grimaced as he observed the ugly bruise swelling on her right cheek area.

Federico and Aurelio sat down on a willow bench outside Elena's cabin for a few minutes, before heading over to the cabin they shared a short distance away.

"Well, *Paisano*, as long as drugs keep moving through Mexico like a river, people like her," signaling toward Elena, "will always end up a victim. *Pobrocita*. She is too pretty for a place like this," Aurelio sighed, gesturing toward the old abandoned army base.

As the two men continued chatting, five bald-headed men walked by, heading toward the quonset huts across the creek less than a hundred yards away. They were dressed in military camouflage uniforms and toted black leather utility belts with a model of pistol that Federico had never before seen. The men had detached expressions as they walked by and wouldn't even nod as Federico and Aurelio waved at them.

"Who are those guys?" Federico asked. "Where'd they come from?"

"El Gordo brought them in," Aurelio said. "They came in last week to help with the training. They go by the name *Los Pelones,* or the Bald Ones. They are former Special Forces operatives, but now they call themselves 'the New Soldiers,' and that's what their shaved heads are supposed to represent."

"Normally you would see the bald heads just on military recruits," said Federico.

"These guys are anything but that," Aurelio assured. "They are highly-trained, experienced fighters."

"Why do we need them?" asked Federico.

"Well, it's no secret that our men have always been able to

outgun and outfight the Mexican police, but these animals are something else! El Gordo brought them here to show us military techniques and high-powered weapons that not even the Mexican military have. Those pistols they are carrying are called *matapolicias,* or 'cop killers.' Their rounds can penetrate body armor, car doors, and windows." It was obvious Aurelio was awed by the *Pelones.*

"I've heard about the *Zetas* and the *Kaibiles* who give similar support to the Gulf cartels," Federico said. "The *Zetas* are deserters from the Mexican army who have become highly trained, and the *Kaibiles* are former Guatemalan Special Forces. I've heard both groups are extremely violent and are no more than trained mercenary killers. Sounds like they are of the same breed."

"That's right," said Aurelio. "Apparently, the *Zetas* and the *Pelones* fight each other a lot. They enjoy posting videos on the Internet of them torturing and beheading one other. I'm glad we won't be here more than two weeks."

"It figures that these are the kind of people the boss would want us to emulate," sighed Federico.

"Wherever they go, there will be trouble, and heads will roll . . . literally," Aurelio said with a shudder. "I hear they have killed people as far north as Dallas, Texas."

"Does El Gordo plan on outfitting us with those cop killer guns?" Federico asked, knowing this would be information the Brotherhood would benefit from, in addition to everything else he had learned about the *Pelones.*

"That's part of the boss's plan," Aurelio confirmed. "He wants whatever will cause the most damage. Since only the armed forces can get good guns like the .357 magnums or 9 millimeters in Mexico, the *Pelones* pay 'straw men' in the United States who have clean records to purchase better guns. El Gordo also has contacts with American street gangs that rob gun stores in towns along the border."

"The boss enjoys violence at its best, doesn't he?" Federico remarked.

"Yeah," Aurelio agreed. "More than anyone else I've ever known. Let me show you something. Take a walk with me."

They walked through the residential area that consisted of log cabins. Even at midday, the air was crisp, signaling the approach of fall. They crossed a foot bridge over a small creek and entered the same area of the compound where they had just seen the *Pelones*. This area contained the three metal buildings shaped like half-cylinders with rusted, pitted surfaces, indicating many years of abandonment by former military operatives.

Aurelio led Federico into one of the metal buildings, where they noticed weight-training equipment, rubber mats for practicing martial arts, ropes for climbing, and a boxing ring. A few trainees were sweating profusely as four of the *Pelones* they had seen walking by were hollering out cadences and blowing whistles, pushing the perspiring young men to what seemed to be their outer physical limits.

"The reason you're here today, Federico, involved in some of the more important details, like this one now with the Guzman girl, is because you flew through this kind of training. Many of these young kids want to quit the first time they throw up. But they know they can't just quit. El Gordo wouldn't let them just leave us and compromise our security . . . our methods. Instead of letting them quit, the boss makes sure they get lousy job assignments—cleaning toilets, chopping firewood brought down from the mountains, doing laundry—until they are thrown in here again for a second chance. If they don't make it the second time, they 'disappear,' if you know what I mean." Aurelio's lips creased slightly into a subdued smile. "Come with me." Aurelio motioned for Federico to follow him toward a corner room isolated from the rest of the area, where he cautiously opened a wooden door. A strong barnyard smell escaped, assaulting the men's nostrils immediately.

Federico stepped through the door quickly, as Aurelio closed it behind them. "Phew!" Aurelio said. "I've smelled chicken manure before, but not that strong!" No sooner had the words left his mouth than the two men were facing a strange sight.

Federico looked momentarily stunned upon discovering he was in a room full of live red roosters flying around, disturbed by the intrusion of not only Federico and Aurelio but three young trainees and the last bald-headed man. The three trainees were standing at attention in front of the *Pelon*, who had a whistle draped around his neck over his green military style T-shirt.

Aurelio immediately recognized Manolo Barto, the new trainee he had contacted for information about the Guzmans. Observing the scrawny wisp of a young man, he knew it was doubtful he would ever endure the training. Nevertheless, the information he had furnished helped the Vultures secure the Guzman girl, so he felt Manolo deserved a chance to prove himself.

Manolo also recognized Aurelio and nodded slightly at him. The fear in the young trainee's eyes was obvious.

Aurelio quickly approached the bald-headed drill instructor and whispered in his ear that he and Federico were there solely as observers. The soldier barely nodded and turned back to the three trainees as he brought the whistle up to his lips and blew it.

Instantly, the three trainees went after the chickens. Within a few seconds, each one had a rooster by its feet with one hand, securing their heads with the other. Two of the boys raised their prey to their mouths and, to Federico's astonishment, bit off their captured rooster's head.

Aurelio glanced toward Federico, smiling. "You didn't have to do that, did you, Federico?"

"No way!" answered the younger man. Federico grimaced as he observed blood dripping from the mouths of two of the trainees and from the headless necks of two of the roosters. As the trainees spit out the heads, Federico's stomach began pounding.

The two trainees who had succeeded in their assignments were wiping the blood from their mouths with the sleeves of their camouflage uniforms. Manolo Barto had yet to stuff the chicken's head into his mouth. He was just holding it to his face, making guttural sounds that signaled his readiness to vomit. The instructor was furious. "*Dale, cobarde.* Do it, you coward!"

Each time the reluctant Manolo would get the rooster's head near his lips, he face grew ashen. He averted his head as the bird kept trying to peck at him. "*No puedo!* I can't!" he finally uttered. The *Pelon* acted as though he had been personally insulted. He struck the trainee in the stomach with a long hardwood baton he had hanging from his utility belt for just such occasions. Then he dragged the hapless trainee outside the rooster pen and into a dark corner where he signaled two of his companion *Pelones* to join him.

The three men beat Manolo mercilessly with their wooden batons. Federico wanted to intervene. He was certain the young man had no idea of the extent of the cartel's expectations when he had solicited employment with them. But Federico knew that intervening would blow his cover as an informant, which would result in a beating of his own, if not death. He owed it to Tito, and to the Guzman girl, to stay out of it. "Is all of this really necessary?" Federico asked quietly.

"According to the boss, yes," Aurelio said. "He wants his men to be as mean and as unrelenting as he is. He wants them to regard violence and killing as no more than tools of the trade."

"Looks like he's getting the job done," Federico observed flatly, as his stomach continued to roll.

As Aurelio and Federico walked back to their cabin, Federico glanced over to where Elena was being held. Lucky for her, the young woman was still sleeping, oblivious to what was happening around her.

CHAPTER SEVENTEEN
THE STRIKE FORCE MEETING

Lieutenant Peter Green had secured the conference room at the San Diego Police Department for an emergency meeting regarding Elena's abduction. He briefed the task force on the effort to locate Elena. The FBI was well represented by "Big Bob" Brady, Special Agent in Charge of the Bureau's San Diego office. Since there was evidence of kidnapping and drug cartel involvement, the FBI had primary jurisdiction.

Historically, Enrique Guzman extended his help to local police agencies in the San Diego area in their drug investigations, charging their subjects with federal violations when the amounts of recovered controlled substances met the federal guidelines. Now with Enrique going through this ordeal, the local authorities wanted to reciprocate and were more than willing to turn over all their available resources to help find his daughter.

Enrique noticed a lot of officers there who could qualify as senior citizens, including Special Agent in Charge Brady, who had been given an extension on his mandatory retirement age of fifty-seven and was now pushing fifty-nine. Another was Jim Jones, a career Border Patrol officer who supervised the San Ysidro checkpoint. He was there because he knew Elena had probably been taken through San Ysidro. The two detectives from the San Diego Police Department who were assigned full time to Elena's case—Henry Cottle and Cesar Perez—were also present. And seated next to Enrique Guzman was his best friend, Mark Madden.

"Gentlemen," Lieutenant Green began, "I know we have a lot of ground to cover this morning, but first, on behalf of Chief Ranford and the rest of the SDPD, allow me to express our condolences to you, Mr. Guzman. We know you've already been through unspeakable tragedy with your son, and to hear this has happened to your father and your daughter was indeed a shock to all of us. We all mourn your loss and commit our resources to you."

A tear slowly worked its way down Enrique's face from underneath his glasses. He wiped it away and stood up to shake Green's hand. "Thank you, Lieutenant. Thank you very much. As the first order of business, I have brought copies of the ransom note I found in my father's journal early Sunday morning for each of you. The perpetrators obviously knew it would be found immediately, since it was in the book my father had been reading just prior to his death." Enrique passed a copy to each man present.

The officers studied the note carefully. "This note was written by El Gordo Diaz, the leader of the Vultures!" Green exclaimed. "We have seen other correspondence, mostly demand notes, that the gang has sent to other victims they have extorted. El Gordo almost always does his own writing. In fact, he's probably one of the few of these deadbeats that can write."

"That's where we have been wrong in the past about these younger gangs, lieutenant," Mark advised. "I think we've underestimated them. They have brains working for them. With unlimited resources, they are bringing in intellectual firepower, skilled attorneys, and enforcers and debt collectors. They're recruiting young talent from the ranks of American youth gangs."

Lieutenant Green jumped back in. "Elena's abduction is part of a trend. There are several hundred kidnappings each year in Phoenix. Most of the victims are illegal immigrants or are otherwise connected to the drug trade. The kidnappers trade the life of the victim for drug money owed. Elena's Guzman's abduction is not an isolated incident, but the motive behind it, including using her as ransom to release drug traffickers, is definitely a new twist."

"That's the problem here," Mark Madden pointed out. "Those examples just don't wash with Elena's disappearance. The perpetrators really believe they can get away with not only using Elena for ransom but that they can also coerce Enrique into resigning his position and backing off his prosecutorial mission.

"The stark reality is that the thrust of the cartel prosecution doesn't lie with just Enrique any more than it does with any of us individually. They are hedging their bets that Enrique, as the strike force attorney who has wreaked havoc on them now for so many years, can suddenly just turn off the spout. If they are naïve enough to think that taking Elena away will allow them to operate with impunity on both sides of the border, they must be crazy!"

"What is the Mexican government doing about all this?" Detective Cottle asked.

Mark responded. "As far as influencing or preventing the actions of the cartels in this country, such as Elena's abduction, they can't do much of anything. The most important issue is what we can do about it on *our* side of the border . . . starting right now!"

Detective Perez, a younger detective with limited experience, was chomping at the bit to ask a question. Unlike all the others in the group, he raised his hand first and was acknowledged by Lieutenant Green. Somewhat nervously, he posed a question directly to Enrique. "I was just wondering if any consideration has been given to the Brotherhood in Sinaloa being responsible for what has happened to Miss Guzman. After all, isn't it true that over the years the Hammer and his son, Tito, have repeatedly attempted to recruit you to their side?"

A pall of silence fell over the group as everyone tensed, realizing how Enrique Guzman might take the green investigator's remarks . . . especially under the circumstances. *Surely he has offended Enrique!* everyone thought. Lieutenant Green scowled at Detective Perez.

"You know, Detective Perez," Enrique answered without

malice, "that's a fair question. You haven't been around long enough to understand the age-old relationship between my family and the Brotherhood. I'm sure your lieutenant will explain it more in detail later, but I want you to know that the relationship is almost unbelievable, and even more so, considering that one of the groups of 'bad guys' we've been after is related to me and to Elena. Fortunately, because of that relationship and the obvious potential for conflict of interests, I have always been instructed not to pursue cases where the Brotherhood is suspect; however, I have, in every instance, referred those cases to prosecutors in my office whom I trusted would pursue them with vigor. Does that answer your question, Detective Perez?"

"Yes, sir. It does. I hope I didn't imply anything . . . dishonorable," Detective Perez responded timidly, looking away from the other officers present.

"To the contrary, Detective. It's a good question," Enrique assured him. "You should also know that my relative in the Brotherhood has promised that he would never in any way deter me from my work or try to influence my decisions with regard to my prosecutions, and he hasn't to this day. He has never given me reason to believe he would behave toward me any differently. My contact with him is extremely limited."

Detective Perez blushed, the embarrassment evident on his face. "Thank you, Mr. Guzman," he said sheepishly. He placed his elbows down on the table and gazed down directly between them. He could tell by the way the more experienced officers were looking at him that he had been out of line.

Mark weighed in again. "Regarding the apparent bribery issue, none of the Mexican police know where Elena is being hidden, or if they do, they're not reporting that information. If any of them have seen her, they've been paid off handsomely to keep quiet."

Mark continued. "Okay, gentlemen, let's talk about the specifics of how we can find Elena and what we're willing to negotiate when that time arrives. First, Jim, I'm wondering if you might have any thoughts about how Elena was transported over the border undetected."

Jim Jones raised his eyebrows. "Are you asking whether they could have taken her into Mexico by paying off someone on the border?" Jones paused, looking as though he was trying to filter the words his tongue was pushing through his teeth. Mark had never heard the man swear, so it came as a relief when Jones continued with a simple, resonant, "Yes. It happens all the time. I deal with this sort of thing over and over. The drug runners have endless funds to make sure certain people keep their mouths shut. When Elena was taken across the border, there were lots of officers looking out for victims in her particular situation, especially with all the human trafficking going on. Could she have been brought through without us knowing? You bet. We have officers positioned all along the border, and we've even put out horseback patrols again, like in the old days. In spite of all our efforts, however, sometimes we all feel like throwing up our hands and admitting the system just isn't working."

Mark spoke again. "The job you have at the border is a nightmare, Jim."

The FBI boss, "Big Bob" Brady, arose slowly and methodically, withdrew from his mouth the Havana cigar that he habitually gnawed on, but never smoked. "Gentlemen, we need to turn this conversation one hundred percent over toward finding this young lady and returning her to this fine man and his wife," he said with authority. "It's time to stop postulating."

All eyes turned to Brady. "Gentlemen, you all know me by now, and you know that I'm often accused of having a 'take no prisoners' attitude on these issues. Yes, I often quote General George Patton, whose philosophies I fully endorse." He wiggled the cigar from one side of his mouth to the other as he became even more enlivened. "I happen to think we've had about enough of these cartel folks jumping across the line and having their way with our people. I mean, give me a break! Three billion dollars lost in uncollected taxes. Two hundred million dollars lost in American wages. Millions of dollars lost annually in American hospitals due to uncompensated medical care. Illegals taking up space in a third of our prisons. If we don't put an end to it soon, what is happening in Mexico will happen here. Dozens of people down there are killed daily by these thugs. These drug lords kill just to flex their muscle." Brady pointed out the window, clenched a calloused, meaty fist, and exclaimed, "Let's start kicking butts and taking names!"

Inwardly, Enrique thanked the Lord for this man's motivation and enthusiasm. SAC Brady hadn't once laid eyes on his daughter, but he seemed predisposed to go to great lengths to secure her safety.

Agent Brady lit the fire, and Lieutenant Green fanned the flames. "Our homicide and narcotics squads will coordinate with your agents, Agent Brady. We have all the evidence from the crime scene at Julio Guzman's residence, including some blood samples, the .223 caliber rounds taken from the deceased's upper body, some blood splatter reports, a few strands of black hair—not Mr. Guzman's or Elena's—which we can check for DNA, and a couple of latent prints taken from the rear door. We also have the interviews with the neighbors who saw the perpetrators leave with Ms. Guzman after they heard shots fired."

"It's imperative that we contact all available informants that cooperate not only with the Bureau and the San Diego Police Department but also the Border Patrol and United States Customs," Mark added.

Lieutenant Green ordered the Detectives Cottle and Perez to obtain Elena's most recent photograph from Enrique and circulate an APB to the San Diego police officers and the police departments in surrounding areas with her description and account of her abduction. He also told them to distribute copies of the witness statements to the FBI along with all evidence reports and photographs.

"Gentlemen, as I answered Detective Perez's questions regarding my personal relationship with the leaders of the Brotherhood, it brought to mind the need to contact Tito. This may sound like a very unorthodox approach to solving a case like this, but you may be aware that the Vultures have been at odds with the Brotherhood for over three years now regarding the drug trade going over the border. Before the Vultures became so greedy, they dealt only in marijuana and meth. The Brotherhood wanted nothing to do with meth because of the danger of mixing it and the increasing number of deaths caused by it. For three years now, the Vultures have been muscling in on the Brotherhood's cocaine traffic with the Colombians, promising more successful deliveries based upon their continuing contacts with the border youth gangs. There is bad blood between these two groups, so I am going to contact my relative and see if he will help us. I've heard that both groups have infiltrated each other in an effort to stay a leg up. In spite of our differences about how to make a living, my nephew has maintained a cordial albeit distant connection with my family over the years. I feel he may cooperate to help Elena."

Big Bob smiled at his favorite strike force prosecutor. "Go for it, Henry!" He was the only one who wouldn't call Enrique by the Spanish version of his name.

"What's the most recent update on the Sinaloa cartels?" Mark asked.

"Our sources in Sinaloa say two of the cartels there, the Sinaloa Cartel and the Vultures, are involved in a lot of violence while smuggling drugs," Brady said. "Oddly enough, Tito Guzman and the Brotherhood seem to be running their business with very little violence. It's not like the old days when the Crocodile and the Hammer ran everything with iron-fisted mayhem. Our informants say the Brotherhood has mellowed, but they don't know why. They're still trafficking high volumes of coke and marijuana, but they aren't spilling blood."

Enrique Guzman knew why and rejoiced inwardly as he contemplated the powerful influence that Fonseca, Ruben's daughter, had wielded on him after her conversion to the Mormon faith. Although Enrique knew his nephew, Tito, operated possibly the most powerful cartel in Mexico and that he was still deeply involved in the drug trade, he was gratified at his transition toward avoiding violence whenever possible.

Over the years, Enrique had learned far more about the Brotherhood's secret sources of power previously used to perpetuate their drug business than he had ever chosen to reveal to the family. Enrique recalled the chilling feeling of evil when his father had alluded to the secret oaths, words, combinations, and covenants the Brotherhood had previously used to embolden their operatives and carry on their business. *It's unbelievable that as blood relatives, our lives have gone in such different directions,* he thought.

Enrique recalled his father sharing with him some accounts of the sinister characteristics of the original Brotherhood organization and the man called the Maya who allegedly had access to supernatural powers that benefited the Brotherhood. *I'm sure that part of Ruben's affiliation with the Maya was so dark that Papa decided not to publish the true nature of it to other family member's.* Enrique thought. *By doing that, we were able to preserve some level of positive feelings toward Ruben.*

Mark Madden closed out the meeting with a concluding comment. "Well, we may not have General Pershing or General Patton with us. Under our current administration, their hands would be tied anyway. But we've got Big Bob Brady, which is as good as Patton reincarnated." Laughter erupted while the big FBI chief stood up and took a bow.

Mark continued, "Okay, as soon as someone comes up with something concrete on Elena's case, we'll meet back here again."

Everyone got up, shook hands, and exited the room. Outside, Agent Brady stepped into a bullet-proofed Bureau sedan. Before the car pulled away, Mark walked up to the driver's side and motioned for Brady to roll down his window.

"Thanks for giving Enrique a glimmer of hope, Bobby." Mark was sincerely grateful to Brady as he reached through the window of Brady's vehicle, compressed the cigarette lighter, and offered to light Brady's cigar.

"You know, Madden, I like you. You're the only Mormon I know who would offer to light my cigar, but you know darn well I don't smoke them. What are you doing?"

"You need to give more of us Mormons a chance, Bobby. And like I've always said, and believe you me, you join up with us now and we'll give you something a lot better than a cigar!" Both men laughed as Brady waved and drove away.

Mark went back inside the police department and approached Enrique, who was finishing a conversation with Lieutenant Green.

"I felt in my heart this morning that of all the planning, your suggestion to contact Tito was the water that would get out to the end of the furrows," Mark told his friend. "I know you know there are two people with your Heavenly Father now who will be there for you in the future with their arms outstretched—your son and your father. Those low lives that took out Miguel and Julio will be dealt with. We are going after Elena, and we are going to get her back. I promise!"

"Thanks, Mark." For the first time in days, Enrique smiled with renewed hope.

CHAPTER EIGHTEEN
THE HOSTAGE

THE TRAINING COMPOUND
2:15 MONDAY AFTERNOON

ELENA AWOKE AND found herself lying on an army cot with a frayed green woolen blanket over her and a dirty pillow under her head. From the angle of the shafts of sunlight penetrating the cabin through one solitary window, she figured it was about four-thirty in the afternoon. It was obvious by the noxious smell that neither the blanket nor the pillow had been washed recently. Her jaw was swollen, and a tooth on the lower right side of her mouth was loose.

Elena still wore the white blouse and black skirt she wore two days before at the youth conference. The blouse was stained by blood that had trickled down from her nose. The silence of the cabin was shattered by staccato blasts of rapid gunfire coming from nearby. The noise exacerbated Elena's throbbing headache. Elena realized the pain in her head was partially a result of the blow she'd received Saturday night, but she also had a vague memory of a needle being stuck into her arm en route to her current location, just before she and her captors reached the Mexican border. Elena was sure she had been tranquilized.

Elena got up from the cot and cautiously peered out through the dirty window. Stacked underneath the window were half-filled gas cans, the fumes of which made Elena even dizzier. Across a dusty yard, she saw several men dressed in camouflage, firing automatic weapons at some paper targets. Others were disassembling their firearms and cleaning them. Just then, a tall, heavily built man carrying a very large weapon walked past the window without looking in.

As Elena considered her predicament, she saw it again . . . the ghostly image of Hector's hand slipping beneath the surface of the water, descending down into the dark depths of the river.

Then the second haunting image came, the one with Miguel's car exploding into flames with him and his wife in it. These were the same demons, which acted as a harbinger of something bad to come.

When circumstances were uncertain, as they were that day, these two apparitions persisted in haunting her. She had an ongoing fear that her future was as uncertain as her Uncle Hector's was before the Allen brothers attacked him.

Elena suspected the guard just outside her door was watching her around the clock. She figured she could possibly take him on with her karate skills, but she also knew he had a hand-held radio to communicate with others nearby. And he was also heavily armed.

Elena was not patient by nature but was now becoming aware that patience was necessary for her survival. *All I can do is sit it out,* she thought. *All these guys have to be trafficking drugs. What else would a bunch of men dressed in camouflage and firing weapons like this be up to?*

Elena figured she'd stumbled into the middle of a drug cartel, but she knew immediately that it couldn't be her cousin Tito's. She didn't know him well, but Abuelito said he'd always been friendly with her family. *He wouldn't kidnap me, would he?*

As Elena stood unsteadily next to the dilapidated cot, pain continued shooting through her head, and she struggled to maintain her balance. She slowly made her way over to a battered old table. There was a pitcher of water there with a wash basin next to it. She also noticed a wash cloth, towel, and small bar of soap wrapped in coarse paper that resembled the kind found in the bathrooms of cheap hotels.

Elena knew the guard must have been listening for her because he pushed the door partially open and looked into the room. He didn't come inside, but she heard him speaking in Spanish into a hand-held radio.

Elena gently washed her face, neck, and arms and then dried off with towel. She kept a wary eye on the half-opened door, hoping the guard would not walk in on her. When she finished washing herself, she walked gingerly toward the door with an old torn screen and opened the screened section.

From this new vantage point, she saw twenty Hispanic men clad in green camouflaged uniforms less than sixty yards away. Several men lay on the ground, firing rifles at targets raised onto plywood backings a hundred yards further away. The targets had successive circles with bull's-eyes imprinted in the centers. Being fluent in Spanish, Elena understood the cadences the men were firing to, as a man who appeared to be a range master shouted, "Ready on the right. Ready on the left. All ready on the firing line! Fire!" His instructions were followed by loud bursts of automatic weapon fire.

Not far from the range was an obstacle course where several individuals climbed over logs, lifted one another over barriers, and strained to climb fifteen-foot ropes and touch the logs at the top, before descending, hand-over-hand. She noticed some would get to the top but lose control and slide down, angrily cursing the rope burns on their hands.

Elena counted several old rusted vehicles placed at intervals with rocks and posts for cover in front of them, obscuring the presence of men with shotguns and rifles. Whenever the whistle sounded, these men rose up from their prone positions, fired rounds into the vehicles, and then quickly advanced to the next firing station.

Where am I? Elena wondered, the panic setting in. *What have I gotten myself into? And* Abuelito? *I heard the gunfire when I was abducted. Have they killed him?* She hoped they hadn't, but she knew there was no reason they would have left him alive as she recalled the violent intrusion. Then the demon memories of Miguel's and Uncle Hector's death again played through her mind. She shook her head and put her hands to her eyes in an effort to shut the visions out. Sometimes it helped.

Elena knew simply by the fact that she was still alive that she was being held for some reason. Feeling desperate, Elena collapsed back on the filthy bed and sobbed, uncontrollably at first, as the frustration of her circumstances set in. After a few minutes of self-pity and overwhelming anxiety, her despair was suddenly displaced by anger. Elena wanted to hit something. Hard. In her indignation, she didn't care anymore about herself. She yelled at the guard in English, "You tell me where I am, mister! Tell me now!"

The guard looked at Elena with confusion, betraying the fact that he hadn't understood a word she said. He motioned for a younger man at the obstacle course to come over and assist him. As long as she could remember, Elena's parents spoke to each other in their native Spanish, and in an effort to infuse their rich traditions into Elena, they engaged her in Spanish conversation while at home, so Elena understood what her guards assumed she couldn't. Choosing to speak English hid that fact from her captors.

"I see the girl is up and about, and she is already yelling at you," the man from the obstacle course said sarcastically. "What's the matter? Can't you handle her?"

"She was screaming at me in English!" the guard yelled. "Of course I can't understand her, *estúpido!* Go get Federico!"

Realizing she was creating a stir the guards couldn't cope with, Elena felt even more emboldened. After the other man left, Elena continued yelling at her guard in English, knowing how it would frustrate him. It felt good to see the frustration in his eyes. It was a small way to vent her grief and despair.

Elena walked right up to the cabin door, put her hands on her hips, and shouted at the guard again, this time in a much louder voice.

"I asked you a question! I want an answer, and I want it *now!* Where am I, and why am I here?"

When the guard didn't answer, Elena elevated her voice to an even higher pitch, aware that she was making the man very nervous. She continued chastising him in a language she knew he didn't understand while wagging her finger menacingly in his face. "Who brought me here? Why am I here? YOU TELL ME . . . *NOW!*" The guard backed away from her, looking around nervously for Federico, who was supposed to be on his way.

The guard yelled frantically at the man who had gone for Federico. "*Caramba, hombre!* Get Federico over here *pronto!* This woman is *loca!*"

CHAPTER NINETEEN
FEDERICO MEETS ELENA

FROM A NEARBY cabin, Federico again pondered what he had felt when observing Elena and the other youth at the church during the youth conference days earlier. He couldn't hear what was being said, but even from his surveillance position, he felt something warm and good. He knew he'd have to be discreet and inconspicuous in looking out after Elena.

Federico was watching trainees complete the obstacle course when another one of the Vulture employees ran up to him, his eyes frantic. Elena's guard, Jose Morales, needed Federico to translate what she was saying into Spanish. Only then did he realize the girl was yelling . . . in English.

Upon approaching the cabin, Federico told Jose to wait outside, so he could more easily calm the girl down. When he entered the dirty cabin, Elena was ready for him. After the physical abuse and shabby treatment she had received, and after having been tied up in the back of a van for two days, Elena had adapted the mentality of a caged tiger.

"What's the matter?" she asked, sneering at Federico. "The guy outside couldn't control me, so he had to get help?"

Federico, who spoke English reasonably well from spending summers with English-speaking relatives in the San Diego area, put his index finger to his mouth and whispered matter-of-factly in English, not knowing Elena spoke Spanish, "I know you have family associations in the Brotherhood. They have sent me to help you. You must believe me!"

Elena cast a doubtful eye toward Federico. She was confused, but she felt her hopes quicken slightly. "Why would you help me?" she asked.

"Your cousin, Tito Guzman, received a call from your father yesterday this morning, telling him you were kidnapped and the police suspected the Vultures. He immediately called me to find out if I had seen you."

"Why would you help?" Elena repeated, displaying a scowl.

"I work for Tito. How would it benefit me to make this all up?" Federico asked.

Elena couldn't answer that question. She wanted to believe her would-be benefactor. *Maybe he's telling the truth after all.*

Federico continued, "I told Tito that I had seen you here at the Vultures' training camp, unharmed other than some bruises. Tito ordered me to make contact with you. He promises to help you."

Elena's eyes lit up with hope.

"But you must be patient, Elena! You must not provoke these people, especially the head boss."

Elena still had some fleeting doubts regarding Federico's assurances. "How can I be sure about this . . . and about you?" she asked.

"I guess you'll have to trust me," he said. "But you should know: I'm putting my life on the line here. Tito wants me to protect you the best I can, but I need to be discreet in my contact with you. I took a risk hanging out near your cabin today, next to the obstacle courses where I could watch your guard and keep an eye on you. I knew since I speak English, they would eventually need me to communicate with you. That'll give us a good opportunity to get you out of this."

Elena's eyes still reflected some doubt. However, as she gazed into Federico's face, she perceived something much different from the hardened, lustful expressions of the other men at the training camp.

"You have to believe me," Federico entreated. "The Brotherhood, your cousin's organization, pays me to inform them of what these people do. If you discuss this conversation with anyone here or let them know I'm helping you, they'll kill me, and you'll be left unprotected. Do you understand?"

There was something in Federico's eyes that assured her he was determined to protect her, and that's what convinced her of his sincerity. She dropped her guard slightly and breathed a huge sigh of relief.

"Thank you," she whispered. "I'm sorry! I just don't know who to trust. They killed Abuelito, didn't they?" When Federico nodded, she experienced a rush of emotion. She loved Abuelito, and the thought of him being gone was almost too much to bear. She was silent for several moments, struggling to control her grief, recoiling from the brutality of his murder, and trying to cope with the finality of his death.

Federico watched her struggle in silence. He wanted to comfort her in some way, but knowing they were being watched, he simply waited for her to gain control of her emotions.

When she finally spoke, her voice was quiet. "I didn't expect help from our relatives in the Brotherhood. I only learned about my Uncle Ruben and his business from my grandfather, right before . . . " Elena's face reflected the embarrassment and grief of her situation.

"When your guard returns, I'll tell him you were just upset. That's why you were screaming at him. I'll tell him I gave you warning, and you agreed to settle down. You'll need to play along. No one will lay a hand on you because you're too valuable as a hostage. They think your father can get some prisoners out of jail. When the six Vulture gang members are released, they'll release you."

"Six Vulture gang members?" Elena asked. "So, is that what this is all about?"

"Yes," Federico answered. "Two of them are the sons of El Gordo, the boss. You are their ransom."

"That explains why I was able to get away with yelling at that guard. I sensed I was worth something to them. That was it!" Elena said. "My father has no control over those prisoners, even if these people think he does. They will never negotiate the release of those men for me. That would set a precedent the government would never allow."

Elena seemed sure of what she was saying, but Federico was unshaken. "Then we need to think of something else."

Out of the corner of Elena's eye, she saw a bald-headed young man in blood-stained camouflage gear walking unsteadily across the training ground. He looked vaguely familiar. He glanced over toward Elena briefly with a blank expression of unfamiliarity. He carried two rusty buckets full of sudsy water and scrubbing brushes and was heading toward the huts. He half walked, half stumbled, mumbling to himself. Even though the young man's face was bruised and extremely swollen, Elena recognized Manolo Barto, her friend from the *dojo*.

"Manolo!" Elena called out.

There was no response. "Hey, there, Manolo! Manolo Barto!" she hollered again.

Still in a daze, Manolo continued his shuffling gait toward the huts, without any sign of recognition.

Federico told Elena about the beating Manolo had taken from the *Pelones*. Elena cringed and teared up as she told Federico about Manolo having been a friend over the past few years.

"I'm sorry, Elena," said Federico. "I don't think he'll ever be the same. They really worked him over."

Elena felt deep sorrow for her formerly carefree friend but resolved not to let it get her down. She knew she needed to focus all her energy on survival.

As Federico walked away, Elena saw something in her young benefactor that gave her hope. She now knew she wasn't alone—that she had not only Federico's support but also that of her cousin, of whom she had previously always been ashamed. Her confusion outweighed her shame—she'd always assumed her cousins were evil. But didn't her grandfather caution her against judging her cousins in Sinaloa?

Thoughts of her grandfather almost overwhelmed her with grief, so Elena tried to distract herself by observing Federico as he walked away. Her tall, broad-shouldered benefactor had a handsome, kind face with piercing brown eyes that conveyed a sense of sincerity and warmth that she found very rare. She found it odd, indeed, that she could be so impressed with someone associated with her captors. *Could he really be looking out for me?* she wondered. She'd always thought of drug dealers and murderers as scum. *Can Tito actually help me?* Elena thought. *If so, why would he?*

CHAPTER TWENTY
THE ASSIGNMENT

THE TRAINING COMPOUND
5:30 MONDAY AFTERNOON

A FEW HOURS after Federico's initial contact with Elena, he was summoned to El Gordo's quarters. The former officers' dwelling had been decorated with fine carpeting, drapes, and nice furniture that only the rich could afford. And women . . . there were always women surrounding the boss. As Federico approached the door, the armed guard posted outside advised El Gordo that he had arrived. He then opened the door and signaled for Federico to enter.

As Federico entered the refurbished living quarters, El Gordo waved at him clumsily to sit down, not wanting to change his own position of comfort on the couch, where he had his fleshy legs propped up on a stool. Two young Mexican women, both scantily clad, were fussing over him. Empty plates sat on the floor next to his feet, obviously from a main course of *tatemado*—pork marinated in spices and palm vinegar—the drippings of which remained on El Gordo's chin and shirt. In front of the fat man, Federico observed plates of fried meat, enchiladas, and *ceviche* topped with refried beans and served with *horchata*.

As El Gordo motioned for one of the women to hand him an additional plate of food, he addressed Federico in a high-pitched voice that came out in grunts and short bursts, resembling the cadences of a Gatlin gun. The glutton's mouth and cheeks were greasy. *If this is what it's like to be the head of a huge drug cartel, I'd better consider another line of work,* Federico thought.

Although El Gordo was only in his early thirties, he had the appearance of a man much older. He was prematurely bald, and Federico had long wondered how he could even support his immense weight on his short legs. Federico had witnessed first hand that El Gordo was short-tempered and prone to scream at those who waited on him. He also took pleasure in wearing a brown leather shoulder holster that contained a .44-caliber magnum Blackhawk revolver in plain view—an obvious show of force intended to intimidate those around him. It was as though he wanted to compensate for his decadent physical state by rein-forcing a macho air of male superiority.

El Gordo sought to intimidate and control those around him, and there was no doubt he was successful. He surrounded himself with highly paid men with mean dispositions who were always ready to carry out his directives at a moment's notice. That's why he had called upon the dreaded *Pelones* to train his men.

Pointing a fat, greasy finger menacingly at Federico, he ordered, "Valdez, I want you to take over guarding the Guzman girl. You're one of the few people I've got that can speak decent English. I've heard rumors lately about some of the men wanting to get friendly with her, if you know what I mean—especially Ramirez and Soto. Those two baboons will stop at nothing. I promised the girl's father that no harm would come to her as long as he cooperates and gets my sons out of jail. I want you with her from morning to night. I'll have someone else I can trust posted outside her door during the night shift."

Federico struggled to conceal his elation. *This is perfect,* he thought. *I no longer have to search for excuses to stay close by, and now that Elena knows who I am, she'll be comfortable around me.*

He enjoyed being around Elena. She was the total opposite of the women who surrounded El Gordo. In fact, he had difficulty comparing her with anyone he had ever met. From the first time he saw her at the church building, he knew she was different in a way that he couldn't easily define. There was a certain reserved femininity about her, but he had also observed her toughness in the way she stood up to and even intimidated her guard. Not only that, with her light olive complexion, long black hair, and slender frame, she was extremely attractive. And even though he hadn't seen her smile since she stood in front of the youth at the church, he remembered that smile and how it enlivened her features.

"Okay, boss," Federico said. "I can handle that. I'll take care of her." He hoped he didn't sound too excited.

"You better!" El Gordo snarled as he reached for a huge mug of *tuba,* an alcoholic drink made out of palm sap, and prepared to take a bite out of a pastry one of the women held up to his mouth. With his mouth full, he added, "There's only five more days to look after her until the prosecutor meets my demands. If anything happens to her, I can guarantee you two things. My sons will rot in prison, and you'll be dealt with for your negligence. *Comprende?*"

"*Sí, Jefe,*" Federico answered. He knew exactly what it meant to be "dealt with." And with the feelings he was developing for Elena Guzman, there was no way he would allow anything to happen to her. He knew all about the reputation Eduardo Ramirez and Benjamin Soto had with women, especially in a situation like this, where they could easily gain an upper hand. They could be ruthless with their victims as they gave vent to their lusts and appetites. Their cold-blooded murder of Julio Guzman was just one example of their ruthlessness.

Killing Elena's grandfather, who was merely raising his cane in Elena's defense, was completely unnecessary. And they didn't stop with just a couple of shots, either. They each fired several rounds into Julio Guzman's body, when either of them could have just as easily restrained the old man momentarily while the other grabbed Elena. Federico knew those two took everything to the extreme, which was why El Gordo never allowed them into his inner circle. Federico vowed he would keep them away from Elena.

"All right, Valdez, any questions? If not, you're dismissed." El Gordo grunted as he struggled to lift himself off the couch. As he lumbered toward his bedroom for a *siesta,* Federico assured him, "No, Boss, I'll take care of her. Don't worry."

"You better," El Gordo grumbled.

* * * *

Elena went to work on her cabin. After Federico revealed who he really was, that he was there to protect her, the shock of her captivity had diminished somewhat, and she resolved not to just sit in the old log cabin and endure its filth.

She found an old straw broom and rusted-out dust pan and set to work attacking the numerous spiderwebs in the corners and the two abandoned hornets' nests attached to the ceiling. Next, she swept up the accumulation of dirt from muddied boots, along with paper food wrappings and several empty beer cans, and scooped it all up with the dustpan. She carried the mess outside, where she emptied it into an open-top, empty oil barrel located just a few steps away from the front door of the cabin. All this was done under the close surveillance of one of El Gordo's men.

When she walked out of the cabin carrying the dirty sheets, blanket, and pillow case from her cot, the guard stepped in front of her, but she simply pushed past him and moved toward a shallow stream of water she had seen flowing through the training compound. She dropped her load into the water, knelt down on the bank, and scrubbed the items with the hand soap she'd found in the bathroom. Using a smooth river rock as a scrub board, Elena worked soap into the fabric. She then scrubbed the fabrics against one another as layers of sweat and dirt ebbed downstream.

Before Federico returned, she had all the linen and the blanket hanging on a drooping clothesline next to the cabin. She'd even brought out the pillow and mattress and pounded them, creating a huge dust cloud, before leaning them against the cabin to air out.

One by one, Elena moved the gas cans outside. She opened the cabin's one window, left the door ajar, and turned on the dilapidated fan to freshen the air and chase out the smell of mildew and fumes. Only then did she stop to eat a plate of chicken, beans, and tortillas that a middle-aged Mexican woman had delivered to her cabin.

Eduardo Ramirez and Benjamin Soto, who resided two cabins

away from Elena's cabin, were also eating lunch. They watched Elena's every movement, openly leering at her as she worked. They took special note of her youthful figure and swaying hips and made lewd comments to each other as she moved from one task to another.

When Federico approached Elena's cabin, he noticed the two men ogling her as they lounged against their cabin, sharing a bottle of tequila. Federico considered asking El Gordo to move Elena farther away from the two men but immediately thought better of the idea, realizing that the request may constitute an admission that he didn't feel capable of taking responsibility for her. El Gordo would assign someone else as her guard, and Federico didn't trust anyone else. Instead, he resolved to keep a watchful eye on the two men.

When Ramirez and Soto saw Federico returning from his visit with the Boss, Soto yelled out, "Hey, Federico, you got quite a woman to take care of there! Are you sure you don't need a little help? You know, someone with more experience?" Both men laughed coarsely.

"Yeah," added Eduardo Ramirez. "Maybe you could turn the little lady loose for a couple of hours and let her come over and join us for some *tequila,* eh? What do you say, *hombre?*" They erupted in laughter again.

Federico vowed never to let either man within a hundred feet of Elena. As soon as he reached Elena's side, he pointed out Ramirez and Soto.

"You see those two men?" Federico gestured to the two men who were still laughing and pointing.

"You mean the two slimy ones that have been staring at me all afternoon?" Elena asked.

"Yes. You need to be extremely careful around those two. The boss should have fired both of them long ago. They're far more trouble than they're worth."

"Federico?" Elena said with fury building into her countenance.

"Yes?"

"I remember the night I was taken now. I saw them murder my grandfather. You don't have to keep it from me. I saw them do it just before they grabbed me and pulled me through the door."

Federico nodded, confirming her words.

"And the taller one, the one they call Eduardo, still has my scratch marks on his face. He's the one who knocked me unconscious."

"Elena, now is not the time for revenge, do you understand? Don't let those two men anywhere near you. If they start harassing you, or if you feel like you're in danger, you must run to me immediately. Do you understand?"

Elena tried not to scoff. She realized Federico had no idea how independent she was. Her father had insisted she study some kind of self-defense, knowing that in his work prosecuting the cartels, the life of everyone in his family could be in jeopardy. Federico was unaware that martial arts were a major part of her life.

Federico looked around the newly tidied cabin. "I can't believe this is the same place," he exclaimed. "Are you sure you're in the right cabin?" For the first time since her captivity, Federico saw Elena smile.

"It's obvious these people don't care how they live."

Caramba! Federico thought ruefully. *I'm glad she hasn't been in my cabin!*

"Elena," he said. "In a stroke of luck, El Gordo has assigned me as your personal guard. I'll be outside of your cabin from early in the morning to late at night. You don't have to worry about your privacy. I'll keep you posted as I hear about how we can get you out of here."

Elena allowed herself to be a little comforted. Since she arrived in this terrible place, she didn't know what else to do but pray. For the first time in her life, she knew Heavenly father was answering her prayers.

"Federico," Elena said suddenly, "do you believe in God?"

Federico hesitated a moment before answering. "Fonseca Guzman, Tito's sister, told me a lot about the Mormon God. She said we are all his children. I believe that. She said God's church had been taken away and that Jesus, God's son, had brought it back to earth through a prophet. She also said there is a living prophet on the earth today."

"Do you believe all that?"

"It makes sene, I guess." Federico responded. "Fonseca sent two young missionaries to my house to give me a bunch of lessons. I prayed with them and it felt good, but I couldn't join their church and still do what I do for a living."

"But you agreed with what they said?" Elena asked.

"I think so," Federico said. "When I was watching you and the other young people at your church, I felt something really strong and good. But then again, none of this works well with what I do. I can't be two different people."

Just then, Federico's cell phone chimed. It was Tito.

"How's the girl?" Tito asked.

"She's okay, boss. We got lucky. El Gordo assigned me to take care of her since I speak English. They've got her in a shabby, old cabin, but they feed her well, and I'm watching out for her."

"Do you think they know about you yet?" Tito asked.

"I don't think so," Federico answered. "At least, they've given no indication that they know I'm a plant."

"Good," Tito answered. "We've got your location, and we have a plan. There's no way the police can move as fast as we can, nor can they be as effective with all the bribes the Vultures pay them here in Sinaloa, so don't expect help from them. We'll take care of it ourselves and let the police . . . clean up." Tito sounded committed and confident. "Take good care of Elena," he continued, "and keep me posted on any further developments."

"I will, boss," Federico responded enthusiastically.

Back in Sinaloa, Tito took note of something in Federico's response that assured him the young man might have another motive for taking extra good care of his cousin. He smiled.

"That was your cousin," Federico said as he pocketed his cell phone. He smiled at Elena. "They have a plan."

CHAPTER TWENTY-ONE
ELENA FIGHTS BACK

THE TRAINING COMPOUND
12:00 MIDNIGHT, TUESDAY NIGHT, SEPTEMBER 28, 2010

TUESDAY PASSED WITHOUT incident. That night, Juan Gomez, an elderly man in his late fifties who was a confidante of El Gordo, relieved Federico of his watch duty.

At midnight, Eduardo Ramirez staggered past Elena's cabin, pretending to be drunk. As Juan Gomez got to his feet to watch him more closely, Benjamin Soto came up behind the late-night guard and placed a cloth laced with chloroform over Gomez's nose. After a moment of struggle, the older man slumped to the ground without making a sound. Satisfied that the guard was out of the way, the two men pushed the door open and quickly entered Elena's cabin. The sound of their entry awakened her, and she cried out as Soto and Ramirez rushed her cot and tried to force themselves upon her.

Federico was approaching his cabin some distance away when he heard Elena's screams. He immediately sprinted back toward her cabin, a pistol drawn in his right hand. When he got to the door, he heard the sounds of a man in agony mixed in with Elena's screams. Federico stepped over the unconscious guard and threw open the door. Benjamin Soto clutched the side of his head trying to stem the flow of blood. The pain of having his ear partially bitten off was a pain he had never experienced before.

Elena fought like a tiger. Although the two men had tried

everything within their power to remove her clothing, they had succeeded only in tearing her shirt. In a matter of moments, the attackers' lust was overcome by anger. As Soto nursed his injury, Ramirez pulled out a switchblade and inched his way closer to Elena, the six-inch blade extended toward her throat.

At that moment, Ramirez experienced the singular sensation of his cranium cracking as Federico brought the full weight of the butt of his pistol down on the back of the assailant's head. Once Ramirez was on the ground, Elena caught Soto with a full round-house kick to the groin. Even the excruciating pain of his nearly severed ear took a back burner to the agony he felt then.

The chloroform wore off, and Juan Gomez arose from the ground. He looked inside the cabin and immediately saw what had happened. He opened his cell phone and dialed El Gordo's number.

Within minutes, a wheezing El Gordo entered the cabin with his two bodyguards. One of them turned on a light switch, and under the dim glow of a single, bare bulb, the fat man took in the situation—the young woman trying to hold her torn shirt closed and the two intruders, one unconscious, and the other crouched in a fetal position, rocking back and forth and bleeding profusely from a wound in the side of his head.

The Boss looked with disgust at both of them.

"*Idiotas!* What are you doing here? You know full well the girl's well-being is the only trade-in value I have for my sons and the others. Just look at you, Soto. She practically bit your ear off and there you are, crying like a little girl." Just then, Ramirez moaned, coming to, and clutched the back of his skull. "And you, Ramirez! You just stood there while Federico got the drop from behind! Give me one good reason I shouldn't kill you right now!" He held his pistol in his hand and waved it menacingly at the two of them. But instead of shooting them, El Gordo stood over them and spat on their cowering bodies, waiting for a response.

The men remained silent, refusing to look at their boss.

"You'll stay with the Vultures, but you've just lost yourselves two weeks' pay. Lucky for you two, I need your guns and your experience; otherwise, you'd be dead by now. You'll never set foot near Señorita Guzman or this cabin again. Now get out."

The two men got up from the floor and slinked out, Soto with a hand over his bleeding ear, still slightly bent over, and Ramirez pressing a hand against his bloodied skull. Federico, who stood next to El Gordo by the door, caught the full impact of their sneers as they walked by, escorted by the late-night guard.

As one of his bodyguards closed the door behind them, El Gordo looked at Elena with unwelcome interest. "I'm sorry for the behavior of those imbeciles, my dear," El Gordo said with a leering smile. Federico needlessly translated his words to English. "They have no manners. You will not be bothered by them again."

Elena answered in English and Federico translated.

"Those were the two men who killed my grandfather," she said. "An innocent person who did nothing but try to protect me, and you punish them now for trying to rape me with only two weeks of suspended pay? But what can I expect from the man who murdered my brother? You are no better than they!" Federico was reluctant to translate that comment, but he did.

El Gordo was furious.

"Watch your tongue, little lady," he seethed. "I'm the only thing standing between you and the likes of Ramirez and Soto, and you'd do well to remember that. But I can see you are not reasonable and have no appreciation for your benefactors. Do not think, even for one second, that you are immune from the same fate that befell your brother!"

Elena's head jerked up involuntarily. That statement answered a question Elena had carried in her heart for two years. She trembled with anger. She'd always known El Gordo was behind her brother's murder. She stared contemptuously at the fat man as he lumbered away with his protectors.

Before leaving Elena's cabin, El Gordo cast a warning glance toward Federico. "Don't you dare let anything else happen to her!" El Gordo hissed, as if it were Federico's fault Elena had been assaulted. Casting a final, disdainful look at Elena, El Gordo muttered some profanities and left, slamming the door behind him.

Finally losing her composure, Elena burst into tears, pouring out her sense of frustration to Federico without even noticing she spoke in her native language. Federico placed a calming hand on her shoulder while marveling at her fluency in Spanish.

"So, you can speak Spanish, eh? And you have hidden it from me?" Federico scolded with mock incredulity.

"It was one of the only weapons in my arsenal, Federico." Elena said, wiping her eyes.

Federico looked into Elena's eyes. "What else is in that arsenal?" he asked. "You have teeth for biting off people's ears and a painful karate kick from the looks of things." He smiled when Elena offered a tiny chuckle.

He immediately grew serious. "You need to calm down some, Elena," he warned. "I get why you hate El Gordo for what happened to your Abuelito and your brother, but for the next few days, he is the key to your survival. If he decides he doesn't need you, he'll reassign me, and you'll have no protection, or worse yet, he'll make you disappear."

Elena placed her hand momentarily on Federico's. "I know, Federico. . . . I understand." She looked into his eyes. "Thank you . . . for everything."

* * * *

5:20 WEDNESDAY MORNING, SEPTEMBER 29, 2010

When Federico woke up early the next morning, his first item of business was to apprise Tito of the night's events.

Since first talking to Federico, Tito had gathered as much information as possible about the Vulture's training compound. As he assured Federico before, he had the location of the compound and was hard at work formulating a plan to rescue his cousin safely.

After Federico finished his account of the near-tragedy, Tito struggled to keep his emotions in check. "Thank you for looking after my cousin, Federico," Tito said. "Those two, Soto and Ramirez, are no good. They are lucky they have such a long history with El Gordo or he wouldn't have hesitated in killing them. They were two of the first people El Gordo recruited when he took over the Vulture clan and were his drinking buddies for years before that. Flaco Diaz would never have hired the likes of them."

"They are lucky to still be walking after Elena finished with them," Federico said proudly.

"It sounds to me like you're becoming somewhat attached to your young charge, Federico," Tito said, and from the lack of response on the other end of the line, he was sure he caught Federico by surprise.

Federico previously had no idea that he had betrayed his personal interest in Elena. He only breathed again when he heard Tito's muffled chuckle on the other end of the phone.

"Well, we Guzmans all have a natural inclination toward fighting," Tito declared.

"How does it look for Elena?" Federico asked, no longer bothering to hide his concern.

Tito responded. "According to Enrique, the strike force held a preliminary meeting, but they don't yet have any solid ideas of how to rescue Elena. When he called recently asking for our help, my uncle was sure of two things: first, they would never negotiate with the Vultures for El Gordo's sons' release; and second, the strike force had no viable plan for getting Elena back. He told me we may have to operate independently of law enforcement. They all know about the strange relationship Enrique has with me. They're going to let me help."

"Well, we have until Sunday at noon," Federico said. "So far, things are stable here, but that can change quickly. At the very least, we don't have to worry about Soto and Ramirez anymore, and when word gets around about them taking a beating and a pay cut, I doubt anyone will want to bother Elena again."

"Let's hope not," Tito agreed. "Enrique's wife has been worried sick over this, but Enrique has taken comfort in knowing you're looking out for Elena, so don't disappoint me. I will tell Enrique that his daughter is safe. His wife needs that knowledge. Keep me posted."

"I will, boss," replied Federico. He snapped shut the cell phone and set to work cooking some *chorizo* and eggs for his and Elena's breakfast.

CHAPTER TWENTY-TWO
WOODCUTTING REVELATIONS

THE TRAINING COMPOUND
9:30 WEDNESDAY NIGHT

AURELIO AOSA, ONE of El Gordo's confidants and gang leaders, knocked on the boss's door and waited for permission to enter before doing so. "Well, boss," Aurelio began, "it's just what we've heard before. The judge refuses to set bail."

El Gordo flinched. "This can't be real! What was his reasoning?"

Aurelio was hesitant to furnish even more bad news. He knew the boss needed to stay on top of the situation, but he also knew that his information would only upset him more. "It's the way we used those gringo boys to strap on the packets and walk over the border. The authorities found out it was us, and well, they're really upset. They're afraid if they set bail, no matter what it is, you'll pay it. They're afraid you'll take your boys and hide them here in Mexico, keeping them safe from prosecution."

El Gordo was fuming. "Why should the border authorities and the judges care whether we give it to our own people or to those stupid *gringo* kids? It's all the same!"

"It's something the American prosecutors call 'enhancements,' boss. It means the crime is more serious if you use teenagers or school-age children to transport the stuff. It's like dealing drugs around schools. The county prosecutor is really angry!"

El Gordo was so angry, he was practically foaming at the mouth. "*Estúpido,* using the American kids was your idea! We're paying them more money for one day's work than their own parents have given them their whole life, and they can't even walk across the border without getting picked up? And you! *You* told me, 'Yes, boss, this is such a good idea, boss!' *Que estúpido!"*

"It would have worked if the crazy *gringo* kids hadn't been wearing winter coats to cover the drug packets in the middle of the summer! It was a hundred degrees that day!" Aurelio said in his own defense. "How could the border patrol not have discovered them?"

"Well, *this* plan better work better than your last one. If Enrique Guzman doesn't unlock the county jail and free them, his daughter dies . . . and you, Aurelio, will make sure it's an ugly—a very ugly—death!"

Aurelio knew that if his plan went wrong, El Gordo would make a graphic example of Elena Guzman so that there would be no confusion about what happens when the boss doesn't get his way.

"Yeah, boss, I know." Aurelio stood and walked toward the door of the fat man's den, feeling the cold glare of his boss's contempt pierce his back.

* * * *

MOUNTAINS NEAR THE COMPOUND
7:15 THURSDAY MORNING, SEPTEMBER 30, 2010

Before being assigned guard duty, Federico Valdez shared in the work of maintaining the premises of their training camp for the six weeks the members trained. One of his responsibilities included gathering firewood. The cabins were unheated except for small wood-burning stoves, and at the higher altitudes, the night's chill required heat.

Aurelio Sosa needed a break from El Gordo's abrasive personality and pervasive threats, at least for a day. After leaving El Gordo's cabin, he asked Federico if he could join him in gathering firewood the next day and Federico agreed. He wanted an opportunity to stretch his legs and would be glad for the help with his chore.

Federico made arrangements with another young man he had befriended—someone he trusted—to guard Elena for a few hours in the morning. He promised Elena he would be back no later than noon.

As the two men drove into the country, Federico asked, "So, Aurelio, you needed to get away, eh?"

"*Caramba!*" responded the older man. "El Gordo is obsessing over whether this Guzman girl will be the ticket in springing his stupid sons and the others!"

"They are morons," replied Federico. "El Gordo's sons have always been a liability to our success. For them, as spoiled and arrogant as they are, they think all of this is a game and that they can do whatever they want without consequence. They know their dear papa will get them out," Federico said, frowning with disgust.

"That's the problem—even I was sold on the idea of using the *gringo* kids—and it worked . . . for a month or so. They were anxious to take our money. At first, we taught them how to dress and act discreetly. Then El Gordo's sons, Pedro and Lorenzo, took over the responsibility of running that program. It was basically a free-for-all. Without training, these idiot kids were dressing for winter in the middle of July . . . and well, you know the rest."

Their pickup groaned in protest as it made its way up a rutted dirt road through the heavily wooded hills. Dense stands of birch trees popped into sight through heavy thickets fed by a small stream, and the terrain eventually gave way to a pine forest. The high-altitude air offered some refreshment as the pickup pulled into a flat area off the right side of the road where pine beetles had killed off several trees that Aurelio decided to take down.

"I heard that the boss's sons and the four others made it worse by crossing over into the States through San Ysidro to party in San Diego about the same time the American kids were squealing," Federico said.

"It's true," Aurelio confirmed. "The kids even pointed out

Pedro and Lorenzo's car to the police along with the car the other four guys drove. Their two sedans were stopped by county officers about five miles down the road from the motel where they were staying, and they've been in jail ever since. *Que estúpidos!*"

Federico took the chainsaw to three trees, quickly felled them, and cut off the limbs. He then lopped the trunks into two-foot lengths, while Aurelio lugged the pieces thirty yards to the pickup and stacked them neatly in the trailer. Although it was still early morning, the sun had fully risen, and Aurelio's lack of physical conditioning was reflected in his labored gait and the beads of sweat cascading down his face.

When the trailer was half full, Aurelio said, "You're an animal, Federico! Let an old man get a few minutes' rest. Besides, you're only doing the cutting. I'm carrying!"

After a few minutes of drinking ice water and eating some jerky that Federico brought, Aurelio finally spoke up. "Things are looking bad for the prosecutor's daughter."

Federico tried to mask the apprehension he felt. He knew his most important job was to protect Elena. And since speaking with Tito the last time, he was convinced he now had feelings for her. Aurelio's statement troubled him a great deal.

As the two men stowed away their ice water and Aurelio took a weary inventory of the large space remaining that still needed to be filled in the wood trailer, Federico decided to get more information. "So what's really the story on the Guzman girl?"

"If her old man refuses to arrange the release of El Gordo's sons, she'll be snuffed out for sure," Aurelio said.

"Do we know if Mr. Guzman even has the authority to arrange something like that?"

"No. But you and I both know that El Gordo doesn't bother with the details. He's made it perfectly clear that if he doesn't get his way, he expects me to make an example of her."

Federico was sure Aurelio was right. He had personally observed how El Gordo treated his men while in fits of rage. He knew reason and mercy didn't enter into the fat man's way of thinking. More than ever, Federico fully understood the need for him to personally intervene on Elena's behalf—not only to fulfill

CHAPTER TWENTY-THREE
BENNINGTON'S BLESSING

MARK MADDEN RECONVENED the strike force for a final briefing regarding Elena's status.

"As we all know, it's been three days since the assault on Elena by two of El Gordo's men," Mark began. "Still, our reports from Enrique's source in the Brotherhood have been favorable. The Vultures are unaware that the El Gordo's choice for her guard is actually one of the Brotherhood's operatives."

All heads nodded enthusiastically with that news.

"Unfortunately, as a unit, our hands are tied. We have no jurisdiction in Mexico, but the Mexican government has made a concession. They have authorized Agent Brady and I to travel to Mexico City and operate under the authority and auspices of the US State Department, through our FBI legal attaché office there. Once SAC Brady and I arrive in Mexico City, we'll hook up with three of the FBI agents stationed there and contact a contingency of the Mexican National Police who will meet us in Culiacán on special assignment.

"We know the Vultures have many of the Sinaloan police on their payroll, so we'll not contact them. The plan is for us to raid the Vultures training compound and to extricate Elena."

Agent Brady spoke up. "Our major concern once we arrive at the compound is the potential hostage situation."

"That's just it!" said San Diego Police Lieutenant Dick Hines. "As soon as they see you, they'll know you're not releasing the six prisoners. The girl's life will be at stake!"

Enrique countered. "There are more cards at play than you know about. I have good reason to believe, based upon the intelligence I'm receiving from the Brotherhood, that Elena may be evacuated prior to Mark and SAC Brady arriving there with the Mexican police."

"I don't get it," Lieutenant Hines said, his confusion evident. "Sounds to me like we're relying just a little too much on a pack of drug traffickers."

Enrique raised his brow. "You know, Lieutenant, this is my daughter's life we're discussing, so I'm taking full responsibility for the successful outcome of her rescue. It's true that this is a most unorthodox arrangement, but the involvement of my nephew in Elena's rescue may be Elena's only chance for survival."

Lieutenant Hines had no further comment.

Agent Brady followed up. "Madden and I leave early tomorrow for Mexico. If, for any reason, our project moves toward our border here, you'll all receive ample notice. Any questions?"

There was silence.

Mark concluded the meeting. "Okay, gentlemen, thanks for being here. We'll adjourn until further notice."

★ ★ ★ ★

SAN DIEGO
1:30 FRIDAY AFTERNOON

Enrique was fully prepared to defend his request to become personally involved in his daughter's rescue, especially because he didn't expect his boss to sanction his meeting with his nephew Tito, at least not at first. After all, Tito was the leader of a drug cartel whose operatives his office had been prosecuting for years.

But Enrique was hounded by the troubling conviction that if he was not on the scene to coordinate Elena's rescue, it would never happen. He had called into the office early that morning, letting them know he would be in that afternoon to discuss an urgent matter with Shad Bennington. When Enrique walked into his boss's office, Bennington was clearing off his desk, getting ready to go home.

"Well, Enrique, you're just arriving, and I'm just leaving. How was the meeting?"

"It's a 'go,' sir. Mark's leaving tomorrow morning with SAC Brady for Mexico City." Enrique briefed Bennington on the details of the meeting. "But there's one more thing, boss."

Bennington looked at Enrique with raised eyebrows, waiting.

"I need to be there."

For a few moments, the head United States Attorney was very pensive. "Look, Enrique, I don't know if I can let you do this," he said. He knew Enrique wanted to protest, so Bennington held up a hand, cutting him off. "Think about it. You know the possible repercussions of doing something like this. Can you even imagine what would happen if I sent a representative of the United States Department of Justice—the person specifically authorized to prosecute Mexican drug cartels—to Sinaloa, the province most responsible for the presence of illegal drugs in this country, for the express purpose of collaborating with the operators of possibly the largest cartel in Mexico on a project that the Mexican government has only unofficially authorized? And even if all this weren't the case, you're obviously too close to the situation emotionally!"

Enrique nodded his head respectfully but said, "I understand, boss. I fully appreciate your position, and I know this could even put your appointment by the President at risk. But, sir, there will be a day when I'm on my deathbed, evaluating my life, and the only thing that will matter that day will be my family. No offense, but I won't be wishing I'd been a better government prosecutor or that I had dotted every 'i' and crossed every 't.' At that moment, I'll be wishing I had been a better husband, a better father.

"Sir, if I don't meet my nephew and help coordinate Elena's rescue, if I don't do everything in my power, I may lose her, and I can't live with that regret. I'm prepared to offer my resignation.

That way I'll be on my own, and it won't reflect on you or the department."

The United States Attorney stared at Enrique with great respect and admiration, but he was plagued with a keen sense of his own dilemma. He couldn't afford to lose the man who had unmatched rapport with all the federal, state, and local law enforcement agencies working the border. There were even key informants on both sides of the border who would only meet with Enrique. The man was a golden goose.

"Enrique," Bennington responded in obvious surrender. "You know I've cut you miles of slack on other politically high-risk operations, but this one, my friend, takes the cake. Still, this department can't afford your resignation, so I'll need just one promise from you. If you go down there, regardless of the outcome, this conversation never took place. You can't ever, under any circumstances, reveal that you succeeded by collaborating with a drug cartel. Are we clear?"

"We're clear," Enrique said, shaking his boss's hand with enthusiasm. "Thank you, sir!"

****

SAN DIEGO
8:35 SATURDAY MORNING, OCTOBER 2, 2010

The next morning, Enrique told Mark he was heading down to Mexico on his own. He promised Mark he'd stay in close contact but that no one else, except possibly SAC Brady, could know of Enrique's presence and actions there. Mark was elated. When Mark advised the SAC that Enrique was going in person, Big Bob Brady exclaimed, "You've got to be kidding me! The DOJ approved that?"

Mark looked at Brady, smiled, and said, "Of course not!"

Big Bob returned the same look of amazement, winked at Mark, and said enthusiastically, "I like it! It's always easier to get forgiveness than permission." Then he stuck his trademark cigar back into his mouth, unlit, and savored it all the way to the airport.

* * * *

EN ROUTE TO CULIACÁN, MEXICO
1:15 SATURDAY AFTERNOON

For the first time since Elena's abduction, Enrique finally felt his despair diminish a little at the promise of being personally involved in his daughter's rescue. He had no idea what he would do, but just knowing he would be there was reassuring. He sat back in the seat of the plane and searched for warm, reassuring thoughts. Almost immediately, he considered the pure beauty of Christ's teachings he had found when the Mormon missionaries first visited his family in San Diego.

* * * *

Enrique was visiting his parents during spring break. Julio and Maria lived in a basement apartment and were barely scraping by with their wages from farm work.

One of the missionaries who knocked on his parents' door immediately caught his mother's attention because he was also of Hispanic descent. Julio was reluctant to allow them in because he was always exhausted from a hard day's labor, but Maria felt differently. She invited them in and made the two young men some sandwiches. As they ate, Maria found Julio napping in the bedroom and Enrique studying, and she all but commanded them to come greet their guests.

Reluctantly, they shook the missionaries' hands, sat down, and upon Maria's insistence, listened to what they had to say. *Just this once,* they had thought.

When the Hispanic boy, Elder Perez, asked for permission to open the discussion with a prayer, Enrique became uncomfortable and even a little perturbed. Nevertheless, as the elders bowed their heads and his mother followed suit, Enrique and his father went along with it.

The prayer made an impact upon the Guzman family they would never forget.

The other missionary, Elder Craig Morley, an American missionary, offered the prayer. Enrique and his parents immediately noticed that speaking was an extreme challenge for this young man as he stuttered incessantly throughout the prayer. As the Guzmans sat across from the missionaries, straining to grasp each word that Elder Morley uttered, they marveled deep in their souls that a young man was brave enough to enter the homes of strangers, struggle with such an impediment, and willingly submit himself to whatever people might think of him.

They also considered the Hispanic elder. He came from Guatemala to a foreign country and struggled to learn a new language, all for the sake of a religion. When they discovered the elders served for two years at their own expense, the family was even more astonished. They couldn't imagine such a sacrifice. They'd never met anyone quite like these two young men. They decided that whether what they had to say was true or not, their commitment and determination were undeniable. They agreed that if these two young, twenty-year-old missionaries were doing what they were doing, in spite of the challenges they surely faced, there was something very special about their faith.

As Elder Morley continued with the prayer, the family was touched by what he prayed for. He prayed that the Guzmans would know for themselves if the missionaries' message was true, that "Brother" Guzman would be blessed to be able to finish his schooling, that their tiny home would be a refuge—a place of happiness and safety—and that the family would have all they needed to be secure. The three were all touched by the young man's heart-felt supplication.

Brother Guzman? Enrique thought. *Brother Guzman. That's the way it should be. Brothers and sisters. . . . of course!*

After a few moments, the Guzmans no longer noticed the stuttering or the stammering. A peaceful feeling—something warm and joyful and fulfilling—eclipsed that sound. It was a conviction that seemed to be independent of the missionaries, or even of the Guzmans themselves, an assurance that stood on its own. Before the prayer was even over, the Guzmans knew they both wanted more of that feeling. It was something Enrique knew he needed and wanted—even more than a diploma.

Each time Elder Perez and Elder Morley came with another

lesson, Enrique grew less concerned with his studies and more anxious to learn all the young men had to share. Enrique and his parents were baptized into The Church of Jesus Christ of Latter-day Saints six weeks after the missionaries' first visit.

At the end of the semester, Enrique transferred to Brigham Young University. A year later, Enrique put in his mission papers, served faithfully in Bolivia, and met his wife, Belinda, during his first year at BYU law school.

★ ★ ★ ★

As the plane continued on to Mexico City, Enrique fell into a deep, peaceful slumber for the first time in a week.

CHAPTER TWENTY-FOUR
FAMILY REUNION

CULIACÁN, MEXICO
4:00 SATURDAY AFTERNOON

ENRIQUE MET HIS nephew, Tito, at the airport in Culiacán, Sinaloa. It was the first time the two had ever met in person. Their previous contact had been mostly limited to Christmas cards or brief messages directed through third parties. The first time they communicated directly had been when Tito called Enrique to notify him of his son's death. The second time they spoke was just a few days before, when Enrique contacted Tito to request his assistance in trying to locate Elena.

As soon as Enrique stepped through the outside door of the airport, Tito embraced him. As the two men embraced, they felt something that transcended the boundaries of their totally disparate forms of livelihood—a familial connection that seemed to eclipse all their differences.

"I've looked forward to this day since I met cousin Miguel. I always knew that one day we'd come together. I'm so sorry for the circumstances and the tragedy of Grandfather Julio's death, but I think we have the ability to rescue your daughter . . . even if the authorities cannot."

"Thank you, Tito," said Enrique. "I would never have requested such help were it anyone but my daughter, but she's all that Belinda and I have left. Your aunt and I will be eternally grateful for all your help."

On the ride to Tito's estate, Enrique filled Tito in on the FBI's plan to hit the Vultures' training camp with the aid of the Mexican National Police that evening. He expressed his overriding concern of saving Elena from her captors on a timely basis—before she could be hurt.

"Don't worry, Uncle," Tito assured Enrique as he patted him on the back. "I have something in mind to take care of this problem." Then he smiled and said reassuringly, "And you will never believe where I got it!"

★★★★

Enrique, Tito, and several of the Brotherhood sat around an ornate walnut table in the conference room of Tito's residence outside of Culiacán. A brisk, cool breeze wafted through the shuttered windows, signaling the advent of fall in Sinaloa.

Enrique truly enjoyed meeting Tito and his family. He was caught off guard by the wary but friendly reception of the operatives of the Brotherhood—the same genre of characters he had so aggressively pursued as a prosecutor. He was struck by the stark contrast in the attitude of appreciation and admiration swelling up within him for Tito and the three Brotherhood foremen who sat planning his daughter's rescue and his feelings of contempt and disgust for other cartels, particularly the Vultures, since the death of his son, his daughter-in-law, and his father.

Everyone in the room seemed united in purpose as they focused on their unusual undertaking. For these unlikely helpers, it was a quest that felt like an act of redemption. There was electricity in the air—a rare and welcome excitement about doing something noble.

Tito spoke first, "Enrique, we have forty additional people at our disposal. According to our informant, there are only twenty-five to thirty people at the Vultures' camp. This is what we propose.

"I have a book that Miguel gave my father when he was a missionary here. It's called the Book of Mormon, but we usually refer to it as 'Miguel's Holy Book.' Are you familiar with this book?"

Enrique chuckled in spite of himself and assured his nephew

that he was indeed familiar with the Book of Mormon.

"I myself have not read it, but my father read some of it to me prior to his death. My sister, Fonseca, has also read it. I'm impressed with one of the stories that my father passed on that outlines a plan we'll use to rescue Elena."

Enrique's head jerked up. "What? A plan from the Book of Mormon?"

"Exactly," responded Tito. "It tells of an ancient people who were taken captive by some wild enemies. They made a gift of wine to their captors—enough wine to put the guards to sleep, allowing the captives to escape. It was as easy as that. We'll want to do the same thing.

"The Vultures love their tequila and probably drink more of it than anybody we know of. They purchase huge quantities of it from Benito's Tavern, just outside of Culiacán, but not usually during their training sessions. Well, we've arranged for Benito to deliver ten cases tonight, compliments of La Familia Blanca, the Vulture's major cocaine purchaser in San Ysidro. By midnight, most of the Vultures should be drunk or close to it, and we will have surrounded their training camp, ready to move in.

"If all goes well, we'll rescue Elena without shedding any blood, unless absolutely necessary. We should be able to subdue the Vultures and leave them for the Mexican law enforcement authorities who will have warrants for their arrests."

Enrique's mind reeled. *All this from the Book of Mormon! Incredible!*

"We're confident this plan will work," Tito said, a broad smile covering his face. "After all, it's right there in Miguel's Holy Book."

"The boss here has told us the Mormons had many wives," one of the Brotherhood foreman said. "Maybe if we do well, we can join up and receive that blessing, eh?"

"Careful, Alejandro," the man sitting next to him said. "First you must learn to handle the one you already have!"

Subdued laughter rippled around the table.

For the next few hours, the men poured over typographical maps of their target area, hashing out the details of infiltrating the

Vultures' camp. When Tito was satisfied, he dismissed the group.

The Brotherhood leader looked around the table. "Please pass on these instructions to your men. We leave tonight at 9:00. We should be in place and ready to move in by 11:30."

CHAPTER TWENTY-FIVE
THE RUSE AND THE RAID

MEXICO CITY, MEXICO
4:30 SATURDAY AFTERNOON

FOLLOWING A MEETING with the regional offices of the Department of State, the DEA, and the CIA to coordinate the planned operation with the Mexican National Police, Mark and Brady met three FBI agents from the legal attaché office in Mexico City. Since the state department was responsible for overseeing all US law enforcement activities in foreign countries, it was necessary to follow proper protocol. After SAC Brady explained the rescue scenario to the agents at the legal attaché office, he immediately encountered resistance.

The head legal attaché, Charles Evans, reacted first. "You're telling us we're going in with the Mexican police to take down a drug cartel and that our backup is another drug cartel? With all due respect, Agent Brady, if Bureau headquarters knew about this, you'd be out of a job in five minutes. So what if the victim is the daughter of some US Attorney who prosecutes drug cartels?"

Brady pulled out a fresh Havana cigar and calmly stuck it in his mouth. He chewed it for a few minutes in silence, never taking his eyes off Evans. When he stood, he towered over Evans.

"Look, Charlie, you haven't even heard the best part."

He took a matchbook out of his pocket, struck a match, and

to Mark's amazement, lit the cigar, and blew circles of smoke in Evans's direction.

"There's a catch, Charlie. Tito Guzman, the leader of the Brotherhood, is Enrique Guzman's nephew. How do you feel now?"

Evans's eyes were wide as saucers. A quick breath escaped his lips as he tried, unsuccessfully, to utter a profanity. Instead, he coughed from the smoke of Brady's cigar. "I still think the FBI will have your hide for this, Brady."

"Is that a fact?" Brady retorted. "Read this!" Brady handed Evans a copy of a letter printed on official FBI Headquarters' letterhead stationery that authorized the proposed operation and took another drag on his cigar. "There's your copy, Evans."

Evans looked at the letter incredulously. "You gotta be kidding me. The Director of the FBI signed off on this? The same organization I work for?"

"That's a fact," Brady confirmed. "The same organization you will *no longer* be working for if you don't give me the three men I need and make the appropriate arrangements with the Mexican National Police to accompany us to Sinaloa."

Evans threw the letter down on his desk and said, grudgingly, "Take whoever you need. I'll call the Mexican authorities."

"Smart move, Charlie, my boy." Brady extinguished his cigar inside one of Evans' fancy beer steins, stuck it back in his mouth, and continued chewing it.

****

Federico was not surprised when the gray pickup, loaded with ten cases of tequila, showed up at the training compound. Tito had already contacted him by cell phone with the plan for Elena's rescue. Federico was struck with the simplicity of such an idea. Historically, every move that either the Vultures or the Brotherhood had carried out against one another was executed with force, brute strength, and violence. Federico had never heard of this kind of cunning strategy. He was intrigued with the idea and wondered how the boss had come up with it.

Eduardo Ramirez and Benjamin Soto were the first to respond

to the delivery of alcohol. They'd both been drinking heavily since El Gordo had put them on probation and had pretty much exhausted their supply of booze.

Ramirez and Soto approached the pickup, instructed the driver to unload the cases of tequila at the central eating area, and had one of the men deliver the gift note from the Blanca family to El Gordo, who sent an operative back with explicit instructions from the Boss to deliver a full case of the tequila to his cabin. Within minutes, word of the delivery had spread through the entire compound. The eating area filled with men noisily filling cups and flasks and pouring the liquid down their throats with abandon.

With each drop of tequila, the celebrants grew more and more lax. Many left their rifles and shotguns stacked inside their cabins, so as not to encumber themselves as they made merry. Although the men became extremely raucous and obscene in their celebration, not once did El Gordo or anyone else try to deter or interrupt their revelries. El Gordo fully expected that his sons and the other four men would be released later that evening, since he had allowed Elena to speak with Enrique over a cell phone earlier that day to assure him of her well-being. Furthermore, Enrique had promised the men's release in the order El Gordo had proposed, through the San Ysidro checkpoint.

When the time for guard shift change came at 10:00, Juan Gomez was there promptly with a cup of tequila in one hand.

"Hey, Juan," Federico said happily. "You know I don't drink, right?"

"Not even a little?"

"Not a drop. I can't afford it. Even if I did, getting drunk gets in the way of training and exercise. But hey, it looks like it's on the house tonight. You might as well cash in while there's still plenty left. I can watch the girl a couple more hours."

"*Muchísimas gracias!*" Gomez said. "I owe you a favor. I'll be back at midnight."

"Enjoy yourself," Federico said. "I'll see you later."

Once Gomez was out of earshot, Federico went inside the cabin and explained the scenario to Elena. "I don't know where the idea of getting the men drunk came from, but I think it'll work well enough that we can get you out of here tonight."

Although Elena hadn't been one to read scriptures that much, she recalled Abuelito telling her the story of the famous rescue of some people he had referred to as the people of Limhi who escaped from a wicked king, once their guards became inebriated. Excited, she explained to Federico how the plan for her delivery was described in detail in the Book of Mormon.

"That makes sense," Federico said. "I know Tito read from that book from time to time and that Fonseca was also enthralled with it. Tito must have been convinced this was what needed to be done . . . and it's working. The Brotherhood is coming at midnight. Hopefully we'll find a way to get you out of here before then, when everyone is drunk."

He tried to sound hopeful, but Federico could tell by looking into her eyes that she was anticipating the worst.

"Federico, what if I *do* get out of here safely? What about you? If they see you helping me, what happens to you?"

Federico had been concerned about his own well-being along with Elena's, but it was overshadowed by the obvious concern that Elena had just voiced for him. More and more, he sensed her affection for him and had a growing hope for the possibility of a future together.

"There shouldn't be a problem for either of us . . . especially considering how these men are taking care of that tequila."

It wasn't until 11:30 P.M. that the noise started subsiding, and a few of the Vultures were seen staggering toward their cabins or passed out on the ground.

By 11:45 P.M., the noise had almost completely abated, and most of the cabin lights had gone out. Federico went back inside Elena's cabin.

"We need to get out of here," he said. "The Brotherhood will move in here within the next few minutes. We'll hike up the pass behind El Gordo's cabin to a ridge where an old timber-cutting road passes through. We can wait there and call Tito to come get us. Are you ready?"

"I sure am," she said, trying to sound cavalier. "I've already been here a week too long." Still, Elena was more than a little anxious.

As the pair moved toward the front door, they heard a drunken Juan Gomez returning for guard duty . . . ten minutes too early.

"Okay. . . . Freder . . . Frederic . . . Federico," Gomez said with a belch. "I'm here to take over. Y-you . . . can go now. Everything's under c-control."

The older man came to the door with his shotgun slung over his shoulder and sat down in the old wooden chair just outside the door.

Federico looked at his watch. It was 11:54. As he looked around, he noticed the remainder of the cabin lights had gone out—all except the cabins of Eduardo Ramirez and Benjamin Soto and El Gordo's cabin. Just then he noticed a damp rag on the ground of Elena's cabin. Ramirez had dropped it in the aftermath of his attempted assault. Federico retrieved the rag, noticing it was still slightly doused in chloroform, and laid it over Gomez' face, holding it firmly over his mouth and nostrils. When combined with the tequila Gomez had consumed, the chemical quickly put the old guard to sleep, and Elena and Federico ran for the pass behind El Gordo's cabin.

This time the chloroform didn't stay in effect for more than a few seconds. Gomez woke up from his doze and caught sight of the fleeing Federico a few feet behind Elena, less than thirty yards away. Gomez brought the shotgun to his shoulder and pulled the trigger. Federico felt pellets penetrate his shoulder and blood trickled down his back.

Within five seconds of the gun's report, the compound was flooded with light from pickups and vans surrounding the train-ing compound, as armed men with shotguns, M-16 rifles, and semi-automatic handguns ran out into the compound, entering each cabin, pointing guns at the occupants. The Brotherhood had no problem subduing the inebriated Vultures. Before they fully awoke from their drunken stupors, they found themselves lashed to their beds with the same nylon ropes that they had used for rappelling training.

Once the Vultures were secured, the Brotherhood set to work

securing the weapons and searching the cabins. In each cabin, they tacked a poster to the wall containing the following notice:

Con los complimentos de la Hermandad y Al Cooperar Al Maximo Con Los Gobiernos de Mexico Y de los Estados Unidos!

"With the compliments of the Brotherhood, and on to cooperate to the maximum with the governments of Mexico and the United States!"

* * * *

As Federico and Elena continued running toward the pass to make their escape, they approached El Gordo's cabin. By now the occupants were on full alert. El Gordo, Aurelio Flores, and one of El Gordo's bodyguards were leaving the house. They ordered the three drunken women that were there with them to stay behind. Eduardo Ramirez and Benjamin Soto had escaped to El Gordo's cabin just after the Brotherhood arrived.

Soto and Ramirez spotted Federico and Elena as the passed by and drew down on them with shotguns, ordering them to stop. El Gordo and his bodyguards were just climbing into a van parked outside the house, but upon seeing Federico and Elena, El Gordo ordered Soto and Ramirez to force them into the rear of the van. Then they sped away as El Gordo and his men emptied their guns into the barrier of vehicles of the Brotherhood.

El Gordo's van broke through the barrier with little problem, since Tito had given specific orders not to fire into any dwelling or vehicle where Elena might be present for fear of harming her.

From the back of the van, Federico struggled to listen as El Gordo and his men babbled away in drunken Spanish. They spoke of a nearby safe house where they could hide out temporarily and "take care" of the girl and the "traitor." Federico knew he had to find a way to save Elena from certain death and that he had to do it quickly.

Federico recalled Elena's prayer for rescue. Sheltering Elena's body as they crouched on the floor of the back of the van, Federico followed the girl's example, bowed his head, and spoke out in a voice that was almost inaudible.

"Heavenly Father . . . I've never done this before, so excuse me if I don't do it right. Can you please help us? Please help me to know what to do. Please don't let these men hurt Elena anymore . . . or me. Please! In the name of Jesus Christ, amen."

A familiar warmth washed over Federico. It was similar to what he felt when he observed Elena bear her testimony at the youth conference. In spite of the danger they were in, somehow he knew that, no matter what happened, everything would be okay.

Better yet, Federico knew how Elena felt about him. He aspired to be with her . . . always.

* * * *

Tito and Enrique were the only people on the scene who saw Federico and Elena get whisked away in the gray van. They followed the van in Tito's four-wheel drive Suburban from a distance, just close enough not to lose sight of the vehicle but far enough away to remain undetected.

* * * *

When Mark and Agent Brady arrived at the Vultures' training compound at approximately twenty minutes past midnight, accompanied by a contingent of one hundred Mexican National Police, they encountered a quiet village that—just minutes before—had been raided and secured by raiders from the Brotherhood who had since vanished into the darkness.

Mark exited the vehicle, looking out onto an eerie sight. Wisps of smoke rose from the chimneys of the cabins. All the lights were on. Cars and pick-ups were parked outside of every cabin. *If I didn't know better,* Mark thought, *I would swear we're walking right into an ambush.*

Suddenly, Mark's phone rang. It was Enrique.

"Mark, Tito and I are in pursuit of El Gordo and four of his men. They have Elena and the Brotherhood's informant, Federico Valdez. They're moving in a gray van. I have the GPS coordinates."

Once the directions were given, Enrique asked, "Where are you?"

"We've just arrived at the target location. Everything's lit up, but no one's moving. It's like they're waiting for us. Brady is frothing at the mouth, ready to bust down doors. He's wearing his pearl-handled revolvers."

"Not to worry, Mark. They're in there waiting for you . . . signed, sealed, and delivered." Enrique knew Mark and Brady would love what had been left for them by the men of the Brotherhood prior to their convenient disappearance. He knew many of the Brotherhood had warrants out on them.

"Oh, that's too bad! Big Bob was looking for some action."

"Go check it out, Mark. They're all there except the five we're following. Should be about twenty-five of them, compliments of Tito Guzman and the Brotherhood. According to Tito, most of them are wanted men, either here in Mexico or up in the States."

Mark quickly briefed Brady with this new information.

"All right, Enrique. How many men do you have with you at El Gordo's safe house?" Mark asked.

"Ten with Tito, plus me. That's it, Mark."

"Okay," Mark said. "The Mexican police are arresting and processing everyone now and seem to have everything under control. Most of the detained are too drunk to even remember their first names. We'll grab our three FBI agents and meet you up there shortly to back you up."

"Sounds good, brother. We'll keep you advised of our location," Enrique said.

Once Tito and Enrique arrived within sight of El Gordo's safe house, they pulled into a grove of trees nearby, and Enrique approached the house on foot.

Enrique checked his revolver. He carried it with him only occasionally when he had received threats over the past years. He ejected some rusty rounds that had been in the gun way too long and inserted some fresh loads. As he worked his way toward the safe house, Tito remained parked in the woods adjacent to the rear driveway.

Inside the safe house, El Gordo was barking out orders. "What value is there in holding onto these hostages now? It's obvious they are not going to turn over my sons or the other four. Guzman would have contacted me by now. He's broken his word, and he's most likely conspiring with his relatives in the Brotherhood.

"Soto! Ramirez! Take the girl and the traitor here to the Red Rock Cliffs. And take him with you," El Gordo commanded, pointing to one of his bodyguards. "After you put a hole in their heads, throw them over the side. I never want to lay eyes on either of them again. Move!"

As they drove the bound captives away, Soto noticed Tito's white Suburban parked behind the rear driveway, eighty feet back into the trees. After driving the van out of sight of the Suburban, Soto motioned for Ramirez and the bodyguard to stay quiet while he double-backed to the Suburban on foot. He exited the vehicle and drew his gun.

Once he was directly behind the Suburban, Soto crept up to the passenger side and fired at Tito through the glass window. Enrique, who had been returning to the vehicle, saw Soto and returned fire, hitting him twice in the upper body. Soto staggered away from the van, leaving his gun on the ground, bleeding profusely from the craters in his chest that he was trying to cover with his hands.

Enrique hurried to the driver's side of the Suburban and opened the door. Tito, grazed in the head by Soto's shot, slumped into Enrique's arms. His hair was full of glass from the shattered window and a wide streak of blood streamed from behind his right ear.

"Tito! How bad is it?"

As Tito looked up at his uncle, who was holding him carefully in his arms, a faint smile appeared on his lips. "It's not real bad. I'm glad, Uncle."

"About what, Tito?"

"I'm glad I've helped with this. I'm glad that as an organization, we've finally done something good and noble. You know, Uncle, I've invested well. I own much good land. I have many options. I could get out of this rat race." His words slurred as he lost strength. When his eyelids closed and his breathing grew labored, Enrique called for emergency personnel.

****

It had been five minutes since Soto left for the white Suburban with his gun drawn. Ramirez slid into the driver's seat and told the bodyguard that if Soto wasn't back in thirty seconds, they would leave without him.

Suddenly, a wide-eyed Soto came careening through the grove of trees next to the van, grasping his chest and hemorrhaging blood from his mouth. In one desperate, last-ditch effort, he lunged to the driver's side window, looked at Ramirez as if to say something, then slid down the passenger door, streaking it with blood as he crumpled to the ground.

"We're getting out of here!" shouted Ramirez as he gunned the van onto the road and toward the cliffs, a quarter of a mile away.

****

Once all the Vultures at the compound were secured, Brady was informed by one of the agents on loan from Mexico City that the Mexican commandant wished to thank the FBI for their cooperation in bringing down one of the most violent cartels in the country. Agent Brady responded with a line that was translated through the commandant's official interpreter: "It ain't over until the fat lady sings, sir."

The interpreter responded by asking, "What does that mean, señor?"

"It means we've still got work to do up here! You know, Commandant, I'm kind of a rare bird in the FBI," he said, pausing so the interpreter could find a translation for "rare bird."

"I get involved in stuff that most administrators in my organization sometimes like to avoid. I'm from the old school, where we like to kick butts and take names!"

The interpreter stared at Brady with a puzzled look.

"Do you need some help translating that?" Brady asked pleasantly. "No? Okay . . . you see, General Patton was my hero. I even carry two pearl-handled revolvers like he did." The big FBI boss pulled his jacket aside, displaying his hardware.

Brady continued, "I've always felt that the FBI was the top

act when it came to 'taking care of business.' However, tonight, Commandant, in terms efficiency, forethought, raid planning, and downright ingenuity, I believe all of us have received some schooling from a group called the Brotherhood . . . a group of *bandidos* at that."

Hearing one of the most respected agents in the FBI give credit for an operation to a bunch of individuals, who, in their minds, were no more than sophisticated drug traffickers, the FBI agents from Mexico City looked stunned.

Brady didn't stop there. "So, Commandant, you're thanking the wrong guy for those tidy packages you've got tied up there. Wish I could take the credit, my friend, but no cigar."

The Commandant looked at the interpreter. "Did you understand all that?" he asked.

"Well, uh . . . maybe half, sir," answered the translator.

As the contingent of Mexican police headed back to their booking facilities with over two dozen prisoners, they also transported huge caches of weapons that the Brotherhood had neatly stock-piled for them, including rocket-propelled grenade launchers, M-16 fully automatic rifles, shotguns, .50-caliber sniper rifles, and two light anti-tank guns.

CHAPTER TWENTY-SIX
DEFINING MOMENTS

RED ROCK CLIFFS
1:20 SUNDAY MORNING, OCTOBER 3, 2010

UPON ARRIVING AT the Red Rock Cliffs parking area overlooking a drop of over two hundred feet into a river gorge, Ramirez ordered El Gordo's bodyguard to get out and determine the best spot to dump the bodies. He wanted to be sure they would reach the river.

Ramirez reached for a sidearm secured in his shoulder holster. As Ramirez turned toward his intended targets, Federico sprang forward suddenly from the backseat, and in a flash he looped his hands over Ramirez's head, trapping the would-be assassin's neck between the ropes securing his hands. "Get out, Elena!" Federico yelled. "Get out, now!"

Elena opened the side door, rolled onto the ground, sprang to her feet, and crouched down out of view of the bodyguard. The bodyguard had his pistol out and was pointing it at Federico but hesitated to fire for fear of hitting Ramirez.

Federico had a death hold on Ramirez. Before he lost consciousness, Ramirez thrashed about frantically, stomping in his panic on the accelerator and revving the engine, which was set in neutral. Once the bodyguard had a clearer sight on Federico, he walked slowly and deliberately toward the front of the van, firing round after round into the windshield. Federico dropped to the floor of the van, and with the bodyguard now directly in front of the van, Federico pushed open the passenger-side door, wrenched the gearshift into drive and rolled out onto the ground as the van moved forward.

With Ramirez's foot still on the gas, the big van shot forward toward the cliff, its wheels churning the dirt beneath it into a dusty cloud. The bodyguard had no time to leap out of the way. His body thumped sickly over the front of the van and stopped on the hood, face to face with its incapacitated driver as the van went off the cliff and into the air. In its descent, it bounced twice off rocky outcroppings, exploded in a ball of fire, and plummeted with a fiery splash into the river.

In the dim light of the approaching dawn, Federico and Elena peered over the cliff and watched as the charred remains of the van bobbed on down with the current.

As Federico and Elena worked on untying each other, Elena noticed the bloodstain on Federico's shoulder. "You're bleeding!" she exclaimed.

Federico took Elena into his arms and held her close. "It's only a couple of small pellets," he assured her. "They sting a little, but once they're removed, I'll be fine. Elena, I prayed today for the first time, and my prayers were answered. I want you to know that."

Federico had never held his head up higher. The significance of his arrest as a naïve teenager meant nothing now. He had saved Elena's life, and in so doing, he had helped rid society of some of its worst dregs. He had redeemed himself. No longer did he feel the need to limit his aspirations.

Elena and Federico turned from the cliff, and in the dim light, the two began walking warily along the open road back toward the safe house. Suddenly, a dark blue van appeared with the letters SWAT written on it. Elena recognized it as the same van her captors drove. Another dark sedan was directly behind it.

Federico and Elena dove off the road and ran into an expanse of open field, hiding themselves in some brush.

The van stopped, and a Brotherhood operative, in fluent English, announced through the van's public address system, "Elena Guzman, you are running from your relatives. Federico Valdez, you are running from your boss." When Federico and Elena heard chuckling coming from the loudspeaker, they left their hiding place and came forward. One of members of the Brotherhood, who knew Federico, got out of the van, greeting Elena and offering Federico his hand.

In the black sedan following the van was Elena's teary-eyed but exultant father. Enrique was out of the car even before it came to a stop, holding his open arms toward his daughter. "Elena . . . oh, my Elena!" Within seconds, Elena plunged into her father's arms, tears of relief streaming down her face.

* * * *

El Gordo was growing impatient and suspicious. *What's taking them so long?* He walked out of the house, looking for his men and wondering why they hadn't returned. He trudged heavily up the dirt road toward the cliffs a quarter of a mile away. When he got within a hundred yards of the cliffs and realized no one was there, he immediately thought the worst. *My own men have double-crossed me! They have killed the couple, dumped their bodies somewhere, and ran off!* The fat man was sure he had been betrayed and was boiling with anger as he turned to make his way back to the safe house.

Before he could get there, El Gordo's men, including the remaining bodyguard and Aurelio Flores, found themselves trapped in the house by several men of the Brotherhood, Mark Madden, Agent Brady, who was brandishing his two pearl-handed revolvers, and the three FBI agents from Mexico City. Brady picked up a bullhorn and announced their presence.

"You, in the cabin! Come out immediately. You are surrounded by the FBI and the . . . the . . . uhh . . . well . . . the FBI!" Even Bob Brady was at a loss for words. *How the devil do I tell them they're surrounded by us and another pack of drug traffickers?* he thought. *Oh, well,* he rationalized, *it's the result that counts.*

The FBI boss raised the bullhorn to his mouth again. "You have no chance of escape. Come out slowly, with your hands behind your heads!" A bilingual Brotherhood operative was translating each of Brady's commands into Spanish. The men outside had positioned themselves into an "L" formation around the dwelling and were kneeling behind the protective cover of their vehicles.

Meanwhile, El Gordo approached the safe house through a cow pasture on the west side of the dwelling. In the rapidly receding darkness, he could see the house was now surrounded by a group of Mexican men and American agents wearing FBI raid jackets. He crouched as far as his corpulent frame would allow and advanced cautiously. When he got closer, he recognized two of the men as members of the Brotherhood. The sight of his arch competitors surrounding his cabin was more than El Gordo could handle. Then, to infuriate him even further, he noticed Tito Guzman, his most hated enemy, with a bandage over his head, standing next to a big man with a cigar in his mouth and two pearl-handled revolvers on his hips, screaming orders into a bullhorn.

"All right!" Brady warned. "This is your last chance. We'll give you fifteen seconds, and then we'll send in gas." The time expired as Brady looked at his wristwatch.

El Gordo crept up behind Mark Madden, one of the Brotherhood men, and Brady with his big handgun drawn. There was no way to hide in the pasture, and with it getting lighter every moment, the fat drug lord knew he had no chance of retreating without being seen or heard. His half-mile hike to the cliffs and back had completely exhausted him; he'd walked more in the last forty-five minutes than he had in the entire year. As he contemplated his next move, El Gordo was convinced he would never survive in Mexico's prisons among all his past enemies. With furrowed eyebrows and a feeling of total resignation, he decided he would surely die . . . but not alone. He inched up further toward the Brotherhood operative. *I'll kill that filthy dog first,* he vowed, *and then the Americans.*

When Aurelio Flores and El Gordo's bodyguard still refused to surrender, Brady's patience expired. "Remember," he told his agents, "if those guys inside bring their weapons up to level, don't hesitate to blow them away. Now, take that door down and toss in the gas!" One agent immediately kicked in the door while another lobbed in "flash-bang" smoke grenades. When they blew, it sounded as though the world was coming apart.

Another agent tossed in a volley of gas grenades, and before long, the dwelling was completely engulfed in smoke and gas. A torrent of profanity erupted inside the cabin and, choking and gagging, El Gordo's bodyguard and Aurelio Flores stumbled out of the cabin with their hands high over their heads. Mark and the two FBI agents took the defenseless men into custody and handcuffed them.

In the confusion, Mark and the Brotherhood operative moved out of El Gordo's line of fire. However, now the fat man was only a few steps behind Agent Brady. Determined now to kill and be killed, the enraged El Gordo raised his handgun and moved out from a clump of bushes, intending to shoot Brady in the back. Instead, he stepped into a pile of fresh cow manure and felt his foot slip from beneath him, causing him to fall heavily onto his side. His pistol discharged, but the round went well over Brady's head.

Pulling out both pearl-handled revolvers, Brady whirled around to see the huge man wallowing around on his back in the pile of slick manure, trying without success to regain his feet. Big Bob Brady leveled his weapons at El Gordo and ordered him to drop his gun. Instead, the drug lord raised his weapon, and Brady responded by quickly firing two rounds from each revolver. The bullets found their mark and, after struggling for a moment, El Gordo's huge body sagged and lay still.

"Hey, Mark!" Brady called. "Is this the big guy? It's got to be El Gordo, right?"

"Yeah, Bobby," Mark answered. "You nailed him. Nice shooting."

Brady calmly holstered his weapons and rolled his cigar to the other side of his mouth, savoring it, as though nothing extraordinary had just happened.

Mark stepped to the side of his old FBI friend, put his arm around Brady's shoulder, and said, "Someone was looking out for you, my friend, and I hate to disappoint you, but it wasn't General Patton."

As the FBI agents loaded Aurelio Flores and El Gordo's bodyguard into the backseat of one of the vehicles, Mark heard a radio

CHAPTER TWENTY-SEVEN
THE RECONCILIATION

SAN DIEGO,
11:20 TUESDAY MORNING, OCTOBER 5, 2010

TWO DAYS AFTER Elena's rescue, US Attorney Shad Bennington stood at the head of a long table in the conference center of his office in San Diego. Seated in front of him were Tito Guzman, wearing a bandage that covered most of his head; Federico Valdez; and twenty-three of the forty men from the Brotherhood who had been involved in Elena Guzman's rescue. The other seventeen had failed to appear.

Seated at Shad's left was Enrique Guzman, and on his right was Mark Madden. All the men of the Brotherhood, including Tito, were shackled and under the careful scrutiny of several United States Marshals. Tito, upon Enrique's request, had convinced the twenty-three men to travel from Sinaloa voluntarily and turn themselves in to American authorities. Each of the men had been identified by American authorities months, and, in some cases, years before, but they had always managed to elude arrest. This was due largely to the contacts with the Mexican and American authorities that the Guzman family had established over previous decades. Their bribes had been most effective. Tito had effectively placed his future and the futures of his men entirely in Enrique's hands.

"Gentlemen," Bennington began, "this meeting may go down in American legal history as one of the most unusual of its kind. None of you have been arraigned before a federal judge yet, although you have all been arrested and processed through the US Marshall's office. Your official arraignment date is tomorrow. None of you have spent a minute in jail, and the only reason you are in custody today is because you have submitted yourselves voluntarily, at the request of your leader, Tito Guzman."

The men all looked at each other approvingly, nodding their heads in agreement as the court interpreter, a Hispanic woman, translated the proceedings.

Bennington continued. "Now, I would say you have some good things going for you. In the past few years of your employment, you've avoided any charges for serious crimes, such as homicide, assault, or extortion, which is very different behavior from your competitors. Other cartels are shedding blood almost on a daily basis along the border. We understand that in the Brotherhood, the violence started its downward trend as an integral part of your leadership, Tito, and your call for change in collection activities in the last couple of years since your father's death. Although I don't fully understand the reason for this, I must say that it is commendable."

Upon hearing the translation of these remarks, the men of the Brotherhood smiled approvingly at what they took to be a compliment.

"Now, it behooves us to make a recommendation to the federal judge assigned this case as to our next course of action. Drug trafficking is an extremely serious crime. It is poisoning the people of this country. Your livelihood over the years has killed countless users, put thousands of people out on the streets, caused broken marriages, ruined careers, and wrecked lives. You have played an integral role in one of the most insidious and devastating invasions of America that has ever occurred."

There were sounds of negative muttering and disapproval among the Mexican men as they realized they were taking blame for the illicit appetites of the Americans . . . for their cravings for the fruits of the fields.

"I assure you, we recognize that this is not a one-sided matter. Your American clients are also to blame. It takes individuals on both sides of the border to bring about a drug transaction. I know that Americans have been sending guns and money down your way that help you carry out your criminal activity.

The Brotherhood members turned toward Tito, their faces taut and wrapped in concern and apprehension. Fear was setting in as the men questioned whether they would be able to return to their homes in Sinaloa and whether they had made a mistake in trusting Tito.

"Now, gentlemen, what I want to do is have Enrique Guzman, our head strike force attorney, address this group. Although he is the dynamic force behind the prosecution of Mexico's drug cartels and the one who has put more drug traffickers in prison than I can count, today he is assuming a very different role. Today, he is your benefactor and will speak in your behalf. He will make recommendations that I understand both Special Agent in Charge Robert Brady of the Federal Bureau of Investigation and Regional Homeland Security Coordinator Mark Madden have approved and support. We now hear from Enrique Guzman."

Enrique rose slowly and cleared his throat as he looked over the group.

"The recommendations I will make in your behalf today have been reviewed by the federal strike force here in San Diego, who was assigned to investigate and apprehend operatives of illegal drug cartels working both sides of our southern border. To a man, every member of the strike force has approved my recommendations.

"I might mention that this is a unique position that I find myself in, since I have some vested interests in your leader, who happens to be my nephew. I had doubts that I would be given this opportunity to speak for you since my position isn't necessarily neutral, so I'm honored by the confidence and trust of my colleagues in being granted this opportunity to litigate in your behalf. It is my hope that we can prevent justice from being distorted and avoid any negative ramifications."

Enrique's introductory statement was met by complete silence. The men of the Brotherhood sat on the edges of their chairs with their hands clenched together as they looked anxiously up at their benefactor.

"To be frank, these are serious charges that have been leveled against you," Enrique continued. "And, yes, you have no idea of the serious negative influences you have had on the lives of countless thousands of people over the decades by administering them the poison you call the 'fruits of your fields.' "

The men seated at the table grew extremely anxious. Some actually started looking around, as if searching out an exit to flee through.

"But, in all fairness, I'll have to say this," Enrique said. "As of this day, the Brotherhood has agreed to give up its pursuits in the drug trade, putting an end to what has probably been the oldest and most powerful drug cartel in all of Mexico. This is something that our local, state, and national law enforcement has spent decades trying to accomplish, but before today, we have been largely unsuccessful. So, we can truthfully say that by your own actions, you have eliminated a great threat to America, and you have done it voluntarily."

The men seemed to relax ever so slightly.

"Second, you helped bring down the Vultures that night at the compound, effectively eliminating the threat of another dangerous cartel that had also operated for many years. This is a very rare case, indeed, but one that I feel, especially after talking to Mr. Bennington, deserves a very rare resolution.

"Third, you saved the life of my daughter by supplying intelligence that neither we nor the Mexican authorities had available. The Mexican government has already reduced all pending charges against you for your efforts in making their jobs a lot easier. They've levied some hefty fines against your boss, Tito Guzman, but have only fined each of you a small amount and are placing you on probation." A surge of welcomed relief passed through the men of the Brotherhood.

Enrique concluded his remarks to the twenty-three men. "In view of the fact that neither Mexico nor this task force no longer considers you a threat, I am recommending to Mr. Bennington here, that the US government follow Mexico's example. It is my suggestion that he not recommend incarceration when you are arraigned tomorrow, allowing each of you to return to your homes in Sinaloa. I further recommend a five-year probation period, during which time each of you would report in person to probation officers in San Diego once each year and by telephone every thirty days. In addition, Tito Guzman has agreed to personally assist you in keeping the conditions of your probation and has agreed to provide continuous employment for you, at least for the next five years.

"Regarding you, Tito, it is my recommendation that you not be prosecuted by US authorities and that the charges against you be dismissed without prejudice. But understand that if for some reason you or your men return to drug trafficking or otherwise violate your probation, Mr. Bennington has the power to charge you with your previous crimes.

"If both parties agree to these terms, the only punishment you would suffer will be what was already administered yesterday when the Mexican authorities placed you on probation and seized half your assets and land holdings."

Listening closely, Tito expelled a sigh of relief.

"Gentlemen, because of you, the Vulture clan has been disbanded, and those men will be incarcerated for many years, many of them for the remainder of their lives. Because you have done so much to aid justice, it is my opinion it would truly thwart justice to incarcerate you."

Enrique sat down, and Bennington again took over the meeting. He asked Federico to stand, and he did so, with hesitation and much apprehension. He looked over at Elena, who had been invited by her father to attend the hearing. She was seated in a chair against the wall of the large room.

"Young man," Bennington began, "it has been brought to my attention that you are directly responsible for saving Elena Guzman's life, while risking your own life in the process. It has also been documented that during your work with the Brotherhood and with the Vultures, you never participated in crimes of violence. In addition, you were the key informant who supplied the information used to neutralize and destroy the Vultures drug organization." Federico's apprehensive expression became more relaxed.

"For those reasons, I am recommending to the judge in this

case that we drop any charges against you and that your record should remain clean. Congratulations."

Elena stifled a cry of joy, ducked her head, and smiled her relief.

"Gentleman," Bennington concluded, "I intend to follow Prosecutor Guzman's recommendations before the judge precisely as he has articulated them. I'm completely confident the court will follow my recommendations. That's all for today, gentlemen."

The room came alive with chatter, everyone grinning and nodding their approval.

As Elena rushed to Federico's side and took his hand, he experienced a rush of joy. Tears welled in his eyes, and for a moment, he was unable to speak. Then he approached the US Attorney. "Thank you, Mr. Bennington," he said quietly, his voice breaking slightly. "Thank you very much!"

As Tito left the conference room with his uncle, he felt overjoyed, but he couldn't help but worry about the ramifications of his probation. He would honor his commitment to help his men uphold their end of the agreement, but he had no idea where to begin with such undertaking. *How do I help them comply?* Tito wondered. *How do I keep them employed? Where do I go from here?*

Then Tito grinned, as he recalled his cousin Miguel and the night he and Elder Jones had come to dinner as missionaries. Tito recalled his cousin's response when Tito expressed an interest in Miguel's CTR ring: *As long as I remember to wear the ring each day, I will remember to do only those things that are proper and to avoid evil.*

I can take care of these men, Tito thought with confidence. *As long as they wish to stand by me, I know that together, we can produce other fruits of the field.*

CHAPTER TWENTY-EIGHT
THE A TO Z SERMON

SAN DIEGO
JANUARY 2011

THREE MONTHS HAD passed since the blessed reunion of the Guzmans with their daughter. During that time, Stake President Mark Madden resolved to deliver the final sermon prepared by the faithful stake patriarch Erwin Granger.

Brother Granger had summoned Mark to his hospital room Wednesday evening, just a few hours prior to his passing. With his final strength and breath ebbing away, Erwin Granger anxiously discussed the details of his last Sunday School lesson with the stake president. The lesson he now knew he would never be able to present.

"I have truly enjoyed serving with you, Mark. Both as your mission president, all those years ago, and as the stake patriarch." He held Mark's hand firmly as the younger man sat quietly at his side.

He continued. "I'll be gone soon, Mark . . . very soon. I'll be joining my Helen, and that thought thrills me. Although life is always good, it's never quite the same without your sweetheart."

Mark smiled affectionately at his old friend, mentor, and role model—the man from whom he'd sought advice and wisdom for decades.

"Erwin," Mark assured softly, you'll be missed here more than you can possibly imagine." Tears ran freely from the eyes of both men as they discussed the past and future for over an hour. As the older man's voice became weaker, Mark felt the grip on his hand tighten.

"Your last lesson will go not only to our class in the Naranjas Third Ward, Erwin, but to the entire stake," Mark assured his dying friend. "I know that I could never present it as well as you would, but I'm sure your spirit will be there with me."

Mark made mental notes of every detail of the lesson as it left the patriarch's lips. Catching the importance of the message, Mark had never before been so anxious to address the members of his stake.

The two longtime friends visited for just a few more minutes until the old patriarch slowly loosened his grip on Mark's hand, closed his eyes, and smiled contentedly as the pain medication took its course, helping him drift off to sleep. Mark stood up, leaned over, kissed his friend softly on the forehead, and quietly left his room.

****

The stake center was filled almost to capacity. All the folding chairs available had been set up earlier that morning, and as the prelude music wafted softly through the air, even the seats on the stage were being filled.

After the stake business was conducted, several other speakers concluded their remarks, and the congregation sang an intermediate hymn, President Madden went to the pulpit, prepared to take the last hour of the meeting.

President Madden smiled as he looked out, first at his wife, Katie, his children, Harley and Amelia, and then at the hundreds of people assembled before him, each poised and ready to hear his counsel.

"Good morning, brothers and sisters! We appreciate your presence here and your sacrifice in making the effort to join us this fine Sabbath morning. We have been well fed spiritually by the speakers, and I hope to add to that feast." Even the children quieted as the stake center became silent. The stake members took note of the zealous and animated expression on the face of their spiritual leader.

"As most of you know, Patriarch Erwin Granger was recently taken from us to join his dear wife, Helen. He was my great friend as well as yours . . . a spiritual beacon to all of us. Brother Granger was an unusual man in that he had that rare ability to say exactly what was in his heart without fear or hesitation, and he could do it without giving offense."

Subdued laughter rippled through the congregation as those present fondly recalled how the old patriarch could so successfully dodge bullets while walking the fine line.

"I loved the way Brother Granger got right to the point and refrained from dancing around important issues. He never used the occasional swearing technique that might be typical of a J. Golden Kimball, nor did he lace his message with so much sugar you couldn't taste the cereal. Simply put, he just communicated!

"Shortly after Sister Elena Guzman was abducted just over three months ago, Brother Granger presented an amazing Sunday School lesson in the Naranjas Third Ward, addressing the huge moral problems that have created such a spiritual vacuum in our nation. More specifically, he called our attention to the secret combinations, oaths, covenants, words, and signs that ran rampant throughout ancient Nephite history as described in the Book of Mormon. He rightfully pointed out that these evils were at the root of the Nephites' eventual annihilation and explained how these same secret combinations are the base and source of power of many evil networks and organizations in the world today, including the Mexican drug cartels that are currently creating chaos and havoc along our southern borders.

"As we all know, these organizations, with little regard for anything but power and wealth, have been responsible for almost ten thousand deaths in just the last year and a half. These brutal atrocities, committed by competing gangs and drug cartels, have, for the most part, been perpetrated south of the borders of California, Arizona, and Texas. But recently, the violence and mayhem have crept north, into our own communities.

"Brother Granger had some strong convictions regarding the evolution of evil, but he wasn't able to cover all that he had to say before passing on.

"He entitled his presentation 'From Point A to Point Z' and discussed the details of that lesson with me in the hospital just a few hours before he died. I felt his sense of urgency that you good people hear his message. So today, brothers and sisters, I'm presenting the essence of Brother Erwin Granger's last Sunday School lesson.

"There are four pivotal steps that cause people, even church-going people, to devolve from Point A, a state of righteousness and innocence, to Point Z, a state of absolute moral decay.

"The first step is forgetting how good we are. All human spirits are essentially good, being created in God's image and born with the light of Christ. But being mortal, we are living in an inherently evil environment that has an effect on us. The Book of Mormon teaches that 'the natural man is an enemy to God.' We know that our immortal spirits are temporarily housed in corruptible, imperfect physical bodies that are subject to the temptations of the flesh. This is an essential part of the plan of salvation—to demonstrate to our Creator that we are willing to and capable of resisting evil and thus qualify for a return to His presence.

"Before Brother Granger passed on, he told me that after giving patriarchal blessings to hundreds of you over the past decades, he knew most of your hearts pretty well. He worried that we tend to judge ourselves too harshly, as a result of feeling the influences of our natural bodies. If he were here today, he would say, as only Brother Granger could: 'So, you have a desire to bash someone's head in once in a while, huh? So what? So you have some sexual stirrings that you worry about, or maybe even some same-sex attractions? So what? Maybe all you think about is food. Maybe you find it difficult to wait from one meal to the next. Big deal! So you really want a car just like the one Brother Brown drives and really think it would be fun just to grab it one night and take it for a joy ride. What's the big deal?'

"He would tell us, and I agree, 'Brothers and sisters, none of those feelings or sentiments really matter unless they nest in our thinking until we permit them to drive us to action.'

"As long as we're dwelling in earthly bodies, we will have earthly feelings, but that doesn't mean we're bad. Nevertheless, many of us become overwhelmed by our natural state, only because we don't understand it. And tragically, we give in to the evil we feel, believing that's just the way we are and that there's nothing we can do about it. In short, many give up, right out of the gate. We forget how good we are.

"The second step in the corruption of the human soul is giving into pride. How does this happen? Pride is manifest when we love what we own, what we wear, and who we are more than we love others, including our own families. Another danger is easily taking offense and carrying hard feelings toward one other, rather than being courageous enough to approach the offender, determine his true intent, and forgive him. Another step in the wrong direction happens when we form cliques and exclude others, thereby withholding our companionship, our blessings, and our righteous influence from those within our reach. Pride limits the scope of our blessings and our Christianity.

"As we discussed during that Sunday School lesson in the Third Ward, pride is present when we minimize the accomplishments of others in order to build ourselves up.

"Brother Granger observed these things happening in our midst and was saddened by it. There is a saying that I heard my father, Harley Madden, use once in awhile. It went like this: 'There's so much good in the worst of us, and so much bad in the best of us, it behooves none of us to speak ill of the rest of us.'

"We need to remember that churches are hospitals for sinners, not havens for saints. We need to regard the gospel as the ambulance that takes us to the hospital to be healed. We need to share that ambulance with those in need and not judge who should ride and who shouldn't. We can look at the cannibal and judge him. We can look at those people in far off places involved in rituals that disgust us, and judge them, but can we safely judge anyone, without the risk of being judged ourselves? Of course, we are all born with a conscience and the light of Christ, but our environment far too often plays an overpowering role in creating the foundation for our behavior and ensuing actions. People can only be judged for what they know is right and wrong.

"Recently, Elena Guzman's life was preserved when she was

rescued by some people who most of us here would never, for one moment, want to be associated with. People who some of us wouldn't want to even give the time of day to. People who would make you shudder if you thought your children were anywhere near them. You may have felt the same way about the Apostle Paul, Alma the Younger, or the sons of Mosiah, prior to their conversions.

"President Hinckley always said that the gospel makes bad men good and good men better. Can we really accurately judge anyone?"

"The third step in descending to Point Z is listening to the wrong signals. This is another point where many of us drop out of the race. This happens after our moral fiber is decimated by forgetting that we are inherently good and from surrendering to pride.

"When we listen to Satan, we forget the role the Savior plays in our lives. We believe in Jesus as the Messiah, as the Redeemer, and as a perfect being whom we should follow, but we don't believe Him when He promises He can and will forgive our sins. We believe that forgiveness is only for others, but not us. We feel we have gone too far and surely are beyond help. Then we give in, indulging our appetites and lusts, all while thinking, *What's the use?*

"We lose sight of the fact that we can be forgiven for any sin we have ever committed, with the possible exceptions of shedding innocent blood or denying the Holy Ghost. And how many have shed innocent blood? Or denied the Holy Ghost?

"The bottom line here is that we can be forgiven of almost every sin if we earnestly seek forgiveness and truly desire to repent. However, when we listen to the wrong signals—the voices that tell us we're too far gone to be forgiven, we give up and descend toward Point Z, Soon, we're unwilling to change, either because we love our sins too much or because we don't really believe we can be forgiven. What a tragic misjudgment!

"At this third point, we can be persuaded to sin if we are influenced sufficiently by our social system. Today, we're experiencing changes in age-old virtues of national policy. Brother Granger was extremely troubled by this new form of society, and he let us know it . . . often." Again, there was subdued laughter.

"Brother Granger was troubled by the direction our country is going. He was afraid that gargantuan social challenges are softening our morality, negatively influencing our behaviors, and making us spiritually vulnerable as a people. He spoke out about the potential danger of these issues and how they could drag us down towards Point Z." As Mark looked out on the congregation, he was pleased to note many individuals were busy taking notes.

"The patriarch believed that as a nation, we are collectively sponsoring abomination by endorsing any form of abortion with our vote. He personally expressed to me that, with the exception of rape or protecting a mother's health, tolerating abortion and endorsing it in the voting booth could make us a party to the annihilation of millions of unborn spirits, unless we change our position. He was adamant in his belief that Heavenly Father does not look upon abortion with the least degree of tolerance.

"Brother Granger was deeply concerned by the kid-glove approach the government takes toward administering justice . . . particularly the way we coddle criminals and allow terrorists full Miranda rights after they've killed thousands of Americans out of their hatred for us. He believed our military was being weakened, making us vulnerable to foreign threats. He was disappointed that we would apologize to foreign governments for our behavior, when many of those same governments would not exist, were it not for the protective hand of the stars and stripes.

"The patriarch condemned promiscuity and immorality as it is glorified in the media. He feared the concept of marriage between a man and a woman would one day no longer be considered relevant. He worried that the intent of our Founding Fathers as embodied in our Constitution is being changed by jurists trying to rewrite it.

"And, of course, the issue of illegal immigration struck home when Sister Guzman was abducted by violent drug cartel operatives out of Mexico who had entered the country illegally, and he felt vindicated for all that he had said about the inherent threat in not securing our borders.

"Brother Granger felt the current form of governmental evolution has definitely contributed to many people washing out at the third step after listening to the wrong signals.

"The fourth step is surrendering virtue. At this juncture of human degradation, Satan has whispered into our ears and convinced us we are no good and have no way of being forgiven. We believe him and become part of the problem, just as the Nephites did when they threw in the towel and joined up with the Gadianton robbers and his evil plots and schemes, which resulted in the destruction of the Nephite nation.

"At this point, people may surrender to the rule of secret combinations, complete with their oaths, covenants, and signs that are at the base of so many of the evil organizations throughout the world today. Human beings sinking to these depths are individuals with a disposition to commit murder and other forms of mayhem. They shed innocent blood in order to obtain power and wealth. They go beyond the point of no return.

"Brothers and sisters, recent events, such as Elena Guzman's deliverance from unexpected sources, even by individuals who most of us would have written off, tell me that good will always prevail over evil and that our Heavenly Father is very much in charge. I choose, personally, to carry that belief with me throughout the rest of my life.

"Today, we have been warned, though posthumously, by a good friend and a great patriarch, regarding four steps he believed could take us from Point A, a state of happiness and righteousness, to Point Z, a state of degradation and despair. If he were here in person, Brother Granger would plead for the people he loved to take his warning to heart and make the needed course corrections."

Those present in the congregation never forgot President Madden's remarks, and Erwin Granger, from a distant place was smiling ear-to-ear.

CHAPTER TWENTY-NINE
THE RESULT

THREE YEARS LATER...

THE FRUIT FARM operation outside of Culiacán was a beehive of activity. A sea of orchards engulfed the traffic on both sides of the entrance to the Guzman operation. The welcoming sign was huge, written in Spanish. Translated, it read: FRUITS OF THE FIELD: APPLES, PEARS, TOMATOES, AVOCADOS, AND MANGOS. Then in smaller print below: "Guzman and Associates."

Enrique and Belinda Guzman and their traveling companions, Mark and Katie Madden, pulled off to the side of the two-lane country road, just so they could breathe the fresh country air and take in the furor of activity common to the fall harvest.

Men drove modern air-conditioned tractors with tinted glass windows and listened to Latin music on the radio as they steered their way through their assigned sections of the orchards, pulling carts laden with fruit. State-of-the-art irrigation systems set up on computer timers had effectively carried the necessary water and nutrients to their targets, enabling the fruit to mature and ripen to perfection.

Advanced science and educated planning were obviously manifest in the end result of the harvest. The owner of this farm, Tito Guzman, was wholesaling "the best of the best" to major grocery chains throughout Mexico, in addition to expanding his markets into neighboring Guatemala.

The two couples had been invited the year before to come and visit Enrique's nephew in Sinaloa to check out his new business. Neither couple had any inkling that they would discover an agricultural endeavor of such magnitude.

"Can you believe your eyes?" Enrique asked Mark.

"I knew he had some money carried over from the old Brotherhood drug operations, since only half his holdings were confiscated, but I had no idea what the other 'half' represented until now."

Enrique winked as he added, "I think Tito might have had a few dollars tucked under the mattress. It also helped that the Mexican government built dams near here. A number of Mexico's largest agrarian operations are headquartered here in Sinaloa now. From the looks of all this, I'd say Tito runs one of the best of them."

"I think Tito had all this figured out before that raid three years ago, because he had already bought up this land," Mark said.

"When Tito told us he was selling apples and pears, I was thinking maybe a store or some fruit stands," Belinda said, the amazement evident in her voice. But just look at all the buildings we've already driven by with Tito's name on them! When Elena came back from Federico's baptism service, she said nothing about this being a major wholesale operation."

Katie Madden interjected her thoughts. "I think Elena and Federico had other things on their minds. But now that they are engaged, I'm sure Elena will become very curious as to the dynamics of the farm operation, since Federico will be working for Tito as a field foreman."

"That's right," said Enrique. "Federico told me Tito offered him an extremely generous starting salary . . . something like sixty thousand dollars. He'll have enough to pay for his education in agricultural science and to start a family. Anyway, let's travel on. We're almost there. When I spoke with Tito, he said they would have dinner ready for us in about an hour from now."

As the couples drove down the road leading to the Guzman estate, they observed a most interesting sight. Lined up in a parking lot next to the company headquarters, located approximately a mile from Tito's home, were about thirty, late model luxury cars.

"Wow!" exclaimed Katie Madden. "That looks like a combined Cadillac and Mercedes-Benz dealership. They must pay their employees really well."

"It's an interesting story," said Enrique. "Remember the night the Brotherhood helped us rescue Elena?"

Mark and the women nodded affirmatively. "Well, when they did that, they put everything on the line. They had to take Tito's word that they wouldn't be hauled off to jail once the Mexican police arrived."

"Right," responded Mark. "That's why, as soon as the job was done, they just sort of disappeared into the woods." He was smiling.

"Exactly," said Enrique. "Tito promised each one of those men that if they took that risk, he would stand by them the rest of his life. He had enough money to offer them each some shares in his fruit farming operation. Since they were all unskilled and uneducated for the most part, he gave them jobs driving tractors and doing farm labor but has paid them handsomely for it, as you can see."

"Where do we sign up?" asked Mark.

Katie laughed. "Neither one of you would last on a tractor. You're too old!"

Mark and Enrique looked at each other. *We could never win this argument,* they thought.

"Did you notice those guys coming off the tractors weren't wearing their Jesus Malverde necklaces?" Belinda said. "You know . . . the ones Miguel had written home and told us about?"

"No, I didn't," answered Katie. "What brought on the change?"

"Elena told us that after the meeting with Bennington in San Diego, Tito called everyone into the old residence in Culiacán and told them he would no longer permit his employees to wear those necklaces, since they were no longer trafficking drugs. And guess what else?"

Mark took the bait. "I give up. What?"

"Are you ready for this?" Belinda was bursting at the seams

to tell them. "Tito asked Enrique where Miguel had gotten the CTR ring he wore as a missionary. Enrique gave him the information for the nearest church bookstore.

"The next day, Tito ordered one for himself and one for each of his twenty-three men. Wearing the rings became a prerequisite for their continuing employment. Tito told them that 'CTR' meant to always 'choose the right' and that they should never deviate from the terms of their probation. Tito said the men have worn the rings ever since, and not one of them has violated their probation."

"This is all too good to be true!" Katie remarked. "CTR rings on reformed drug traffickers!

****

After arriving at the Guzman residence and exchanging *abrazos*, the guests ate a sumptuous meal of seafood *paella*, freshly cooked tortillas, and hand-squeezed lemonade. Tito was gushing with excitement as he exclaimed, "The newly engaged fiancées have an announcement to make."

Federico motioned to Elena to stand up with him. "Elena flew in two days ago with her friend, Anita, from San Diego, who is going to be her bridesmaid. We have chosen April twenty-third for our wedding." Looking straight at his future father-in-law, Enrique, his friend Mark, and their spouses, he asked, "Could you please be there with us?"

The couples enthusiastically accepted the invitation. Speaking for all of them, Mark said, "Thank you. It will be our honor."

Federico continued, "Tito and his family will have a reception here for us after the ceremony. But we have one more announcement."

Every one glanced up with curiosity.

"When we are blessed with children, the first son will be named Enrique Madden Valdez!" Both Enrique and Mark beamed with pride. "And the second son will be Tito Valdez!" Tito was equally touched and fought to hold back a tear.

After dinner, Tito pulled Enrique aside and, looking into his eyes with his hands on his shoulders, exclaimed, "Uncle, I feel so fortunate that, even with all of my wrongdoing while leading the Brotherhood, not once did I shed the blood of another man, nor did I ever order an assassination. Because of this, and after I have made everything right, one day I will go down into the waters of baptism."

"Yes, Tito. I'm glad for that." responded Enrique.

"And, Uncle, it is my prayer that you would be the one to baptize me."

Enrique looked admiringly at this man as he considered the great change that had come over him. "It would be such an honor!"

****

Light, wispy clouds covered the setting of the sun, causing bright rays to shoot heavenward from the gardens outside the Guzman home. The orange and pink horizon became a backdrop for a long-lasting embrace for Elena and Federico, who had separated themselves from the other dinner guests, as they contemplated their future together . . . a future of farming fruit and raising children in the valley at the confluence of the Tamazula and Humaya rivers.

Sleep came easily for Elena that night . . . a sweet surrender to long-awaited peaceful slumber, so different from prior years of anguish and fighting off demons . . . the recurring intrusions of her brother's murder and Uncle Hector's watery death. Since her rescue from her near-death scenario at Red Rock Cliffs, Elena's heart had been softened. Her anger had diminished. She was a woman at peace.

Dreams came. Not the tormenting kind that had caused her to awaken angry each morning. These were dreams sweetened with a measure of hope and positive anticipation. Federico's love for her eclipsed the need to work out her anger through karate. Her presence in the *dojo* meant little to her now. Federico loved her and would be there for her in the vast array of tomorrows. As her eyelids closed, harbingers of happiness swept into her subconscious as she drifted away into deep sleep orbit.

The dream took on new life. It centered on a river, large and flowing slowly. It appeared more like a lake, wide and placid. There was no wind to form waves. The mirrored images of cumulus clouds on the surface made it resplendent, as the sun fought its way through, casting warmth and light on a small inlet, bordered by cattails and hollyhocks.

The surface of the water broke, causing a circle to spread out in every direction. This time nothing descended downward into dark depths, as it had before. Instead, rays of sun flashed onto fingertips ascending with vigor upward. Next came the hand, followed by the full arm, extended, reaching up, grasping for the sky. Then came the head, neck, and shoulders of a young Hispanic man with a peaceful smile on his face.

As Elena slept on, she envisioned the young man swimming briskly and determinedly to the shore of the inlet, anxiously parting the cattails and running through the hollyhocks, heading toward a glorious light that emanated from the horizon and filtered out in his direction.

Another dimension appeared in Elena's dream scene. There was another light, a burst of flame emanating from an exploding vehicle. But this was different! Out of that ball of fire, both Miguel and his wife, Judy, walked forth . . . first tentatively, and then, upon seeing the same bright light on the horizon, quickened their pace. They reached toward the same light that Hector was now approaching.

Miguel and Judy's paths converged with Hector's. The three held hands and disappeared into the warm glow of the light.

When Elena awoke the next morning, there was no more anger.

The demons were gone.

CHAPTER THIRTY
ON FROM THERE

CULIACÁN, MEXICO

ON THE STREETS of Culiacán, more late-model pickups continue to pull up in front of the shrine of the drug patron saint. Young men packing guns, wearing Jesus Malverde necklaces, cowboy hats, and snakeskin boots exit their pickups. As their girlfriends lay wreaths of roses at the foot of the shrine, the young men order musicians to play loud songs dedicated to Malverde, hoping for another successful trip north into *gringo* Land with cocaine, methamphetamine, and marijuana carefully hidden away in their vehicles.

At the same time, bullets are being fired in all directions at those and by those drug lords-in-embryo, scurrying to form new cartels, to take more secret oaths, and to fill the vacuum left by the Brotherhood and the Vultures.

MIKE MCPHETERS, raised in Ketchum, Idaho, served as a Special Agent of the FBI and a SWAT team member for over thirty years, while also serving four times as a Mormon bishop. He was decorated by the Bolivian government for his role in investigating the killing of two LDS missionaries in La Paz, Bolivia. He also investigated the James Hoffa murder, the D. B. Cooper hijacking, Rajneeshpuram (a commune founded in Central Oregon by a bhagwan from India), major narcotics distributors, and many other significant cases. Mike completed his undergraduate work at Brigham Young University and received Master of Business and Master of Public Administration degrees from City University in Bellevue, Washington.

Mike is a retired member of the "National Association of Legal Investigators," the world's premier private investigator association. He was a Certified Legal Investigator (CLI) with them before he retired. It's a board-certified position held only by approximately 120 investigators world-wide.

Currently, Mike is a cruise lecturer for different cruise lines: Norwegian Cruise Lines and Royal Caribbean Cruise Lines. He has lectured in over twenty countries. He and his wife, Judy, have five children and twenty-one grandchildren. They reside in Moses Lake, Washington.

Mr. McPheters recently authored the bestselling book, *Agent Bishop: True Stories From An FBI Agent Moonlighting As a Mormon Bishop.*

Visit www.MikeMcpheters.com for more information, or email Mike at mikem@gcpower.net.